"Here's what I k **Morgan took a couple of steps closer to him.**

"They're made by people who are afraid of losing control of a situation. If you give in to them, you feed that sense of control, which emboldens them, and they become more dangerous."

"Fine, I'll take that chance. Face the danger. But not with you."

"Then, okay, I'm fired. And we'll work the case separately." She walked back to her satchel.

No. "Wait."

She shook her head. "I've been working to solve my sister's murder for seventeen years, Blade. If you think you have the power to stop me, you're just..."

What? He was what? He wanted to know. And didn't need to.

She was right. He hadn't brought her into the situation. Or even called her to town. "Someone's playing with me," he said, feeling a smidgen of his usual calm settling over him. "Baiting me."

"Someone who knows that we once hung out together," she added, her brows creased, as though she was studying a difficult puzzle. "They had to know that making a threat to my life would hit you where it hurts."

Dear Reader,

This is a book of my heart in several ways. It's set in a state in which I only lived full-time for two years as a little kid, but that has been a second home to me my entire life. But more, it tells the story of young love that wasn't trusted, got lost and then found again. My true-life story in those few words. It's also the story of fortitude. Of refusing to give up even when life seems to be prepared to deny you forever. A lot of us have been there at one time or another.

It's a suspenseful, twisting and turning mystery that kept me on the edge of my seat, some days literally, as I was writing. I didn't know how it was going to end until it did. The best kind of book to read or write!

But most of all, it's the story of love. True love. In its various forms. This book depicts everything I believe in. The love that is real and strong enough to endure. To win out over evil. To bring us a happiness that far surpasses any other joy we could possibly feel. Love isn't just in the moment, or temporary. It endures. Even if we lose it. If we let it, it will find us again.

I hope love finds you over and over.

Tara Taylor Quinn

HER SISTER'S MURDER

TARA TAYLOR QUINN

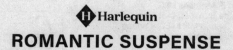

ROMANTIC SUSPENSE

Harlequin®
ROMANTIC SUSPENSE™

Recycling programs for this product may not exist in your area.

ISBN-13: 978-1-335-50254-4

Her Sister's Murder

 Harlequin Enterprises ULC
22 Adelaide St. West, 41st Floor
Toronto, Ontario M5H 4E3, Canada
www.Harlequin.com

Printed in Lithuania

MIX
Paper | Supporting responsible forestry
FSC® C021394

A *USA TODAY* bestselling author of over one hundred novels in twenty languages, **Tara Taylor Quinn** has sold more than seven million copies. Known for her intense emotional fiction, Ms. Quinn's novels have received critical acclaim in the UK and most recently from Harvard. She is the recipient of the Readers' Choice Award and has appeared often on local and national TV, including *CBS Sunday Morning*. For TTQ offers, news and contests, visit tarataylorquinn.com!

Books by Tara Taylor Quinn

Harlequin Romantic Suspense

Sierra's Web

Tracking His Secret Child
Cold Case Sheriff
The Bounty Hunter's Baby Search
On the Run with His Bodyguard
Not Without Her Child
A Firefighter's Hidden Truth
Last Chance Investigation
Danger on the River
Deadly Mountain Rescue
A High-Stakes Reunion
Baby in Jeopardy
Her Sister's Murder

The Coltons of Owl Creek

Colton Threat Unleashed

Visit the Author Profile page
at Harlequin.com for more titles.

For J—the twin of my heart. Our days in the hills, and all the years after, sustain me, still. Love doesn't die.

Chapter 1

Gravel crunched above him in the darkness. Freezing in place, all senses on alert, Blade Carmichael went into defend-and-protect mode. Listening. His eyes were the only things moving as he took in the rim of the eight-foot-deep half-acre hole in which he stood.

Being trapped in a pit, inspecting footers, wasn't something he'd choose to do without daylight, or without others around. But with darkness falling, and his company expanding so quickly, he hadn't been able to get to every site with the sun still shining down on him and with his crew still present.

The sound came again, weight on gravel. It wasn't the rolling sound of a vehicle. Didn't have the normal rhythm of footsteps, either. Was something being pushed by someone on foot? Or dragged?

Whatever was up there, it didn't belong. He'd locked the temporary gate behind him, as he always did when he drove on-site. The plowed and flattened land was clearly marked with keep-out and no-trespassing signs.

There had been a series of weird things happening lately. He'd been pretty sure someone was following him but had no proof—just a blue sedan. Sometimes it was parked down the street from his house with no one inside that he could see. And then he'd seen it outside a restaurant where he'd been eating. Across from his office, twice. And once when he'd been driving, a few lanes over and a couple of vehicles back.

But then, he tended to err on the paranoid side of watching his back. Spending seventeen years wrongly accused did that to a guy.

He hadn't noticed the car as he'd driven to the site, but that didn't mean it hadn't been there somewhere.

His truck was up top in full view.

Someone knew he was down in the pit.

No one was authorized to be on any of his sites after dark. No one. Ever. A rule that, if broken, cost an employee their job. Or garnered a call to police and a trespassing charge.

Turning off the light strapped to his head, he backed up slowly to the footers he'd come down to inspect, careful to keep his own boot crunch at a minimum. Once there, he leaned back, pressing himself into the dirt wall of the pit. Jeans and his button-down shirt and tie didn't offer much protection. All alone and thinking he was just going to be doing a few quick measurements, he'd left his hard hat on the front seat of the truck.

He hadn't felt real fear for his life in a long time, not since he'd mastered both target shooting and martial arts. His heart pounded, and he didn't welcome the sensation of snakes slithering in his gut. He reached slowly for the Glock 9 mm holstered to his belt, legally allowed in Michigan if it was visible, and by his concealed-carry permit if it wasn't. He'd never used the pistol, other than to shoot targets.

He'd never killed anything.

But the world thought he had. Even though he'd never been formally charged, and had a completely clean record.

More gravel turning. Crunching. Getting closer. Was someone coming to get revenge? The paranoia that he'd been fighting fairly successfully in recent years suddenly surfaced with a vengeance. There was nothing on the lot to steal.

Nothing there at all but dirt, some rebar cemented into footer framing and him.

The sound was definitely scraping. Or dragging.

Dirt?

Was someone moving a large mass of dirt?

To bury him in his own pit?

Horror clawed at him. After so many years full of dread, were the death threats he'd received finally becoming reality?

No, he had to get a hold of himself. He was a grown man running a successful business in a town where his past wasn't an issue.

The investigation had been thorough seventeen years before and as soon as he'd been released from custody, he'd immediately, and legally, dropped the McFadden from his name. Leaving Blade Carmichael McFadden behind, he'd hoped.

The only evidence against him had been circumstantial— strengthened by the fact that there were no other viable suspects. But even though the DA had decided not to press charges, public opinion had been swayed against him.

But not in Rocky Springs. Not in the small Michigan town where he'd made a good name for himself.

Was someone from the past on his lot? Had they come to make him pay? Knowing he had nowhere to run? To hide?

Struggling against the unhealthy thoughts, he tried to focus on the sounds above him.

The scraping sounds were coming closer. He was a standing duck.

What if someone local had heard about his past?

The only way out, the stepladder he'd brought down with him, was all the way on the other side of the pit.

And climbing up would do nothing except make him an easy target.

No matter what was going on, someone was on his lot, illegally, in the dark.

Gun in his hand, safety off, he listened and watched the rim, waiting for the first sign of whoever was up there to show itself. His only chance was to stay alert and get a shot off first.

A feat he should be able to accomplish. He'd been on high alert since he was seventeen years old.

Maybe getting to the ladder was the best bet. He could climb slowly. Crouch down. Get a look at his would-be assailant before they got to him.

Blade was already acting before he'd finished the thought. Moving softly, sliding quickly along the dirt floor, he kept himself crouched and balanced as he leaned into the wall of dirt his crew had dug.

The sound was closer. Almost directly above his head. He wasn't going to get to the ladder in time. He stopped moving and pressed himself into the dirt with all of his strength. Gun in both hands, barrel pointing upward, he slid his head backward an inch, then two, attempting to see without being seen.

Throat dry, tight, he couldn't swallow. But mixed in with the fear, surprising him, was a bit of relief. No more dreading that this day would come...

But it still might not have come. He had to stay calm. Focused. Deal with the moment, not the past.

He hadn't killed that sixteen-year-old girl. But he hadn't hung around to make sure she made it back to camp safely, either. Not that he'd invited her to the party, or even that she'd have left with him if he'd asked. She'd been having too much fun hanging out with the others. But he'd been a senior camp counselor. She'd only been a junior...he shouldn't have left while there was still a junior there...

He shouldn't have been there at all. None of them should have been.

The dirt against his back reverberated slightly. From weight on the ground directly above him. Had to be right at the rim of the pit. He couldn't see a thing but dirt and sky. No moon. No stars. And no assailant visible to him.

But someone who knew he was in that pit was right above him. Illegally there.

Bracing for a load of dirt or a bullet that would bring searing pain, he kept his eye trained above, arms and hands set to use his pistol at the first sign of movement.

Tense, ready, he waited.

The one thing he had going for him, a man thought to have murdered a sixteen-year-old girl when he'd been just seventeen himself, was that he'd never, ever physically hurt anyone.

Before he had time for another thought, rocks and clods of fresh dirt started to tumble around him, hitting his head, his shoulders. Some were big enough to bruise him and obstruct his vision. He couldn't see anyone up above. But he couldn't just stand there and die. He'd learned long ago he had to bear his own load. Cocking back his pistol, he pointed the barrel to the sky, and pulled the trigger, not to kill, but to warn, to scare and then, if necessary, to defend.

Before the bullet had even reverberated through the air, a body landed on the dirt at his feet.

* * *

Former FBI agent turned private detective Morgan Davis had dread in her gut as she entered Rocky Springs just after sunrise. She'd gotten the call in the very wee morning hours and had been instantly up, showered, dressed in black pants, a white cropped blouse and black flats, and was out the door, making the two-hour drive from Detroit in record time.

Maddie, I've got him...

The internal words started before she realized their intent. No. She wasn't going back there. Not to the time. Or the false hope.

She wasn't a sixteen-year-old youth camp counselor anymore. She'd lost her youth the night she'd lost her identical twin sister. Murdered by someone she'd thought was one of her closest friends, the only guy she'd ever had a serious crush on. The only one who'd ever shown any interest in someone as straitlaced and serious as she was. The only guy who'd asked her to be exclusive with him.

Maddie had been the vivacious one. The honey that drew everyone to them. And kept their attention when they arrived. Morgan had the same perfectly aligned features, striking blue eyes, blond hair and slim, long-legged build, but she'd rarely been noticed. And, introvert that she was, she'd been perfectly content to sit in her sister's shadow, watching out for the both of them, planning their futures.

Until that last summer at camp. Maddie hadn't wanted to be there. They'd heard the school counselor talk about a need for counselors at the summer youth camp, alighting Morgan with interest. Interest she'd known her twin wouldn't share, just as Maddie hadn't been paying attention during assembly that morning. During the rest of the mandatory meeting, while her sister kept exchanging looks with a boy across the aisle, Morgan worked it all out. They'd spend their first summer apart. Maddie going to cheer camp and Morgan being a counselor at the youth camp they'd attended for years. It would be good for them...they could text every morning and every night...and have so much to tell each other at summer's end.

As it had turned out, their overly strict, older parents had jumped on the guidance counselor's call for help. The twins had started counselor training that very afternoon...

And that had been the end of life as they knew it.

Following the prompt from her dark blue SUV's navigation system, Morgan turned and then turned again. She'd never been to Rocky Springs. The beach town hadn't had any crimes calling for FBI presence when she'd been with the Bureau.

And Sierra's Web, the nationally renowned firm of experts she'd joined the year before, hadn't sent her there, either.

She wasn't there on official business. Yet.

She was there because a non-FBI law enforcement acquaintance had fulfilled a promise.

Blade Carmichael's name had shown up in a crime scene report that made it over the unofficial BOLO wire across the state. Word of mouth traveled fast when a guy showed up dead in a ditch at the feet of a suspected killer. Morgan's acquaintance knew she'd want the information.

According to the report that had been read to her so early that morning, Carmichael had been in a new-build basement dig. The body had landed at his feet from up above. He'd heard footsteps. One set. And then nothing. The form had been unmoving, lying with a leg bent underneath it and both arms splayed out. He'd immediately dialed 911, then ran to a ladder and climbed to the rim of the pit. He saw no blood, no sign of anything, except for a strip of dirt that looked like some kind of heavy box or blanket had been dragged across it, cutting a path on the newly cleared land.

He'd made a quick perusal of the site and headed back down to the body.

Male, based on the dark pants, he'd told the operator on the line, and light-colored dress shirt. Short hair, mostly dark. Gray tinges, perhaps from the moon's reflection? The guy was face down. Carmichael couldn't get a feel for age.

He had checked for a pulse and said something about flesh not yet cold to the touch of his fingers.

The lack of pulse was evident, though. He'd been touching a dead man. No bleeding profusely from a killer's bullet. Not bleeding visibly at all, and not pooling from beneath him, either.

The suspect—she couldn't not think of Blade that way—hadn't been arrested when law enforcement arrived. There hadn't been sufficient evidence against him to warrant doing so. But Morgan knew better. Blade Carmichael was someone whose alias—Blade Carmichael McFadden—might not show up in official police records. But it was definitely at the top of the suspect list in her personal memory.

He'd grown up in another beach town—South Haven. Another town she'd never visited. One he'd vacated abruptly when it had become known that he was a murderer and his father's business had tanked. The family, just him and his parents, had moved to Grand Rapids, and then, upon his high school graduation, to Florida. He'd returned to his home state to attend the University of Michigan, graduated with a degree in business management and settled in the burgeoning, if still small, beach town of Rocky Springs.

Why he'd gone to all the trouble to change his name and then return to his home state, she didn't know. Except that, even as a teenager, he'd loved the state. The Great Lakes.

The vast outdoors. The seasons. Those were the kinds of conversations he'd had with Morgan years ago.

While Maddie had talked constantly about getting out and seeing the world, wanting to move to California or New York, Morgan had loved Michigan, too. The natural beauty of forests and streams, bound by the Great Lakes and a lot of wide-open country.

It felt right to think about something good as she prepared to enter hell.

Her phone rang. Slowing, she saw Jas's ID on her dash screen, pulled to the shoulder and picked up.

"Hey," she greeted her ex–FBI team member and close friend. Because she knew if she didn't pick up, Jasmine would go into full agent mode.

"I heard about the murder, Morg. Tell me you aren't headed to Rocky Springs."

Glancing at the Carmichael Construction sign on a stick stuck in the ground just ahead, she figured, since she'd reached her destination, she wasn't headed anywhere. "I'm not."

"You're there already, aren't you?"

She wasn't going to lie. Silence was the only other option.

"It's not good for you." FBI Special Agent Jasmine Flaherty knew, more than most, that Morgan was somewhat obsessed with getting her sister's killer behind bars. Legally. Rightfully. Forever and ever, world without end.

It was partially why she'd left the Bureau.

"The dead man is Shane Wilmington. He was another counselor that summer. One who had been at the party, too." An unsanctioned gathering, just down the beach from camp property, reached through a hole in a very old and never very strong wire fence.

She idled at the curb as she explained herself. She trusted her friend with her life—and needed Jas to know she could trust Morgan, too. She wasn't just there because *the name* had unofficially popped up in a new murder investigation. But when the dead body had turned out to be someone else from that night…

What investigator worth her salt wouldn't at least get herself to town and see what she could find out?

"Be careful."

"I will." Morgan's words were confirmation of how she lived every minute of every day.

"And call me. The second you know anything. And when you're headed home."

With a grim face, she agreed to do so and hung up. When she got to the gate, she showed her Sierra's Web private detective credentials to a uniformed guard, and pulled forward onto the lot legally occupied by the man who'd killed her sister.

She wanted to be all brave and strong. Unflappable. She wanted to be the woman who'd earned her reputation as one of the best agents the Michigan Bureau had ever seen. Instead, when she took in the newly plowed ground—the vehicles, some with bubbles, some not, the crime scene tape around a big hole in the ground with a crane hovering just off to the right of it—she started to shake.

Heart pounding, she took a deep breath. Pushed away her need to cry.

The crane was there to remove the body, she knew. The rest of the folks—forensics, crime scene investigators, detectives and officers, she determined by vests and vehicle markings—might wonder why a private detective was on scene.

If the guy guarding the lot had actually read her badge,

recognized it and told anyone who she was, she'd tell them why she was there. Unofficially. Because they might have a serial killer on their hands. One who committed murder seventeen years apart.

As it was, no one seemed to notice as, her Glock at her hip and creds in her back pocket, she made her way toward the scene of the murder.

Chapter 2

Morgan took half a dozen steps and stopped. Carmichael was at the scene. She hadn't expected that. Not nine hours after the crime had been called in.

She started toward the less populated end of the pit. The crane was there, without an operator inside it from what she could see. Closer yet were a couple of crime scene techies wearing gloves, bagging things she couldn't make out. The body was already in the morgue, undergoing an autopsy to determine cause of death.

The body. How jaded she'd become.

She hadn't known Shane well. Hadn't liked him all that much. He'd encouraged Maddie's wild side, rather than helping her rein it in, encouraged her to bad-mouth her parents, agreeing with her regarding their over-the-top strictness.

From what Morgan had heard, Shane had been the one who'd instigated the parties that had gone on after hours that summer...

He'd been a kid then.

And a successful real estate broker on the day he died. A husband and father. A churchgoing man.

She'd been hoping to chat with the lead detective. To find out what they knew so far in terms of the current crime, and to float the Blade-Carmichael-as-a-serial-killer idea.

She hadn't planned on Carmichael's presence. He'd been questioned hours before. She'd been hoping he'd be in jail, on suspicion charges with a forty-eight-hour hold, if nothing else. Not standing in conversation with a couple of suited men.

Did that mean he was getting off again? That he'd managed to commit the perfect crime a second time?

Over her dead body.

Would he know her if he saw her?

Her hair was still blond. Still long. Up in a bun. She still had the long legs, and not a lot of girth on her. But she was at least twice as strong as she'd been back then.

And not the least bit introverted if it came to getting the answers she sought.

When she looked in the mirror, she didn't see any resemblance to the young girl she'd been before Carmichael had murdered her sister. It was the eyes. They used to mirror a soul that was alive. And a life filled with hopes.

Now they just reflected the truths she saw.

And heard.

"He said he shot the bullet straight up from here," one of the CSIs said, shoving a long piece of tube in the dirt, pointing upward. The other calculated an angle for the downward trajectory and they both moved to where the bullet should have landed. She wondered if they already had the shell casing.

Shane's body had been found with a bullet through the side of his head. Entered and exited. But the deadly shot hadn't happened at the construction site. He'd already been dead before he'd been dumped. Blade Carmichael claimed he'd only shot his gun once, from the pit, to defend himself from whatever was above him, but the entire story was too contrived. How would someone else have gotten on-site if the gate was locked? And how had he gotten away without being seen? It wasn't like someone could have just walked on-site dragging a body and then disappeared into thin air. Chances were, Carmichael had already killed the man— probably with a different weapon—then turned over his registered weapon with the one bullet missing. That would explain any gunshot residue that could be found on him— shooting that bullet in the air.

It would also make it look like he'd been in the pit before the arrival of the body—needing to defend himself. An alibi, of sorts.

Along with the late-night inspection, due to a job starting early and thus giving him an overpacked schedule necessitating the after-hours incident.

It was all so clean.

Too clean.

Calling in the body had been a bold move.

Across the way, Blade pulled over a guy in jeans and a T-shirt who'd been headed her way. Had a quick word with him. And then turned back to his other conversation. He'd glanced at her. Gave no indication whether he knew who she was.

She didn't have any idea what friends he currently had. How far up the chain they went. As far or further than his father's friends in the past? Maybe not high enough to save a man's local business, but enough to keep charges from being filed against his seventeen-year-old son.

Just looking at the grown-up version of that seventeen-year-old blew up a host of emotions inside her, and it took her a second to get her bearings back. The shape of his face, rounded head with angular chin, the dark hair that was shorter than she remembered, but still bearing that distinctive wave at the back…those legs. They all found answers within her. Recognition of something she'd once thought to be as hot as it got.

He'd been the only guy she'd known who she hadn't been able to walk away from and forget. *Still was.* But for vastly different reasons. He'd been the first really close friend that her sister didn't share. And the real blow had been that she'd thought he shared her feelings. That they'd been destined to meet. To spend the rest of their lives together.

Right up until he'd sneaked off and partied with her identical twin—and then, in a rage, had killed her.

Probably because while Maddie was a flirt, always up for escapades, and loads of fun…she had very distinct lines she didn't cross. Having sex at sixteen had been one of them. Mostly because their parents had set such strict guidelines for their freedom to come and go and Maddie hadn't wanted to risk losing their trust, or the few benefits they'd had.

And, she'd once told Morgan, because when she entered into that kind of relationship, she wanted to be old enough to live with the guy if she wanted to do so. Not have to do it in the back of a car and go home to bed.

The only saving grace from that night was that Maddie hadn't been sexually violated. She'd fought her attacker. He'd panicked, thinking someone was going to hear them, and had killed her without getting what he was presumed to have been after. And Maddie—the biggest flirt in their school—had gone to heaven a virgin.

The jean-clad man was upon her. She noticed his red bushy beard more than his eyes as he gave her a nod.

She nodded back at him and took a few steps to the side as he climbed up into the crane.

Two similarly clad guys were inside the pit with a CSI, digging in the dirt. Probably looking for the casing of the bullet Carmichael claimed to have shot. They'd have waited until dawn to begin searching for it.

Uniforms had given her good information in the past and said things a detective might not be as willing to share. As soon as the two officers aboveground finished their conversation, she'd head over to them. As she took a step in that direction, two things happened at once. The crane's engine started up and Carmichael turned fully around.

He was looking straight at her. She stared back. Daring him across the thirty-foot distance. To challenge her. To try to convince her that he had nothing to do with Shane's body in his pit.

He started her way. Moving slowly at first, and then more quickly. As he neared her, he called out. Then hollered and broke into an all-out run. Straight at her!

In front of everyone...

When she realized that he wasn't going to stop, Morgan stepped aside, backed up quickly to avoid him, only to have the maniac dive right for her.

His body slammed into hers with enough power to rob her of air and she landed with a bruising force, his body shielding hers from the freshly plowed ground.

A horrible clanging accompanied their fall. And something slammed against the ground just beside them. Hard enough, heavy enough to give nearby earth a jolt.

Heart pumping, Morgan pushed herself away from Blade Carmichael, reaching for her Glock, but didn't get it pulled as she saw all the law enforcement personnel running. Every single person on-site—like a tornado—hurtling toward them.

She sat up. Apart from him.

"Are you okay?" Blade's voice carried what sounded like real concern. And a lack of recognition?

Breathing hard, she couldn't look him in the eye. Didn't want to look at him at all. Or have his touch on her skin, warm and cushioning as it had been. "Fine," she said, staring at the crane's boom, which had just crashed to the ground.

It would have crushed her if Blade hadn't moved so quickly to get her out of the way.

She could have been killed.

Almost *had* been killed.

Blade Carmichael had just saved her life.

And just prior to that Blade had called over the crane operator, given him some kind of instruction, upon seeing her standing there. After which the operator had gone directly to the crane. Put the near-fatal accident in motion.

Had he given the order to kill her? Changed his mind?

Had he intentionally set circumstances in motion to allow him to risk his life to save hers? To divert attention away from him as a murderer?

The theory was a bit much—and yet, a completely believable explanation for what had just taken place.

Even so, as the detectives and officers reached her, all eyes wide, all wanting reassurance that she was okay, Morgan kept her most rancid thoughts to herself.

He'd body slammed a law enforcement official.

Blade stepped aside, giving way to the detectives and officers clamoring to the woman's side, as she showed her credentials.

And then, mouth open, he recognized her.

And understood why she was there.

He'd body slammed Morgan Davis. *The* Morgan Davis.

The cacophony of rising sun, dirt, a crane boom implanted in the ground, his operator climbing down to stand beside him, voices clamoring, fell away. Nothing in his world made sense, and all Blade could hear were the words of a devastated sixteen-year-old Morgan Davis.

Murderer! Get away from me! You killed her! You killed her!

He'd fallen in love with her that summer. Had been certain she'd been falling for him, too. Had gone over to comfort her...

He could still feel the strength of those fists slamming against his chest until the leader of the female camp counselors pulled her away. And the nurse took hold of her. Leading her off.

It was the last time he'd ever seen her...

"Morgan?" He said the word aloud. He hadn't meant to be heard—it just escaped.

He was shocked to see her, and yet...her presence made perfect sense, too.

Shane's death...his body being dumped at Blade's construction site...the tie to youth camp, to Madison Davis's death...

She glanced over at him, almost as though she'd heard him call her name. Their gazes locked. He wasn't going to be the first to look away. He'd done nothing wrong.

Her gaze held the expected hatred. A determination she hadn't had at sixteen.

And something more.

Something indefinable. Deep. Painful.

It was that something that had him not only looking away, but turning his back, too. An officer took charge of him then, asking questions as they walked over to the downed boom together. His operator, Lonnie, joined them. Gave a full account of his actions since he'd first approached the crane that morning. Blade answered questions about inspections. About assembly and disassembly procedures for all six of the cranes owned and operated by Carmichael Construction.

And he kept ex–FBI agent turned private detective Morgan Davis in his sight, at least peripherally, at all times. He hadn't known she'd left the agency to team up with some private firm that had one of the detectives on-site falling all over her.

Her being there couldn't be good. But he shouldn't be surprised, either. He'd known she'd gone into crime solving. Had heard from a friend of his dad's with the South Haven police that she'd joined the FBI. Easy to figure out why. He got all that.

Just hadn't expected her to turn up so early. To have gotten word in the middle of the night and made it to Rocky Springs by dawn.

And now she'd almost died on his construction site, too. Because of a malfunction with one of his cranes. Right after he'd spoken with the operator.

The only thing that made sense about that was if someone was framing him.

But who? And had Morgan just been targeted personally because she'd been at camp, too? Or had the crane incident just been meant to make him look bad? A shoddy contractor with unsafe equipment?

If Morgan was being targeted, who'd known she was going to be there?

All things he had to find out.

Adrenaline filled him. Could it be that his chance had finally arrived? Was he actually going to be able to find the real killer?

Though he'd been questioned a good part of the night, he hadn't been charged with anything.

He figured that the detectives were still looking at him. He'd cooperated fully. Had granted them access to his home, his computer, his business and personal accounts. They'd know soon enough that he worked most of his waking hours. He ate out a lot. Fished when he could. And worked more.

He'd been told not to leave the state.

Like he had anywhere else he'd want to go.

Certainly not to his parents in Florida. Not with this hanging over him. He hoped to God it was done and gone before they ever got wind of it. He wouldn't take them through that hell a second time.

What if, once again, the police didn't find enough evidence? Whoever had killed Madison Davis had managed to get away with murder once. Blade couldn't take the chance that he'd be able to do it a second time.

He couldn't count on the police.

There was only one person he could think of who would be good enough, determined enough, to get to the whole truth.

No matter the danger. Or the cost.

One person who needed the truth as desperately as he did.

A person who—if he'd understood correctly when she'd shown her credentials—was for hire.

The woman who was certain that he'd killed her twin sister.

Chapter 3

Shaken up from the crane incident, Morgan was more determined than ever to insinuate herself into Shane Wilmington's murder case.

But she knew that she couldn't officially do so, not unless she could convince whoever was in charge of the case to hire Sierra's Web. If Blade Carmichael was a serial killer—and she was convinced of that—the FBI could take jurisdiction. Which would make it Jasmine's case. She gave her friend a fifty-fifty chance of even letting Morgan get close to the case, let alone paying a hefty sum to hire her to work it.

She'd offer to work free of charge. Hell, she'd pay the Sierra's Web fee herself. She just had to find someone with the authority to bring her on.

No way she could get this close and not be able to finally find justice for her sister.

Since nearly being smashed by a crane had drawn attention to her presence on-site, as soon as Carmichael was led off by an officer, Morgan went straight to the man who appeared to be in charge. She introduced herself with her credentials out to Detective Chad Larson, a tall man with a mustache from the Rocky Springs Police Department. She met the only other detective in the department, too.

Ramon Gonzalez, who was shorter and stockier but also had a mustache.

"I have an interest in what happened here due to a different case I'm working. I'd sure appreciate any professional courtesy you can give me, any details you can share."

Gonzalez looked her over and glanced at Larson, who said, "We've taken molds of footprints, but don't expect to get anything from them. With all the construction boots worn on the site yesterday, it's pretty well impossible to differentiate, or even get full sets of prints. Carmichael's were all around the bottom of the pit and part of the rim, but they would be, either way. He's already admitted to being on-site, inspecting the footers inside the pit, when the supposed body dump happened. The curious part is the area where the body would have had to go over. There were no footprints, but we found a path of tamped down earth, like a piece of cardboard or heavy plastic bearing a heavy weight had been dragged." The man sounded focused, sincere, but she found it a bit too clean, again.

She was supposed to believe that local law enforcement actually thought that someone had done the body dump and then, what, dragged the cardboard backward as the person ran from the scene, covering his footprints as he went, as Carmichael claimed? The man had said he'd heard footsteps...

And the crane incident? No one had known that she'd be at the site. And no one could have predicted that she'd walk where she had.

But she'd seen Carmichael look in her direction as he'd spoken to his operator. The man had moved immediately to the crane...

And Carmichael had saved her life in front of a gathering of law enforcement.

"It's too coincidental that that boom fell right after a dead body was removed from the pit," she said aloud to the two men.

"Blade's convinced he's being set up," Chad Larson said, and Ramon nodded. Her heart sank as she caught the nuance in that statement.

"He's convinced? As in, you believe he really believes that?" Because if they did, they'd also have to believe that Carmichael knew he hadn't done it. They'd have to believe he hadn't. "Or you think he's using that theory as a cover-up?"

Larson's brows drew together. "It's too early to answer to that," he responded, as though realizing that he was talking to an unknown private detective—albeit ex-FBI who was working for a highly respected firm of experts—and not one of his officers.

His dismissive tone left her completely dissatisfied. She'd wanted to hope that the Rocky Springs Police Department was going to succeed where others had failed. That these guys were going to catch on to Blade Carmichael McFadden, and finally bring him to justice.

With her adrenaline already pumping, dread quickly flooded her, as she saw the past repeating itself. The guy had a way of convincing people that he was, above all else, a good person.

Blade Carmichael's forthright manner, his seeming honesty and unassuming self-confidence had sucked her in, too. Convincing her to open her heart to him even though she'd made a vow to herself that she wouldn't get swept up by a boy during hormonal high school years, like Maddie had, almost monthly, to an inevitable sea of tears every time.

She had to talk to the guy. She wasn't an impressionable

sixteen-year-old kid anymore. Nor did she still instinctively
trust that people were good until they proved otherwise.
Instead, she'd developed a sense for reading people. One
that had served the Bureau, and many clients, well.

"Do you mind if I speak with Mr. Carmichael?" she asked
both men. She had to get her own feel for Carmichael's testimony. It was the only way to find the lies.

They shook their heads simultaneously, telling her she
was free to speak with anyone she liked, giving her a green
light that catapulted her inner drive into full gear.

She was walking toward him with definite purpose.

Blade had just finished with the officers. He'd been told
to be available to the detectives as needed and was free to
go about his day.

He chose to wait for Morgan. The woman exuded power
and he'd be a fool to give her any further cause to tighten
the noose around his neck until he suffocated.

He liked her hair in a bun. It drew attention to the striking shape of her face. And those unforgettable blue eyes.

The look with which she speared him wasn't at all promising. And still, in spite of the obvious antagonism, he considered her approach a good sign. Once upon a time, she'd
shared her soul with him. He'd known her better, on a
deeper level, than he'd known anyone else. Before or since.
Had followed her stellar career with the Bureau, too, as best
he could with a retired South Haven contact as his source
of information.

She hated him. But he knew she'd be fair. That she'd
fight to find the truth. Expecting him to be punished to
the full extent of the law—yes. But if she found the truth,
she'd know he wasn't guilty.

And then he could be done with her. Be done with the

pain of her betrayal. He'd needed her that awful morning. Had counted on her being the one person who'd know he hadn't done the horrible things they were claiming…

"Mr. Carmichael," she called out to him while he was still a few feet away. "May I speak with you?"

He waited silently, an answer of sorts, until she reached him. And then said, simply, "Morgan." He'd never been one for subterfuge. They weren't strangers.

"I'd like a few minutes of your time," she said, not calling him out on his familiar choice of address. Allowing it? Or simply ignoring it?

"As a person from the past who's as concerned as I am about the body that showed up here last night? Or as a detective?"

"I'm both."

Not much of an answer. He needed her proffered conversation to go well. Had been given the opportunity to win her expert help and wasn't sure how to go about succeeding. He could feel her defenses as almost physical pricks to his skin.

"I'm guessing you think I murdered Shane," he said, the words making him slightly sick, and yet, relieving him of pressure, too. He had to get it out to get rid of it.

"As a professional investigator, I see you as a prime suspect."

Okay, then. He'd wanted it out there.

"And personally?" He knew as soon as the words were out of his mouth, they were the wrong ones. On every level.

Just…standing there with her…it was the first chance he'd had to actually have a conversation with her since the morning her sister's body had been found and she'd screamed at him to get away from her.

He'd spoken to her in his mind so many times over the years.

Prior to that godawful morning, their last conversation had been him asking her to be exclusive with him, and her immediately agreeing.

She hadn't issued a comeback to his reference to their past. Acknowledging that they had a personal history. And for the first time since the body had landed in his pit the night before, Blade experienced a dread-free second or two. It quickly vanished. But it had been there.

"I apologize for the question," he said. "It was out of line."

He knew what she thought, personally. She'd screamed it at him loud and clear that last morning. *Murderer! Get away from me*...

But maybe...just maybe...he had a chance to change her mind?

The thought came out of nowhere. He pushed it aside. What she thought of him ceased mattering seventeen years before. But if changing her mind meant he was finally exonerated, maybe he should try.

"I'm fine to speak with you," he said. "But if you wouldn't mind, I'd like to go home and shower first. We could meet in say...forty-five minutes...at the Ellery Café on Blossom Street. It's right on the beach and I'll call ahead and get us an outside table."

Sounded like he was making a date. "That'll give us privacy, and yet we'll be in a very public place where you'd feel safer."

She straightened. "I was a special agent with the FBI, Blade. And am now officially considered an expert in detective work with a nationally renowned firm. I've taken down serial killers and terrorists. I'm not the least bit afraid of you."

He believed her.

Acknowledged her point with an accepting nod. For a second there, he thought he saw a momentary glistening soften her gaze. It was followed so immediately by a return of stone-cold determination that he wasn't positive he'd seen it but rather, had transposed a moment from the past onto a very disturbing present.

He noted the weakness in himself so it didn't happen again. The young man she'd known back then no longer existed.

And the man he'd become didn't need her softening. He needed the determination that brimmed her eyes like shards of steel as she stared him down.

"Can you give me forty-five minutes?" he asked again. He wanted her off the crime scene. Away from detectives. Away from any other Carmichael Construction mishaps that could already be in motion, ready to hang him.

He needed to be able to talk to her, just Blade Carmichael and Morgan Davis. Not as the kids they'd been, but as the honest and hardworking adults they'd become.

Her not quite bitter nod of acquiescence wasn't a good sign.

But it was a reprieve, and he was willing to take what he could get.

Morgan hung around the crime scene after Blade left, looking at the details through her own investigative lens. Letting questions come as they always did when she gave herself to a case, and looking for answers, too. She spoke to the uniformed officers. Most of them knew Blade. They could hardly believe he'd murder someone.

But they weren't ruling out the possibility, which she found encouraging.

And then she left. She typed the café address into her vehicle's mapping system, and, looking in her rearview mirror as she always did, settled back for the ten-minute drive.

Pulling to a halt at a four-way stop, she noticed that a police car had pulled up behind her. It was still there as she turned and turned again. Small towns only had so many ways to get from point A to point B and she was headed to the most popular strip in Rocky Springs. Another car, black and luxurious-looking, a Lincoln or Cadillac she guessed, pulled behind the police car after the second turn. And then the cop turned off.

She hadn't been able to make out which of the officers she'd spoken to had followed her off the lot—he or she didn't get close enough—but she was glad to know that they were prevalent about town. Maybe even watching out for her.

Nine minutes later, she pulled into the café parking lot, her gaze drawn toward the beach and the expansive blue lake beyond. Movement at her side drew a quick glance.

The black car was in the café parking lot. But when she glanced over it suddenly sped up and left. It happened so fast she couldn't make out any of the driver's identifying features. Wasn't even sure if the person behind the wheel had been male or female. She'd seen white skin topped by dark hair. But her own skin was crawling. She was sure it was just her senses on overload, but she made a quick call to Jas, just in case. She told her friend that she'd felt like she'd been followed from the site and described the black car as best she could.

They lived dangerous lives. And had learned not to ignore gut feelings. Yeah, they turned out to be nothing sometimes, but the one time they weren't "nothing" they were thankful they'd listened.

Blade was pulling in just as she ended her call. As she watched him jump down out of his truck...all male and a summer love grown up...she wanted to phone her friend back to report in on another danger that could befall her. And most definitely did not make that call.

That girl she'd been in the past had died right along with her twin. No way she was going to give her any chance at life. Or allow a murderer one second's chance in hell of resurrecting her.

True to his word, Blade had a table waiting for them outside on a patio with enough space between tables to give them privacy. She wasn't hungry, though she should be, so ordered oatmeal and toast with her coffee. Blade had the same. She'd agreed to talk to him for one reason only, to get what information she could. And if he thought he was going to con her...

Neither pretended pleasantries as their waitress left them alone at the table for the first time.

"I need to find the killer," he said, his steaming cup of coffee untouched. "The police couldn't do it seventeen years ago, and I can't let my whole life rest on them being able to do it now. I need your help, Morgie."

She stiffened her back. "Don't you dare call me that."

"I'm sorry." He looked her in the eye as he issued the apology. Didn't try to excuse or even explain his lapse.

"I know what you think of me," he said, continuing to hold her gaze. "I also know I didn't kill your sister back then. And I didn't kill Shane last night. It's pretty clear that the two have to be connected. No way Shane's body ends up in my pit, while I'm there alone, by accident. Or coincidence."

"Especially considering that he lives in Grand Rapids," she allowed. Purely as a fact pertinent to the situation. She told herself not to get sucked into Blade's seeming sincerity.

He'd managed to lure her at sixteen. She'd talked to him about feelings, soul-deep yearnings, other things that she hadn't even shared with her sister.

Not again.

"You've got a vested interest," he continued. "Obviously, you haven't been able to let the past go, either, or you wouldn't have driven through the night to get here."

"If you think you're going to distract me from proving that you killed Shane, you're wrong."

He didn't falter, didn't even blink. He leaned in closer. "I'm telling you, I want the truth as badly as you do."

"I can't just waltz onto a case. I have no jurisdiction or right to even be here. The fact that I was allowed at the scene, and that the detectives chose to speak to me, was professional courtesy. Period."

"But you've been looking for proof ever since your sister was killed, haven't you? It's pretty clear you've put word out or you wouldn't have known to be here less than twelve hours after I called in the body."

He'd always been the smartest guy at camp. Which had partially been what had drawn her to him. That and his maturity.

"You wouldn't be here if you didn't intend to do your own sleuthing. All I'm asking is that you let me help," he said. "Let's do this together. It's clear whoever killed Shane is out to hang me. My life will be an open book to you. Look everywhere. Interrogate me until we're numb. Just find something…"

Was he for real? Or just really good at manipulating people to get what he wanted?

Which would be...absolution from a second murder?

If he'd killed Shane, the best chance she had at finding out why, how and where would be through the open door into his life he'd just offered her.

But more than that...he'd given her what she couldn't invent for herself. The in to officially be a part of the case. "It'll cost you," she told him.

He didn't even blink. "How much you want? Name the price."

Okay, things were moving too fast. He was playing right into what she wanted and needed. Giving her a way in.

He was playing *her*.

She shook her head, but held his gaze, gaining strength as she did so. "It's not my price," she told him. And, reaching for her creds, pulled a card out of the thin leather pouch that held them. "You want me on this case, call Sierra's Web and hire me. You'll need to sign permission forms that allow me access to every piece of evidence, every communication involved with your case. It'll be like I'm your lawyer, only I'm going to shadow every move you make."

She was only taking him on if she could do so officially. With the firm's teams of experts right there with her.

No way was Blade Carmichael going to pull any wool over her eyes a second time. He might be playing her, for reasons of his own. But with her right there, with the firm there, following up on everything she heard, every email, every piece of forensic evidence she brought them, Blade would be the one who'd be played.

Right to the finish line.

At some point, if she was monitoring him, he'd say something, let some little detail slip, that would allow her to prove that he killed Maddie. Because no one, not a living soul on earth, knew her sister's case as well as she did.

When Blade stood, pushing his chair back, and walked away, she cursed herself for being too straightforward, pushing him too hard. Maddie had been the one of them blessed with the art of finesse. It was a gift Morgan could have used to get the man to give her exactly what she most needed.

An in to the case.

She stayed at the table long enough for their food to be delivered, and to let the waitress know she needed to settle the bill. Hadn't even received the check yet when Blade was suddenly back.

"Done," he said, just as her phone rang.

He was eating oatmeal when she hung up from Glen Rivers Thomas, the Sierra's Web forensic partner to whose team she was assigned.

Blade had given the firm an open account, with the caveat that Morgan be the lead on his case. Not just on his case but running it.

If he thought he was going to pull the wool over her eyes with his faith in her then he was setting himself up for a major disappointment.

Pushing her untouched breakfast aside, she leaned forward. "Rest assured, that when I find the proof, whoever killed my sister is going down. Forever." She stared at him with an intensity that had cowed lifetime criminals. "He will not see another day outside of prison walls. There won't be an attorney good enough to get him off." Like the high-priced guy his daddy had hired to keep Blade from ever being officially charged seventeen years before.

"From your lips to God's ears."

Wow. Invoking higher-ups. His statement didn't impress her. But the way Blade held her gaze, his own eyes steady, unblinking...

Either he really believed she'd find him innocent, or he was the most arrogant, self-confident, unconscionable man she'd ever met.

Too bad he didn't know she'd lost her ability to be moved by smooth talk the night Maddie was killed. The night her heart had died, too.

And if he'd managed to amass friends in Rocky Springs, people who'd fallen for him as hard as Morgan had, he could have had someone in a black vehicle follow her from the crime scene. Maybe to make sure she kept her word to meet him at the diner, or to see who she spoke to between leaving the crime scene and keeping their breakfast plans.

And there was the cop who'd pulled out right after her. Did Blade have the town's police force in his pocket, too?

Perhaps he thought the surest way to make certain that any unturned stone she might turn up would be magically destroyed before charges could be filed was to follow her.

Was that why Blade was hiring her, to stay one step ahead of prosecution?

"Tell me about the crane. How does it suddenly just fail at a crime scene?"

He started, sitting straight up in his seat, as she got to work.

Interesting.

He hadn't been sure she'd agree to help him. In spite of how convincing he'd been.

Without pushing for confirmation that she was agreeing to take his case, he started explaining about bolts and pins, assembly and disassembly of booms. Talked about statistical chances of a boom falling, and the most common causes. And ended with, "There's no way that crane failed by accident. Inspection and safety measures at Carmichael Construction are overkill, and everyone knows that a single infraction will get you fired. Period. Someone had to have tampered with the crane." His voice filled with intensity as he continued. "That particular crane was scheduled to be at that site starting today. Any number of people had access to that knowledge. Equipment schedules are posted. No way someone could have aimed that accident at you, but the boom failing—that was no accident."

There was one way it could have been aimed at her. If Blade had instructed his machine operator to make it happen.

He had access to equipment schedules. And clearly knew how to manipulate a boom failure. He'd pulled his operator aside, while looking at her, and given some direction.

Her gut lurched. Part of her, that young woman she'd thought completely dead, wanted, just for a second there, for her to believe he didn't do it.

She didn't trust those kinds of feelings. Most particularly not with Blade Carmichael. She trusted facts. So she regurgitated the ones that had been covered so many times in the past, and in her mind over the years.

"You went to the party. You told me you weren't going, but you did." She'd jumped back a decade and a half. Didn't feel the least bit sorry for the abrupt change in her interrogation.

If she sounded like an accusatory girlfriend with hurt feelings, so be it. She didn't give a damn.

His shoulders dropped, his chin falling to his chest. She grabbed her purse, ready to leave before the bill finally made it to the table. Let him pay for it.

"I was senior camp counselor." His voice stopped her. "Shane was making some off-color jokes about being with identical twins. I didn't trust him. Not knowing that Maddie was going to be there."

"And yet, according to your testimony, you left early. Left her there."

"Because he had. I stayed until he left."

"But you told police you thought he was the killer."

"They asked who I thought could have done it—among the kids at camp."

There was more. So much more. Maddie's class ring found in the pocket of Blade's jeans in his cabin the next morning. The little ribbon cross Morgan had made for him that day in craft class, and that she'd slipped into his shirt pocket herself, clutched in her dead sister's palm...

He'd have answers for them all, she was sure. Had read the reports, and knew those answers weren't the truth.

But she'd get there. She'd hear him admit every step he took that night. In time.

Maybe not right away.

Probably not before she opened up every crevice in his life to find out why and how Shane Wilmington's dead body had ended up in a Carmichael Construction pit.

But she'd get there.

And when she did, he'd have to look her in the eye and... What?

What could he possibly say or do that would ever, could ever, melt the ice she'd been encased in since her sister's horrible death?

Chapter 4

Blade wasn't going to look for any aspects of Morgan's character that could be remainders from the past. Even if her twin's murder hadn't completely changed her, he *knew* it had made him into a person that did not, in any way, resemble the young man he'd been.

The twinge of optimism that coursed through him as he paid the breakfast bill and walked back to his truck—the flood of relief—was only because he now had an expert detective on his case.

The fact that the expert was Morgan Davis was merely a consequence of her having become that expert after Maddie's death.

And that, his gut knew, was no coincidence. Morgan had wanted to be a novelist. A purveyor of stories filled with hope and happy endings. Not a hard-nosed, physically honed pursuer of bad guys.

Before she'd left the restaurant, he'd called his attorney to release his entire client folder to Sierra's Web, a copy of which would be on Morgan's computer within minutes. She was checking in to a local hotel on the beach—her choice—and ultimately at his expense, as the cost would be added to his bill with Sierra's Web. He'd agreed to cover all costs of the investigation.

One of the partners from Sierra's Web would also be contacting local police, asking for access to case files, and would be putting in requests for all police reports from seventeen years ago, too.

Morgan had asked for the rest of the morning and afternoon to peruse the information and consult with her Sierra's Web teams, before speaking to him again.

Almost as though she'd known he'd been up all night and desperately needed some rest before heading full tilt into battle.

They'd be meeting late that afternoon, at the Carmichael Construction office, just off Main Street in Rocky Springs. She'd made it very clear she intended to dig into every aspect of his existence, including his laundry basket, if she determined the need.

And what she said she needed was nonnegotiable. He gave access or she walked.

Every mandate she'd laid down had been followed by a long pause, as though she'd expected him to put up resistance, or at least question her motives. Maybe she'd been waiting to see at which point he'd balk—giving her a clue where to start her search for evidence.

Truth was, he'd give her complete access to every thought he'd ever had, every memory, and the gunk from every drain he'd ever had access to. If it could help her figure out what seventeen years hadn't revealed to him, his high-paid attorneys or the highly qualified law enforcement personnel who'd worked Madison Davis's murder case, he'd give her everything.

He had nothing to hide.

Except perhaps the dirty underwear in his laundry basket. Leaving the clothes he took off in a pile at the top of the basket—she could analyze the hell out of them and he hoped the Sierra's Web forensics team did just that—he cleaned the skivvies out of the basket. He put the handful of items in the washer, and started the small load.

Call him weird, paranoid or just plain comical—he didn't want Morgan Davis thumbing through his various shades and designs of dirty gray and blue briefs.

Let her see them in his drawer, fresh from the dryer, on top of the pile of the others he'd tossed there after laundering them. She'd find them if she did as she'd said she was going to do and went through every drawer, cupboard and hiding place in his space.

He'd been through that particular humiliation before. Having his entire bunk area and trunk searched at camp. And then his bedroom at home. Followed by the rest of the house when nothing turned up in his private places.

Nothing turning up to incriminate him was a great thing. He fully understood that. But trying to prove something with nothing—that was not so good.

Showering with the washer going hadn't been his best decision, so Blade's rinse-off was quick, and then he tidied up his house a bit while he waited to get the clothes in the dryer before he could drop into his chair for a nap. It wasn't like the two-thousand-square-foot ranch home on the opposite end of the beach from town was a mess. But he ran his hands over the countertops, just to make certain there wasn't something sticky there.

And ran the vacuum and a quick wet mop over the floors where appropriate for the same reason.

The dust…it was just going to have to do its best to look good. No way he was taking up that challenge. His once-a-month house cleaning service wouldn't know what to do if he didn't leave the mysterious, floating lint bunnies for them.

Underwear in the dryer, he'd just pushed back in his recliner when his phone buzzed a text. Thinking that it was a foreman from one of his many jobs—or the client/owner of the property that was now a crime scene—he picked his phone up off the table beside him.

And froze as he read.

Not enough that you killed one sister, you're going to involve the other one in your schemes, too?

He hadn't recognized the number. Shouldn't have opened the text.

And didn't know who to call.

Was he wrong to have hired Morgan?

Should he quickly fire her and make certain that nothing about his life touched hers, again?

No. His mind gave him the immediate answer. No, because, just as he'd told her, she'd come to town on a few minutes' notice as soon as she'd heard that there was suspicious activity that could involve her sister's cold case. She'd be there whether he'd hired Sierra's Web or not.

For all he knew, she'd sent the text from some other phone, just to test him. It wasn't like she trusted him, any more than he trusted her to have his back.

Their path wasn't one of soulmates, or even friends. They were two people looking for the same answer. And the need for that absolute truth was what bound them.

Period.

Once he'd reasoned his way out of the hell of dread, Blade forwarded the entire message, including the sender details, to Morgan.

Following her mandate to keep her fully in his loop. He'd do it as long as it served his quest to find a killer.

He'd once thought he'd be spending his whole life telling Morgan all his secrets.

Funny how promises made forever could be so quickly broken.

With the opportunity of her lifetime falling into her lap, Morgan needed her stuff. The laptop computer designated to strictly digital information pertaining to Madison's case. Copies of all reports, lists, investigations she could get her hands on. Case photos. Search links, websites on topics from evidence hiding in dirt, to teenage hormonal behavior. Camp attendee lists. Snapshots of their lives since. And, of course, Blade Carmichael's life history, as far as she could get without a warrant. Then there were her physical case files. A lot of them were copies of hard copies of the digital information.

There was also the scrapbook of photos of her and Madison growing up. It kept her going when she started to lose hope. And the box she still kept that held the mementos of Blade Carmichael from that summer. Not for nostalgia's sake—God no. She needed them to help her cognitive skills pertaining to the case. Reminding her of things he'd said, places on campgrounds they'd visited together...small details that could point to solving the murder when put together with a new piece of evidence.

She had no idea why she'd saved the box at sixteen. Hadn't realized she had, until she'd moved out of her parents' home after college and found the small box in a bigger one filled with her things. And with all her newfound criminal investigation knowledge simmering in her brain, she'd figured she'd possibly found a gold mine.

Morgan was halfway to Detroit when her phone buzzed a text and her automated system read it aloud for her. Signaling an abrupt exit, she took the ramp just ahead of her, and pulled to a stop in the gas station at the end of it. Read the text. And then, sending it to the Sierra's Web team, she called Hudson Warner, the IT expert partner, and asked him to ping towers, as well as the number. She needed to know if there was imminent danger to herself, to Blade or to anyone else.

While she waited to hear from the Sierra's Web home office in Phoenix, she texted Blade, telling him the team was on the text and asking him not to respond. To which he replied with a thumbs-up emoji.

And she had to wonder...had he texted himself? Burner phones were a dime a dozen. Could be purchased at most grocery stores and a lot of gas stations. It wouldn't have been difficult for him to grab one on the way home from breakfast. To further suck her in.

Or prove to her that he was going to keep her in the loop.

He was likely playing her, she reminded herself. Making her pay for turning her back on him the morning after the murder. Granted, she'd been harsh. But she'd been sixteen and had just been told her identical twin had been brutally murdered. And that Blade was suspected of the murder.

They'd questioned her about her relationship with him. Had asked her to try to remember everything he'd said to her the night before...

The inquisition had happened before her parents had arrived. She'd been terrified. And so consumed by grief she'd been unable to process most of what was coming at her.

They'd shown her the cross she'd given Blade the day before, the one she'd made on a whim, showing younger kids what they might do during the craft hour she'd been monitoring. She hadn't known until later that it had been found on her sister's body. But she'd known that the cross had been of huge significance in the midst of the horror of that morning.

Her car's audio system blared with a ringtone. Glen's number popped up on the dash screen.

"Burner phone. From a tower just south of Rocky Springs." The man delivered the news she'd expected, and, thanking him, Morgan got back on the road.

Noting that a tan car that she'd seen behind her for a while before she'd left the freeway was back, a minute or two after she'd reentered traffic.

She hadn't seen anyone get off at the exit. There most definitely hadn't been a tan car at the gas station.

Shaking off the sense of doom, Morgan took a deep breath, and with it, took control of her mind, too.

In her condo, she made quick work of gathering up her things. Some extra burner phones, her main laptop. And, of course, clothes and toiletries. She could buy new, charge them to the case, but why?

She wasn't out to hurt Blade Carmichael. She was out to prove that he killed her twin sister, and then to make certain that he spent the rest of his life in prison.

If she could prove he'd killed Shane, she'd have a great start.

Searching Carmichael Construction's client list would be first on Morgan's to-do list once she made it back to her hotel.

She'd been given several hours between breakfast and meeting up with Blade again, but four of them were being spent driving back and forth to Detroit. She wasn't going to be able to have as much prep work done as she'd have liked. But she knew the case.

Shane was suddenly dead at Blade's feet after seventeen years without new evidence pointing to the murder suspect as a killer. Shane had also been at camp with them, and at the party the night Maddie died. And Blade had specifically pointed the finger at Shane when Blade had been questioned by the police. She had the official report.

Had looked at it again, just before she'd torn out of her condo that morning.

There had to be more between the two men than either of them had ever let on. Shane knowing something from the past...a constant threat to Blade, with Blade having something to hold over Shane, too, she guessed, as nothing else made sense.

An illicit affair at camp that had some criminal or life-changing implications? Something worse?

Considering the young man she'd known, the suspicion was plausible. Shane's egotistical way with the girls at camp, the way he'd left broken hearts and laughed about them, could easily point to the guy having pushed other boundaries too far. And been caught by senior counselor Blade, who'd made it his business to watch over him.

If Shane had told Blade that he didn't care if his secret was told, or had come clean to his wife or police or whoever he hadn't wanted knowing whatever Blade had on him, then the next logical step would have been for Shane to blackmail Blade with the murder information. Or, more likely, go to the police.

That would mean Blade would have to kill Shane to shut him up.

It all made sense. Good, investigative sense, as far as theories went. A starting place for digging deeper.

Energized, with adrenaline flowing more freely than it had in years, Morgan drove the miles back to Rocky Springs with an eagerness to get to work.

She couldn't stop watching her back, though. That was

something else that had become an integral part of her that long-ago summer. The police had questioned her extensively, and she'd figured out that they'd needed to know if someone had perhaps murdered her identical twin sister by accident. Maybe their target was really Morgan.

Unless the murder was solved, that question would always be in the back of her mind. She'd never spoken the possibility aloud. Never even told her parents. Or heard them speak of it.

But there it was, lurking, as she checked her rearview mirror and noticed a camel-colored sedan, nondescript, like a dozen others on the highway with them, a few vehicles behind her. Again.

The entire way to Detroit, she'd had the feeling that someone was following her.

Like the car that morning.

And now, the same tan car?

It made no sense. Her rational brain shook off the sense of doom. Even if someone *was* following her, the idea that there'd be two different someones, or that a person would take the trouble to change vehicles during the task…it didn't point to sound thought processes.

What did kind of gel, though, was the idea that seeing Blade again had just slammed a part of her back into the past—which meant residual paranoia could resurface. She needed to stay on top of that fear, beat it before it got her.

Her years of criminal study, physical workouts, target shooting and working for the FBI had helped her overcome it in the past.

It wasn't far-fetched to think that small portions of that fear still lurked inside her. Enough to jump forward given the right circumstances.

Her job was to make certain she didn't give it a playing field.

And still, she watched. Noted that as she turned from one highway to another the same tan car, or one identical to it, with the exact same hood ornament, followed her off the exit. And was over one lane and four vehicles behind her again.

Pulling out her phone, she opened the camera. Needing to get a photo of the car just for her own peace of mind. She'd look it up later to reassure herself that her instincts had been in overdrive in the moment. Because another person related to her sister's murder had just been killed.

She couldn't make out the license plate. Even when she slowed, the car didn't catch up to her. Which only fed those little mean spears of paranoia.

With her phone to her ear, as though she was making a call, she flipped it out flat a couple of times, got what shots she could. And spent the next few miles attempting to put the matter to rest in her mind.

She was somewhat successful, until she turned off at Rocky Springs. The car didn't follow her. But driving through town, she was certain she saw the black car again.

A team being paid to make note of all her comings and goings? Taking money in exchange for keeping her in sight at all times?

Blade Carmichael was a rich man. He'd had an inheritance from grandparents. And had built a solid, very successful construction company from the ground up. He'd never married. Had no kids.

A guy like that could afford half a dozen teams of people willing to follow a single woman around her life. Reporting back everywhere she went.

In case she stumbled onto something he didn't want her to find? A burial ground of evidence?

Or talked to someone he didn't want her meeting with?

At the moment, it was the most likely explanation. Why would anyone else care where she went, or who she talked to?

Unless, maybe someone she'd helped put away who'd recently been released from jail?

She considered the thought's validity for all of two seconds before mentally adding a task to her Sierra's Web tech expert's to-do list. She would need a search of all her cases and cross-referenced with people recently released from prison.

She'd been planning to send the request upon completion of her first day's work in her hotel room, before going to meet Blade.

A request that flew out of her mind as her phone rang, just as she pulled into her hotel parking lot. It was Glen Rivers Thomas, the Sierra's Web partner who'd hired her.

"Rocky Springs police has agreed to allow us official access to the case," the man reported as soon as she'd answered. Glen was the strong silent type if ever she'd met one. "And we've got our first head-scratcher," the man continued without allowing her time to express her relief. Or gratitude. "Cause of death," Glen said. "Shane Wilmington was shot, but his official cause of death is a broken neck."

Her gasp came out of nowhere, filled her car. Thankful that she'd already parked, Morgan said, "Someone broke his neck, then shot him?"

"You'd think, but no. Shane was shot first, but it was a through and through…"

Damn. No bullet. Blade Carmichael was the luckiest son of…

"He died from some kind of heavy pressure against his neck. Someone standing on it, maybe. Or applying a whole lot of weight to something pressed against it."

"Rage," she said, uttering the first thing that came to mind.

While the thud of her own lead weight hit her gut. She'd figured Shane's death had been the result of a truce gone bad. A seventeen-year secret about to be exposed.

Something like that didn't happen humanely.

It came from a potful, years full, even, of panic-induced rage.

She might not have the bullet to tie Blade's gun to the murder, but her suspicions about him had just amped up off the scale.

And why in the hell was she shaking, feeling any disappointment at all, while bursting with the first taste of victory she'd had in years?

Chapter 5

Blade was seated behind his desk, his own set of case files—and private investigations conducted on his behalf over the years—spread before him, as Morgan walked in late that afternoon. The company receptionist out front had been told to send her back as soon as she arrived. And the young man, Duane, a college student, had buzzed Blade to let him know she was on her way down the hall.

He'd been pacing when Duane's communication had come through, and stood from his armed leather desk chair as she rapped lightly, and let herself in. The king welcoming a business associate to his lair. Or so he needed her to think. It was immature, he knew.

He had no reason to impress Morgan Davis with his success. She was the woman who'd once professed she was his soulmate and within hours had had no belief in him at all.

More accurately, maybe, he was reminding himself that he was no longer that young man whose entire life had irrevocably tumbled in the space of a blink. He'd closed his eyes to sleep, in love and with his future stretching gloriously before him and had been awoken by uniformed men with guns pointed at him, while another slapped handcuffs on his wrists.

That moment had shaped every single one that had come after.

"You've already got all the official reports." He started right in, standing there with his large desk covered in files organized in the order in which he planned to deliver them to her. Picking up the first stack, he handed them over. "These are private investigations I've had done quietly over the years. Unfortunately, none of them turned up anything I could take to the police."

Brow raised, Morgan gave his face a quick glance, and then she reached for the files, her focus clearly on them.

He gave her kudos for that.

And wasn't surprised when she sat down, seemingly immersed, judging by the long pauses for reading and page turning, in the file he'd purposely placed on top.

His seventeen-year dossier of Shane Wilmington. Starting with everything he'd collected over the internet during all that time, followed by private investigator reports.

She didn't comment. Didn't even look up. Eventually, he sat. Watching her.

Assessing.

Not only her reaction to the information in front of her, but her entire demeanor. Straight shoulders, tight chin. Defensive posture.

For a split second, as a shard of remembered fear shot through him, he second-guessed his decision to hire her firm. But he quickly shut down the unwanted drama. It was a skill he'd learned far too young. Trouble had a way of finding him. There was no point in borrowing more.

The antidote to that worry was positive action. Movements, thoughts that steered him away from the darkness, and into the light. Doing everything he could, no matter how long it took, to prove his innocence. Rather than dwell on the fallout from living under a cloud of false accusation.

A new cloud.

Fear shot stronger that time.

And, with his elbows on the arms of his chair, he steepled his fingers, concentrating on the woman seated on the other side of his desk, poring over information.

Looking for that one elusive little piece that could hang Blade, probably. Except that he knew for a fact it wasn't there.

He had not killed Madison Davis.

That was his positive reinforcement. No one would ever find definitive evidence to press charges against him because he hadn't done it.

There'd been no DNA samples taken from the body. Maddie had died a virgin. And nothing conclusive, in terms of fingerprint evidence, taken from her clothes or skin.

Shane Wilmington had been seen making out with her, behind a cluster of trees, at the party. Blade had been the one to break them up, and to warn Shane that he had to leave immediately.

He'd suggested Maddie do the same, but she'd been waiting on a couple of the other female counselors. Girls she'd walked over with. He'd tried to convince all three of them to vacate the area, to allow him to walk them back, but when one of the guys pulled out an outdoor camping projector and a movie, he'd known he'd been fighting a losing cause.

The movie, a popular teen horror flick he'd seen and found…boring…hadn't drawn him nearly as much as his bunk and thoughts of his newly established exclusive status with Morgan Davis. The only reason he'd attended the party at all was to keep an eye on Shane. And with the other counselor back in the boy's camp, with a firm warning that

Blade was going to report him if Shane got anywhere near Madison Davis after hours again that summer—Blade had turned in.

"This dossier on Shane…" Morgan's voice yanked Blade out of the darkness he'd been attempting to avoid. "Who else knows you have it?"

He shrugged. "My lawyer knows I've kept tabs over the years. The PIs I've hired know about their involvement. There's never been anything turned up to report…" He repeated what he'd said earlier.

Morgan glanced up at him, frowning. Studied him for a few seconds and said, "Your lawyer, was he at the scene earlier this morning?"

Lower lip pursed, Blade shook his head. Shrugged, and said, "I had nothing to hide. I was in a ditch when a body dropped over the edge at my feet. I dialed 911 immediately. And stayed put."

She nodded, still watching him. "Might have been good to have him there, just the same."

He disagreed. Calling his lawyer would have made him look guilty. "There was nothing I could say to incriminate myself," he explained, telling her the truth that he lived by. He never even drove over the speed limit.

"You do realize that this…obsession…you've had with Shane all these years…looks bad for you, in light of what happened last night."

Her use of the word *obsession*, the pause…a deliberate move to disarm him? Or had she had difficulty getting the word out? The stone face she showed him gave nothing away.

There was no opportunity at all to read her as he'd been able to do in the past.

He looked her straight in the eye. Steel to steel. "I did

not kill your sister," he said, conviction in every word. "Shane is the only other viable suspect. I don't want to go to my grave a suspect. So I keep my intentions an active part of my life."

He was not obsessed. He was determined. There was a huge difference. "I make trimonthly checks of his social media. And hire a detective once a year," he told her. "And part of that is a conscience thing, so I can sleep at night."

That caught her attention. She turned her head slightly but was still focused on him. "Explain that."

"If the man murdered your sister at sixteen, you think he stopped there? That he'd never lose his temper, or raise a fist to someone, again?"

As she held up the opened file with both hands, Morgan's immediate response was, "It would appear that he's lived a stellar life."

He got that. A privileged, much-loved guy who took deliberate actions to ensure that his reputation shone bright enough that people didn't see a double life, lived in darkness for a decade and a half.

He nodded toward the file she'd laid back on top of the others on her lap. "You see anything in there that would lead to the man ending up dead in my pit?"

She nodded, the movement seeming, maybe, like a sense of concession.

Something got Shane Wilmington killed. And Blade knew for an absolute fact that he didn't murder the man.

"He wasn't just killed." Morgan's words got Blade's complete attention. "He was shot, but the cause of death was a neck broken by deliberate pressure. Like a shoe on his neck." Her gaze couldn't have been more pointed. She was looking for any sign he might give her to indicate some prior knowledge of the fact. Or some satisfaction taken from reliving it.

Knowing anything, and everything, he did, could and would be construed to fit preconceived notions, Blade remained still. Schooling his thoughts, his features, as he'd learned to do his last year of high school.

"Overkill," he finally said, when it became clear that she wasn't moving on without some kind of response.

"You know anyone who had any reason to be that angry with him?" Morgan asked, still pinning him as though her gaze was a microscope with a camera chip embedded inside.

"Besides me, you mean?" he shot right back, without a blink. "If you were to consider believing that I'm not guilty of Madison's murder, then it's conceivable that I'd feel a good bit of rage toward whoever did do it and framed me." He didn't sleep at night by pretending things weren't there. He slept by acknowledging every aspect of everything that happened, so he'd be prepared if and when someone came at him with bogus theories.

He might not be able to exonerate himself yet, but he could do everything in his power to ensure that he wasn't knocked completely off his axis a second time.

"Of course, if you're going with that theory, then we'll at least be on the same page in terms of finding someone who is not me who killed your sister." The words weren't kind. He didn't hesitate at all, or glance away, even for a second, as he uttered them.

"Sierra's Web was given access to Shane's financials," she said then, surprising him. Had he just won a round? Or was she just done with the conversation?

When his brain processed the ramification of what she'd just given him, he sat forward. "And?" A man's financial life revealed everything. And it had been the one aspect of Shane Wilmington's business that he'd never been able to access.

Morgan's headshake depleted his surge of energy. "There's nothing anywhere in his life, not his accounts, his phone records or tax filings that show any discrepancies, or even hints at possible secrets lurking anywhere in the underbelly."

Had that been a note of disappointment he'd heard in her voice?

"By all accounts, building a profile from what we have—and your information really just confirms it—my sister's death was a life-changing experience for Shane. His entire life, his relationships, his family life, even going back to his college days, he was different from the second he returned home from camp. He started attending church regularly. Became studious, where before he was lucky to skate by as an average student. He even started up an antibullying program his last year in high school, and it's grown to multistate proportions. And every year, he traveled to meet with new student bodies around the country, talking about why bullying hurts everyone."

By the time Morgan had finished, Blade felt as though she'd been cramming her thoughts down his throat. Not from her delivery. There'd been nothing but professionalism in her tone and expression. He couldn't really say what was hitting him so wrong.

Until…it occurred to him. The woman was sitting there singing the praises of the only real suspect in her sister's murder—and still pointing her accusatory finger straight at Blade's heart.

Who'd have thought her lack of belief in him, her lack of support, could still rankle so much? Even with seventeen years' distance between them.

Those years, they'd changed all of them. Him included. Meeting her gaze calmly, Blade offered, "Getting away with murder could do that to a guy. Scare him straight. If it was an accidental thing. He didn't mean to do it. He's not psychopathic…"

He let his words trail away, as his thoughts took off silently, and spun in another direction.

If Shane *had* killed Madison, then it did stand to reason that to someone who loved Madison dearly, who'd lost even more than Blade had that night in the woods, there could be a rage-filled need to see Shane pay.

It was human nature to need to find justice. Especially after an act had taken away life as you knew it.

Shane and Blade—victims of justice? The one killed, the other framed for murder. A second time.

Morgan still couldn't seem to let go of Blade's culpability in whatever happened that night. Her dislike of him had emanated off her like hot coals at the crime scene that morning.

Because he'd attended a party to watch over Shane. To protect Madison and the other girls from the egotistical womanizer.

Based on all research and investigations, no one had any reason to kill Shane Wilmington.

Except Morgan Davis, if she'd figured out Shane had murdered her twin.

Morgan's mind flew across the criminal landscape in front of her. Her sister's murder. Shane Wilmington being caught making out with her that night.

Maddie's obsession with Shane.

Maddie's class ring, which she'd been going to give to Shane, being found in Blade's pocket the next morning.

Neither Shane nor Blade having alibis for the time of the murder—within an hour after the unsanctioned party broke up.

The little ribbon cross Morgan had made and given to Blade before curfew that night—a sign of their exclusivity commitment—clutched in Maddie's hand when she was found early that next morning.

And seventeen years later, Shane Wilmington found dead at Blade's feet.

She stared at the man, sitting behind his impressive desk in a business he'd grown from the ground up—and clearly still worked with his own two hands, alongside the more than a hundred people he employed.

If Shane had been blackmailing him, threatening to expose some proof that would put Blade away for Maddie's murder, then why would Blade have killed the man on his own job site? Or dumped him there, and then called the cops?

With all his equipment, and job sites, the man could have easily dug a hole deep enough to make Shane disappear forever.

Unless he somehow thought he could point to the man for Maddie's murder without Shane having a chance to rebut, hoping to clear suspicion from himself...

She gave her head a mental shake. No way he'd do that by planting Shane's body at his own feet, making it appear as though he'd just killed the man. He would at least make it look like someone else had been at the job site. Or plant some proof of Maddie's murder on the body.

Blade had a good life. Had built a new world for himself, in a lovely town, living in Michigan, on the beach, just as he'd always wanted. Why would he mess that up by bringing up the past that haunted him?

As much as her mind needed to believe that he was her sister's killer—needed to believe that she knew who'd killed her sister and her only quest was the proof to put him away—Morgan's gut wasn't completely buying into the story.

Because her mind couldn't seem to back it up with irrefutable fact. Not even in theory.

Blade killing Shane—okay, if he'd killed Maddie, that could be pretty easily argued. The blackmail theory was a solid one.

But implicating himself in the murder?

Unless he'd done so just to throw everyone off track.

Calling the police...hiring her as soon as she'd shown up in town...

He'd walked away from one murder without charges being filed.

Was that his signature? Committing crimes and insinuating himself so fully into the scene from the very beginning, while knowing that investigators would never find proof to convict him?

If she could just outsmart him...find that one little detail he'd missed...something he'd failed to cover up. A signature he was unaware of that he'd repeated at both crimes.

She had to watch his seventeen-year-old interviews with police again. Compare them to that morning's reports.

All she needed was one small, elusive thing to wrap everything up nice and clean and move on. Try to find a good life for herself. One that included her career, of course, but maybe every waking hour didn't need to be spent investigating crime.

She'd been staring Blade down. He'd been staring right back. Getting them nowhere.

"If not you, then who?" She blurted the question that

she'd been trying to push away for hours. Aside from her, Blade Carmichael had spent more time than anyone else investigating her sister's murder. And paying for it, too. She had to know what conclusions he'd drawn. What he told himself that let him sleep at night.

For curiosity's sake if nothing else.

The tension in his face fell away, leaving a bleakness there that shocked her. The expression lasted only a second or two. She could easily pretend she hadn't seen it.

Except that Morgan didn't pretend anything anymore.

Truth and provable facts, and the search for them, were the only things she allowed to occupy space and time in her mind.

Blade hadn't answered. She raised her brows.

"Shane," he said then, meeting her gaze full-on. And then shrugged again. "He's the only person who makes any sense at all."

Other than Blade, of course. But she agreed with him, that if it wasn't him, Shane had to be it. Maddie wouldn't have gone into the woods with anyone else.

And the camp was a secure facility. Surrounded by walls that Maddie had once told their parents resembled a prison. Security cameras had been at every entrance, and triple-checked. After becoming an agent, Morgan had spent hours viewing every minute of every one of those tapes to no avail. Not a single unauthorized vehicle had entered or exited that night, and the approved vehicles that had, had been through forensics, with the drivers all having alibis. No one had walked in. Every camper, every faculty member and staff person had been checked out.

"So why, seventeen years later, is someone getting rid of him and trying to frame you for the murder? Why would someone need to take out both of you?"

His gaze sharpened to points, and then softened. His jaw clenched. A vein in his neck popped out.

"What?" she asked him, heart pounding.

"You said last night's murder was a crime of passion."

"Of rage, yes," she agreed.

"I can only think of one person who'd have reason to carry that much anger inside, who'd maybe given up on the system doing its job. Seventeen years have passed, and the case is no closer to being solved...the culprits are no closer to being brought to justice."

The way he was looking at her...not with meanness, but a definite chill...hit her.

"Someone who's so fed up she quit her job and went into private practice."

She knew exactly what he was thinking. What he was about to say.

Lifting the pile of folders on her lap to her chest, Morgan held on to them, stood and, with one fluid movement, turned to the door.

She'd reached the opening, had turned the handle to complete her escape when, from behind her, she heard Blade's voice.

"Now you know how it feels."

Chapter 6

Morgan was still shaking, inside and out, when she reached her car.

Blade's words reverberated around her as she drove to the hotel, and they were still with her as she let herself into her second-floor beach-view room.

She'd left the curtains open, could see the great Lake Michigan flowing in waves toward the sand and away again.

Michigan's waters had always had the power to soothe her. It was something she and Blade had had in common—communion with their state's natural gifts. A desire to live in Michigan for the rest of their lives.

Now you know how it feels.

It wasn't just that he'd said the words.

Or even that his intent could have been to get her goat.

But he'd concocted a theory in which a law enforcement official might find merit. Leaving her to suspect that he hadn't just been drawing some kind of parallel conclusion to prove a point. He'd been giving her his honest thoughts.

Blade knew she hadn't killed her sister.

But he thought she'd murdered Shane Wilmington? Was that why he'd hired Sierra's Web? To catch her in her own *web*?

Horror washed through her. Again and again.

For herself.

And slowly, as an hour passed into two and she tried to find calm in the sun setting over the water, for him.

Now you know how it feels.

In all the years since Madison's death, she'd never once considered how Blade had felt that morning, when he'd come to her, a look of disbelief and fright filling his face, and she'd screamed at him to get away from her.

She'd thought he'd been going to try to convince her to be his alibi or something. Or something. She had no idea what she'd thought. Only that he represented an end of life.

An end of innocence. Of love.

But looking back, as a mature adult, one who'd seen all the bad the world had to show her, who'd sat with many families grieving for missing or murdered loved ones, having to pour salt in their wounds with the questions that would lead her to their truths, to the justice they'd needed...

That look on Blade's face, if she was remembering it correctly...why hadn't she ever seen it in her mind's eye before?

Had she ever looked?

Allowed herself to let him in that far?

Had his sudden advent into her life, the new shocking lead in Maddie's case, opened places in her mind that had been closed since she'd been told her sister was dead?

Blade had been frightened out of his wits. Looking to her for something. Help? Comfort? Even just the belief that he couldn't have done such a thing?

Now you know how it feels.

She wanted his words to be snarky. An attack. Getting back at her.

They hadn't sounded that way.

Nor did they feel that way.

Did he really believe she could have killed Shane Wilmington?

Pacing her room, she looked to the water, to the few people left enjoying the beach so late in the day, and found... nothing but cold chills. The kind you got when you were sick.

His theory had been pretty well-thought-through. To the point of suggesting that she'd left the FBI due to a frustration with the system.

There'd been truth in that statement. A lot of it. Not geared toward Maddie's case, specifically, but in her inability to go where the wind took her on investigations due to the Bureau's red tape and policies. She'd become an investigator so that she could bring answers, some peace, and hopefully the ability to move on, to families who'd lost loved ones. Or who had loved ones who disappeared. Or were the victims of other crimes that were waiting to be solved.

She'd worked a case with Sierra's Web the previous year. Part of a baby-kidnapping ring. Some of the babies who had been stolen and sold had been shipped to Michigan. Seeing what Sierra's Web had been able to do, which the Bureau hadn't had the means to do...had been a life-changer for her.

In a good way.

And she could see how that life choice, made so recently before Shane Wilmington ended up dead at Blade Carmichael's feet, pointed to the possibility that she'd ceased being a federal agent because she'd needed freedom to get justice for herself. Vigilante style.

What she couldn't see was how to walk away from the case. She didn't know who'd murdered her sister. She thought she knew. Had very real suspicion. But she didn't *know*.

And she didn't even have a good suspicion about who'd

killed Shane Wilmington. She couldn't rule out Blade, not with her head, anyway, but she had questions.

Too many of them.

All without answers.

Plopping down to a love seat on the far wall of her room, Morgan ordered her mind to collect itself. To make a plan and execute it.

She needed to be on Blade's payroll.

And whether he suspected her of Shane's murder or not, he needed her, too.

If for no other reason than because the two of them lived under the shadow of the same nightmare. Neither of them would ever be free to live any kind of normal life until they found the answers they'd both been apparently seeking, separately, for a decade and a half.

Those files that Blade had given her that afternoon… why, if the man had committed the crime, was he still spending so much money to find the proof?

Hiring Sierra's Web that day made sense. He had a fresh murder at his doorstep, pretty much literally. But for the past seventeen years?

Why had he kept such thorough tabs on Shane Wilmington?

And then found him dead at his feet?

She could come up with logical theories for each question, separately. But not one that fit both occurrences.

Maybe Shane had been blackmailing him somehow, like she'd thought, threatening to go to the police with some kind of proof that Blade was guilty in Maddie's murder. And maybe Blade had really been bold enough to kill the man, and then make it look like he was being framed.

But why do that?

Why not just bury the guy? Make him disappear forever?

Unless he knew someone, or something, could tie him to Wilmington?

Now you know how it feels.

Dizzy with the rapidity of her mental circles, Morgan thought about ordering dinner from room service. She glanced around for the menu and was distracted by the pile of files she'd carried in with her. Stacked on the desk. Next to the box of them she'd brought from home, which was on the dresser.

She needed answers.

And, oddly enough, not just the name of a murderer. Or two.

Pulling her phone out of her pocket, she tapped the number she'd put on speed dial, as she always did when she took on a new client for Sierra's Web.

"Yeah." Blade sounded tired. Just that. Bone-deep tired.

"Have you eaten?" Not a business question. But a practical one. She had to eat if her mental acuity was going to return in full force.

"No."

"Can we meet for dinner? We can discuss theories we've come up with over the years." It was the only place that made sense to start.

Brainstorming with colleagues. Even when everyone shared a theory, there were always small differences in perspectives that shone light on small details that oftentimes led to larger truths.

"Considering the text I received after we dined in public today, I don't think that's a great idea. But I could pick up something. Bring it there."

To her small hotel room? He'd overshadow the place.

"How about I come to you?"

"I'd rather be the one out driving at night."

It was a bit late for him to get all macho on her. But his statement flew her back in time, before she'd known she was heading off. She'd been assigned campfire duty at the girls' camp, which meant she had to be the one who stayed around to make sure all flames were out, and all campers made it back to their cabins. Blade had wanted to sneak over and make sure the fire was out. He hadn't wanted her to be standing out there all alone in a clearing surrounded by woods in the dark. Which was ridiculous since the firepit was in the middle of a circle of wooded cabins and other counselors would be out doing cabin checks.

"I'm an expertly trained former FBI agent, Blade," she said, maybe more sternly than necessary. A reaction to the warmth that had momentarily entered her system. "I think I can drive around Rocky Springs at night." She finished with, "I'll be going out alone, otherwise. I need to eat."

And still hadn't landed on a room service menu.

"I'll have dinner delivered," he said then. A compromise. She got it. She wouldn't be out and about making stops.

An unnecessary choice that would cost him a delivery charge. But when he asked her for her preference, she gave it to him. A dinner-sized chef salad with French bread.

And left him to figure out where and how to make that happen.

Blade knew he'd hear from Morgan again. He was the way to her justice. Just as she remained his absolute best shot of clearing his name. He hadn't expected a dinner invitation.

And couldn't find a restaurant in Rocky Springs that served both chef salads and French bread. He ordered the salad, along with his glazed pork loin and vegetables, and then, with only minutes until Morgan would be arriving, he made a quick trip to the grocery around the corner and got the bread. Had to buy a whole loaf. So be it. He wasn't going to give her reason to find fault with him.

A small part of him, remnants from the past, didn't want to disappoint her. Now that he knew that excess baggage was there, he'd get rid of it. He'd promised himself that the past was not going to pollute his future.

And was closer than ever to ensuring that he kept that promise. As unwelcome as Shane Wilmington's dead body had been in his pit the night before, it had brought a whole lot of attention to his case. Expert attention.

More eyes looking for the truth...

He saw Morgan was parked at the light, waiting to turn into his neighborhood. He was coming up the street she'd turn on—the access to his road—from the opposite direction. They'd be turning on his street together. The light change would determine who followed whom.

He was sending strong thoughts for his light to stay green—keeping her stopped, waiting to turn—long enough for him to beat her to his place. Suddenly, he lost all train of thought.

The black sedan a few vehicles behind her and in the straight lane...expensive-looking, tinted windows...he'd seen it before. That morning, parked at the crime scene. The scratch in the tinting on the passenger side had caught his attention. Because he'd been looking for something trivial to concentrate on while he fought the panic that had been threatening his ability to think clearly. He'd succeeded. In seconds. And later, when he looked for the car again, it had been gone.

Turning onto his street while Morgan's light remained red, he took note of his victory, while trying not to over-think the situation.

Only authorized cars had been allowed on the lot. That black car, in his neighborhood…so they were watching him. He'd expect no less.

But the long light allowed him to get his truck into his garage and have the automatic door down before Morgan pulled onto his drive. He met her at the front door after she rang the bell. Ready to take her on.

Until she looked up at him with worry in her gaze, passing him to enter the impressive foyer with shelves built into the wall, one of the home's extra touches that he'd built himself. "Someone's following me."

Her greeting locked up his gut again. "Black sedan?" he asked. He knew better than to look on the bright side of anything he noticed out of the ordinary. You only got kicked in the balls when you expected the best.

She turned, not seeming to notice his house at all, as she held on to the top of the large satchel hanging from her shoulder with both hands. Almost as though she was hugging it, or herself. "And a tan one. I've been telling myself I'm overreacting, but…" She stopped, beige dress pants and white cotton blouse giving her an air of professionalism as her eyes pinned him in a most decidedly nonfriendly way. "How did you know it was black?"

Door locked and bolted behind her, he slid his hands in his pockets, fine to meet right there where he could show her the way out quickly, and said, "Because I saw it on Bellair, a few cars behind you when you were stopped at the light." And then noted her body language was more than mistrustful. He computed the words she'd actually said. "What do *you* mean 'and a tan one'?"

He walked as he spoke, needing to get them to the large dining room table, in what would have been a formal dining room. From day one, he'd pegged the square footage as his case workspace—complete with a wall of corkboard filled with pretty much every photo, every picture he'd ever had of the original crime scene, and the people who'd been at camp that godawful night.

It was also, unusually, a room with no windows. He'd removed them from the floor plan.

"Wow." Morgan stopped at the opened, double-doored entrance, her gaze moving around the room.

"It's the ten-foot ceilings," Blade spewed forth inanely. The entire first floor had them. As she, an expert detective, would have already noted.

Still holding her satchel, Morgan moved slowly around the room. Seeming to study every single poke he'd ever made in the walls. Saying nothing.

He left her to her ruminations, feeling exposed. And willing to take on the discomfort, too. Anything to get the answers he needed.

When she made it back to where she'd started, she turned to the table, moved toward the empty space he'd cleared for her on one end. Set her satchel there. "This is impressive," she told him, including a sweep of the room in her glance.

"It's desperation," he corrected. "Now, back to that tan car?" He didn't remember one at the crime scene.

And grew more and more uptight as she told him about the black car following her to the restaurant that morning, the tan car behind her all the way to Detroit and back.

"I can't be sure it was the same car," she finished. "It was the same model. Same color. Considering that Detroit is the automakers' hometown..."

She met his gaze, and he held on. "You know it's the same car," he said.

She shrugged.

"Had you seen either car before today?"

"No."

Standing upright, Blade made a decision. "You're fired." There was no doubt in his tone. His posture, every sense he had, was filled with conviction.

"What?" She didn't quite yell. The one word came out more like a squeak. Her gaze threw bullets at him.

He wasn't the least deterred. "No way, Morgan. First, I get that text about your dead sister, and now you're being followed? No. You need to leave. Immediately. Don't come back and don't call me. Period. I will not have your blood..." He felt his face drain as adrenaline left his system.

He already had her blood on his hands. Because he carried Maddie's with him every single second of every single day. Not because he'd killed her, but because he'd left her at that party. And hadn't checked to make certain Shane hadn't gone back. Neither of them had been his direct responsibility but reporting the party had been.

As soon as he'd found out about it. And he hadn't done it.

"Here's what I know about threats." Leaving her satchel on the table, Morgan took a couple of steps closer to him. "They're made by people who are afraid of losing control of a situation. If you give in to them, you feed that sense of control, which emboldens them, and they become more dangerous."

"Fine, I'll take that chance. Face the danger. But not with you."

"Then, okay, I'm fired. And we'll work the case separately." She walked back to her satchel.

No. "Wait."

She shook her head. "I've been working to solve my sister's murder for seventeen years, Blade. If you think you have the power to stop me, you're just..."

What? He was what? He wanted to know. And didn't need to.

"...just wrong," she finally finished.

She was right. He hadn't brought her into the situation. Or even called her to town. She'd go forth with or without him. "Someone's playing with me," he said, feeling a smidgen of his usual calm settling over him. "Baiting me."

"Someone who knows that we once hung out together," she added, her brows creased, as though she was studying a difficult puzzle. "They had to know that making a threat to my life would hit you where it hurts."

Maybe. A part of him liked that they were talking about what they'd once said they meant to each other. Making it a thing. As though it had really existed outside of their hormonal teenage existence. Setting it apart as real enough to still call to him, be meaningful enough to serve as a threat, all those years later.

Not because he saw her current point, but because she'd seen it.

"It doesn't have to be someone from the past," he said slowly, watching her. "It just has to be someone who knows that I was the suspect in your sister's murder and have paid for it ever since. Someone who's warning me that the past might repeat itself in the present, with the other twin."

The words were cold. Harsh. Because the truth was.

That was the world in which he lived. The world in which she was currently standing.

But he got her point.

"And whether we work together or separately isn't going to make a difference, in terms of the threat, is it?"

He posed the thought as a question, but he didn't need to see Morgan's headshake to know the answer.

Chapter 7

She'd made a mistake, agreeing to meet in Blade's home. Searching it had been in the plan from the beginning, but having dinner there? Working with him?

What in the hell had she been thinking, suggesting that the phone threat that had come in had been of a personal nature, based on their youthful romance seventeen years before? She blanched at the thought of having said such a thing.

Was beyond embarrassed that her client had had to point out the more likely scenario to her.

He'd been publicly held accountable for Maddie's death. Anyone who knew about the case, had read about the case, could conclude that he wouldn't want the other twin to show up dead. Most particularly not right after the deceased twin's boyfriend had been found murdered at his feet.

"We can't get you out of danger." Blade spoke as though they were no more than professional associates. "But we need to take precautions to minimize your exposure to life-threatening situations."

The statement, while sweet, made her smile. In a professional-only way. "Again, ex–FBI agent here," she said. "I've spent the past fifteen years making enemies of the worst kind. And I'm trained to protect myself."

"So you've reported the tan car? And the black one?" he asked, and any response Morgan might have made froze on her tongue.

She'd given the information to him first...had entrusted it to him before taking it anywhere else... What did that mean?

And even if it meant nothing, what would it mean to him?

She couldn't have him drawing any false impressions about why he was there. Or in any way insinuate that the things she'd thought she'd felt for him in the past were real.

"No. I haven't been able to get license plates. Which is what really bothered me the most. It's like whoever is doing this, if there really is someone, is good enough at it to know how to position himself so that I can't ever get a look at the plate." She came up with the valid answer in time to save face.

Blade sprang into action as soon as she'd finished the words. Taking a step toward her. She backed up, heart pounding, feeling apprehension, not fear, until he turned and grabbed a television control off the table. Clicked it toward a large screen hung on the far wall of the room.

"That black car was on the lot after it had been cordoned off as a crime scene," he was saying as he clicked and scrolled.

She stared at him. Somewhat aghast at his sudden intensity. Not fearful, but not sure about him, either.

"There's a long thin scrape in the tint on the front passenger window," he added.

She continued to stare. Either the man had lost all cognitive ability, or he was about to impress her.

"When I saw the car behind you at the light, I thought it was there because of me. Watching me. I'm home, so it makes sense that they'd be keeping an eye on my neighborhood." He'd brought up security camera screens. She recognized the crime scene. Remembered that the lot was currently under the control of Carmichael Construction. Realized that the cameras she'd seen there were his. Not the landowner's.

He glanced over and said, "I was found with a dead body at my feet, with only my word to verify that I didn't put it there. When everyone started questioning me, I zoned out for a couple of seconds. Stared at the damaged tinting on the window." He didn't even pause for breath as he continued, "The evidence is circumstantial—no one can prove I didn't put it there, or, more importantly, prove that I harmed Shane Wilmington. But, just like in the past, a lot of people will be convinced that I made history repeat itself. That I found a way to commit murder a second time without being charged." His green eyes stayed focused right on her without a flinch.

Morgan, feeling the blow of the words, had to school herself not to show any reaction. Not to recoil.

He was including her in that community of opinion who believed him guilty, not only of her sister's murder, but also of Shane's. She'd spent seventeen years with the knowledge that he'd killed her twin. And wouldn't be honest with herself, or be any kind of decent detective at all, if she didn't consider that the second murder was also on him.

"I can't figure out why you'd kill Shane and stand there with his body and call the police." The words came out of their own accord. A truth that she'd have chosen to withhold at that point, had she been at the Bureau, in an interrogation room or even a conference room.

As opposed to being in the home of the man with whom she'd once thought herself forever in love.

Her past association with Blade, what she'd thought she'd felt, what she'd promised, didn't matter. Had no bearing.

So why did they keep rearing up to blindside her by throwing shadows on what should be clear?

"Why would I kill him at all, after seventeen years of getting away with murder?"

The question came quietly. Introspectively. A question Jasmine might have asked her, putting herself in the perp's mindset as they tried to figure out a case.

Blade's words drew her gaze to him, kept it there as she said, "What if he knew something that could prove that you were guilty of murder? What if for some reason he suddenly decided to confront you with it...some change that compelled him to come forward...say, a real estate deal? There would be a lot of money to be made if the right contractor would take the job and be willing to skate on certain inspections..." The words flowed as they came to her. Holding sound logic.

Believable motivation. Pieces falling together.

But for the first time in her career, Morgan didn't want to follow them to see where they'd lead.

Her words reminded Blade of ones he'd issued to her earlier that day. But somehow they didn't carry the sting they might have. He didn't dwell on the realization. "So what is my reason for calling the police with the dead body in the pit at my feet?" he parried when Morgan fell silent.

She stared at him a minute. And then, eyes opening wider, said, "To throw suspicion off you. Who'd call the police on themselves, and then not confess, right? But that doesn't really work because in your line of work you could so easily dispose of the body in a pit, pour cement for a foundation and be done with it."

For a second there, he was shocked, hearing the words come from Morgan Davis's mouth. And then he was glutted with guilt. The change in her…that a mind that had once danced with butterflies and stories of happily-ever-after would be so quick to fill blanks in dark worlds…just seemed…criminal.

"So why else might I have done it?" he asked, drawing his own mind back to the real world. The question was rhetorical. And yet…not. If he knew what she was thinking, what others would conclude, even if he couldn't get a step ahead of them, he could at least keep up.

Morgan's gaze was different. Not soft, but open. "You tell me," she said, dropping down to a seat at the table.

He sat as well. Taking a second to figure out her new tactic. Decided to take her at face value. To give her what she wanted.

So she could deliver what he needed. The truth.

"The only thing I can figure is, he showed up on-site—and would have had to climb the fence because I'd locked the gate behind him—threatened me somehow. I don't know it's him, I'm not expecting anyone, and suddenly there's a guy there. I pull my gun…he lunges toward me, I shoot. He's still coming at me, I knock him down, put my foot on his neck to keep him down…and panic and call the police…" It all fit.

And Blade, hearing his words replay in his head, felt sick. In body, heart and mind. What in the hell had he just done?

"Why would you have pulled your gun?"

"I did, actually, when I heard the noise up above. That dragging-on-the-gravel sound."

"So a guy's above you, has you trapped in a pit with all kinds of heavy equipment around that he could have used to hurt you, and instead, he stands there and lets you pull a gun and remains in your line of fire to let you shoot him?"

"He came down into the pit to confront me," Blade said, compelled by her attentive look to play along with her.

"Or, what if you weren't in the pit when he confronted you? What if things happened as you say, but aboveground? And then, when you realize what you've done, you drag him as you claim happened, dump him in the pit and then climb down and call the police?"

He shook his head. "I'd been taking photos in the pit. They're time stamped. I was definitely in the pit."

Morgan stared at him. "And he'd only been dead less than half an hour, based on liver temperature."

"Right." Didn't mean Blade hadn't killed the guy, just as he'd hypothetically described. He had photos from ten minutes prior to the body landing at his feet. He hadn't had his maps and location system on. Had no way to prove that he'd been on-site for more than half an hour.

She looked at him, oddly, as though he had something more to tell her. Something he wasn't saying. "So why did you call the police?"

"I had a dead body at my feet." He gave her the only explanation he had.

"Exactly." Morgan stood, paced around the table. He watched. Reminding himself of the one truth he'd always had. He was innocent.

When she sat back down, she did so right next to him. Facing him. Leaned forward until her gaze was only inches from his. "I'm not betting my life on this one, Blade. But if this were any other case, I'd risk my career on it."

"On what?"

"You didn't kill Shane."

He sat there, watching her, a bit confused. Looking for

her angle. Ready to meet her head-to-head as soon as he figured out her direction. And when he couldn't catch up soon enough to suit him, he asked, "How do you know that?"

"Because a man who just murdered someone, most particularly if he'd been surprised by an intruder in the dark, would be in panic mode. Locked on his own job site, down in a pit, he'd conceal evidence, at least long enough to think. And if he was someone who broke laws, who skated on inspections, or had anything to hide, he'd sure as hell at least think about hiding that body. An honest man, on the other hand, one who, for whatever reason, has lived an exemplary adult life, without even so much as a speeding ticket, would automatically dial the authorities."

He looked for the trap she might be setting. To see if he'd fall into it. Didn't see one. Didn't mean there wasn't one. She was an expert. "What about the whole plan to make myself innocent by calling in the body? A ploy to draw attention away from myself?"

Her headshake brought a frown to his brow. "A man who's in panic mode doesn't have the wherewithal to come up with such a plan in the space of time between your last photo and your call to the police. And all of that aside, there was no blood found at the site," she said, reminding him of something he'd known, but they hadn't discussed. The wound hadn't been fatal. Someone could have shot Shane, stemmed the flow of blood, kept him alive for an hour or more, before breaking his neck and hauling him into Blade's pit.

"So I shoot him, wrap him, he's still alive, I bring him to the pit, I break his neck, and then call the police," he said, needing to see it all. What the police might see. Detectives. Anyone and everyone who were going to need to prove that he was responsible for both murders, since the two people dead had been in a relationship years ago.

"And take pictures with his body just hanging out?" She rewound footage he'd paused on the screen—the black car. How had he let himself get distracted from finding the plate?

He had to get the woman out of his house.

She'd stopped the scroll on the screen. And he saw himself, in the pit. Taking photos. No body there.

Weary, he continued to play along until the end. "I left the body up top while I took pictures and then…" His words dropped off as she scrolled again. And stopped the footage. Scrolling forward, and then back, several times.

"Do you see that?" she asked.

Now what? He watched the screen. Once…twice. Paying more attention as she waited for him to figure out which tangent she'd jumped to.

And then sat up. "There's a break in the footage," he said. "The clock shows no break, but right there, it's like…"

"The camera was somehow stopped and restarted, without the clock showing a discrepancy," Morgan said softly. "You could very well have stopped the camera yourself, to allow you to move the body over, and somehow manipulated the timing afterward, but before…there's no break in the clock from the time your men leave until you arrive. And after you arrive, where there's the break in footage, you have time stamped photos on your phone to prove you were in the pit. Not aboveground…"

Glancing over at her, meeting her gaze, Blade started forward, to pull her into his arms. Stopped just in time, but couldn't quell the emotion glazing his eyes for a second, as he heard her say, "You did not kill Shane Wilmington. And neither, by the way, did I."

With that she stood up, walked to her end of the table and started to remove files from her satchel.

Morgan had to retreat to her corner while she tamped down the flood of relief flowing through her as she allowed herself to accept that Blade hadn't murdered Maddie's boyfriend. She'd been struggling to see him responsible for it. Had needed the proof.

And had to get herself in check, too, if she was going to do her job. A job for which he was paying handsomely.

She'd wanted to take his hand as she'd watched truth dawn on him. She'd cared. Personally. And couldn't let that happen, period.

If she found proof that Blade thought she'd never find, that he'd killed her sister, she'd be in the front row in the courtroom, giving testimony as to why the man should be put away for the rest of his life with no possibility of parole.

The doorbell rang. She didn't even look up as he left to answer it. Nor did she intend to move anywhere else to eat. She'd take her salad with files, thank you.

She had to find justice for Maddie. She had no future without it.

And whether she liked what she found or not, she had to be able to see the elusive clue when it presented itself. She had to be 100 percent.

By the time he returned, placing a bag next to her and taking another to his end of the table, she had her focus back on the television screen, going through frame by frame, as she watched for the black sedan to appear on-screen.

The reason he'd turned on the cameras in the first place.

Glancing up at the screen, as though noting what she was doing, he said, "I have wine, tea, coffee or beer."

"I'd like water," she told him. Maybe to be querulous,

to put some walls between them, but also because it was what she really wanted with her dinner.

And by the time he returned with a tall glass filled with ice and water, and a full French loaf overpowering the small cutting board that the bread and a knife sat on, she had the image on the screen frozen again. Pointed toward it, rather than acknowledging that she'd been served.

"Look. I've been through the whole thing. There's no front plate, and the car backs into the parking spot at the edge of the lot, right in front of a line of trees. When it leaves—" she scrolled more "—it pulls forward just enough to back out of the lot onto the street, at an angle that precludes the cameras from catching the plate number."

"A coincidence? Piece of bad luck for us?"

Us. Just hearing the word come out of his mouth, referring to them... No.

Just. No.

"More likely we're dealing with a professional." She focused on what mattered most. Finding the answers that would end one part of a seventeen-year nightmare.

"Everyone had to have credentials to get on the lot."

"I drove in. My credentials weren't checked until I approached the scene. And...to your point, you thought law enforcement was keeping a tail on you. We don't know that they aren't."

Sitting at his end of the table, opening a container that released mouth-watering aromas, he looked over at her. "The black car followed you to the restaurant, and probably here. And the tan car, possibly following you to Detroit and back?"

She shrugged. "As you said, I show up at a crime scene, with no formal invitation, just after dawn, from across the state. The dead man happens to be the pseudo-boyfriend of my deceased sister, and the potential suspect is the man long suspected of killing my twin. I've recently walked off a prestigious job with the FBI—albeit to join an equally prestigious private firm of experts—and it's well-known that I've been investigating Madison's death privately ever since it happened. I'd almost fault the local police if they didn't keep some kind of tabs on me. If for no other reason than to make certain that when I find who did this, I don't go rogue and take justice into my own hands." Hearing her words, listening to reason, Morgan felt some of the immediate tension draining out of her. Opened her bag and pulled out the largest, loaded chef salad she'd ever seen, with meats that were clearly fresh cut, and tomatoes that shone with ripeness. "Where did you get this?" she asked him, figuring she'd visit the place again, if she ended up in town long enough.

"Ruby's," he told her. "On Main Street. I ordered the family portion."

Of course he had. Blade Carmichael had been the guy everyone went to when they needed something. At least among the counselors. He was the always-prepared guy. If he didn't have something, he'd figure out a way to make do with something else.

Which had intrigued her no end. The way he always seemed to have what they needed or come up with alternative solutions. The single most important quality that had drawn her to the younger version of the man. Even more than his steaming-hot looks.

The trait had definitely led him to impressive professional accomplishments. Just looking at the little bit she'd seen of his home, she could understand why Carmichael Construction was such a huge success.

And always-prepared guys, who could figure out ways

to get things done in various ways, would fit the profile of a man getting away with murder.

Ignoring the big loaf of bread for the moment, she took a bite of her salad. Had difficulty swallowing.

Now you know how it feels.

Her gaze moved up and out, landing in his direction without her full consent. He had an empty fork in hand. Was watching her. Frowning. But looked more bothered than angry.

Wouldn't a guilty man get angry when he couldn't convince someone of his innocence? Because that suspicion hanging out there meant he wasn't succeeding. Not well enough.

He looked away. Grabbed a napkin, dropped it—on his lap, she surmised—and took a bite.

"I'm not sure you didn't do it." As soon as she said the words, she wanted to take them back. Hoped that she'd said them softly enough he hadn't heard.

The way his gaze shot back to her put the death to that hope. "Shane, you mean?"

She shook her head. "My current theory is that you did not kill Shane. I don't believe you did," she further enhanced her response. She wasn't positive he hadn't, because she couldn't be, not without the proof.

Which left only one other option. The one that had broken them apart, and because of that, would always be between them. Separating them.

Just because she now knew how it felt, to be suspected of something she hadn't done, didn't mean he hadn't done it.

And still...

"I'm sorry that I didn't at least listen to what you had to say." She put down her fork. Wasn't the least bit hungry.

Picked up the bread, yanking an end off the loaf with her fingers. Needing to get back to work.

To have her focus only on the job. Where it served her, and others, in a positive manner.

Dwelling on the past...sitting with an ache that would never die...weakened her.

Apparently not nearly as off his game as she was hers, Blade continued to eat. Seemingly engrossed in the food, the experience. He hadn't looked up at her at all.

Morgan took small sips from her glass. Letting the cool, clear fresh liquid slide down her throat. Soothing it. Ripped a small bit from the piece of bread she held. Found a note of pleasure in the homemade taste as it rested on her tongue.

"You went to the party when you told me you weren't going to." There. That.

A pain that still had the power to undermine her determination to let it go. She sounded like a jealous high schooler, not a renowned investigator who'd put serial killers in prison. In those moments, some of the things roiling through her, she felt a little like that teenage kid.

Because he'd broken her trust. In himself, and in her own heart, too. A result that didn't live just in the past, but was a very real part of every minute of her life since.

Joining forces with Blade Carmichael had been a logical, professional choice. Clearly not a good personal one. The surge of feelings, of young doubts, of broken trust... she hadn't expected them. Didn't have a plan in place to deal with the onslaught.

Distraction, focusing on the case, her usual cure, wasn't working. Not with Blade sitting there eating in his usual constructive way. One bite at a time. Making his way through his meal to reach a clean-plate accomplishment.

Or a full-stomach one.

He had a reason for everything he did.

So why had he approached her that morning so long ago, reaching his arms out, looking as though he'd seen a ghost?

To beg for her forgiveness?

Or...

Or what? Tell her he hadn't done it? Clung to her as the only person who'd believe him? Because if he hadn't killed Maddie, his entire, well-ordered, constructive world had been crashing around him and he'd had no one who cared to hold him up. To stand in his corner. To vouch for him in any way.

Shaking her head, denying the images springing to mind, she dropped the bread. Picked up her fork.

Didn't matter what he might have said. She hadn't given him a chance to speak.

Maybe if she had, he'd have uttered whatever had been on his clearly stricken heart. He'd have let loose that elusive small clue that could solve her twin sister's murder.

Certainly, if she had, she'd have a key to dealing with the man in the present. Maybe even a smidgen of his trust, something that would lead him to let his guard down.

And maybe, if she hadn't been so filled with dreams of Blade in the past, her first and only love, she'd have noticed that Maddie hadn't been at all her usual, winding-down self when they'd met in the large girls' bathroom to brush their teeth that night. She'd have paid more attention when Maddie hadn't seemed to notice two of her campers hiding in one of the showers, sharing an extra snack, a candy bar, after the no-more-sugar hour had passed.

Maybe, when they'd told each other "Good night, sleep tight," she'd have known that Maddie was planning to sneak out of her cabin as soon as her girls were asleep, not go to bed herself.

Maybe, if she could get her head out of her ass, she could find justice for all of them and put the past behind her.

Chapter 8

Blade finished the meal he cared little about. He'd paid for it, would be hungry if he didn't consume it, and it wouldn't be good reheated.

And then he looked over at the woman he'd alternated between needing and hating during the first couple of years after his life had blown up in his face.

She was eating, but judging by the amount of food left in front of her, she'd barely touched the dinner he'd provided. To her specification. Down to the dressing.

Perhaps there was some lesson in that for him. If he wanted to bother to unravel it.

He didn't.

"I apologize for my parting shot as you left the office this afternoon." He said what had to be said. They weren't teenagers.

And her sister's death, and his having been pegged for the crime, were in no way her fault.

The rest…that was personal.

And they, in their modern-day manifestations, were not.

She'd stopped eating to look over at him.

"It was unprofessional," he said, putting the period on the topic.

He wasn't close enough to be sure about the emotion he thought might have flared in that striking blue-eyed gaze, but found himself hanging there, waiting for her response, when the pealing of her ringtone crashed into the moment.

A move clearly designed by fate, Blade determined as he left her to her conversation, taking his empty dinner container and iced tea glass into the kitchen to dispose of them.

He ended up taking the container, and the bag it came in, to the bigger trash receptacle in the garage, so he wouldn't overfill the smaller kitchen one.

So he could get out of his house, out of the confusion slithering through his world, for a second.

Morgan was still on the phone when he returned. He couldn't make out her words, but the tone of voice didn't sound good. Short. Tense.

Angry? He couldn't tell.

And figured he'd best get back into the dining room and find out. The call might not be about their joint efforts, at all. She had a life.

But it could be...

He got no farther than the double door opening to the room, had a glimpse of Morgan's tight lips as she paced, when there was a loud knock on his front door, followed by the ringing of the bell.

For some reason, a glimpse of Morgan's generous-looking uneaten salad accompanied him as he answered the summons.

Something big was going on.

Dread filled his gut, hardened it as he pulled open the door.

Saw the two Rocky Springs detectives standing there, their faces grim.

And knew better than to turn around, to seek any kind of information or understanding from the woman he heard coming up behind him. That phone call...

Had she known they were about to have visitors?

And hadn't warned him?

Did it matter?

The cops were at his home.

And once again, he was on his own.

Shaking inside, cold, but managing to find her professional distance, too, Morgan followed as Blade led the investigators, one male, one female, into a formal living room she hadn't yet seen. The furnishings, dark leather, were offset by the light-colored porcelain flooring and lighter-colored wool rug. Tasteful. Elegant.

And seemingly completely unlived in. Other than a little dust, she saw nothing that indicated any form of life took place in that room.

There wasn't even a television set.

A shame, too, as it had a lovely bay window overlooking the front of his property, which, she knew, was lined with pine trees. In the dark, the window looked out over darkness and shadows.

Darkness and shadows. Like Blade's life?

As precise as he was about all his choices, she couldn't help but wonder if the design was purposeful. The back of his property had a beach view.

Looking from the window to the man who'd obviously built his own home, she kept her mind as blank as she could. Needing to hear facts, to assess truth, to make sense of a situation escalating so far out of control she couldn't find a starting point. A place to begin investigating.

"Have a seat, Blade," James Silver, the male detective, said. Inviting a man to sit in his own home.

Blade didn't question the police presence in his home. Didn't react to being ordered around there, either. He simply sat. On the chair closest to the room's exit. Facing the window.

Standing back, also close to the door, but within view of Blade's face, Morgan itched to pull out her phone, to record the coming moments. To be able to watch them later. She had no permission to do so.

Life wasn't an instant replay.

The female detective—Kaycee Blakenship, her badge read—took a seat on the couch, the corner closest to Blade, while her partner sat down beside her. Morgan spared both of them a brief glance. Didn't recognize either from the crime scene.

James had called Blade by his first name. Meaning they knew each other?

Wasting less than twenty seconds of her attention on the detectives, she returned her full focus back to the man who was paying her to be there. He wanted her to find the truth.

He could be underestimating her ability to do so. Figuring she wouldn't get to it and would, thus, keep him out of jail. But she wasn't feeling it.

And feelings weren't truth. She couldn't trust them.

"We need to know your whereabouts this afternoon, Blade," James spoke first.

Morgan watched Blade—his face, his hands...looking for any sign body language might give her. She knew what was coming. The next minutes were critical.

"I was here," Blade said. Then, when he glanced between the three investigators who were all looking at him, said, "I left the crime scene, came home to shower and then met Ms. Davis for breakfast." He named the diner. "I was there for fifty-four minutes, left and drove straight home, parking my truck in my garage. I came in, put a load of clothes in the washer, waited for the cycle to finish, put the clothes in the dryer and took a nap. I'd been up almost twenty-eight hours…"

"You washed clothes?" Kaycee's tone wasn't unkind, but it was clearly pointed.

"I did, yes," Blade said. And for the first time, he looked down for a second. Broke himself away from the interrogation he'd been unexpectedly shoved into. Morgan's heart rate doubled. A rapid tattoo spelling horror.

"Mind telling me what you washed?"

Blade didn't have to answer any questions. Hadn't had to let the investigators into his home. He could lawyer up at any point.

In that second, Morgan wanted him to do so. Had to physically restrain herself from interrupting to tell him to do so.

He looked over at her. To get her advice? She took a step toward him, but he'd turned back to the suited detectives on his couch. "My underwear," he told them.

And Morgan stepped back.

"Your underwear." Kaycee's tone held…doubt.

"Yes."

"One pair?"

Oh God, the man had soiled himself during the night's events and this woman was going to drill him about it?

"No." Blade's chin tightened. "The week's worth that were in the laundry."

"You washed only your underwear."

"Yes."

"Mind telling us why?" James's tone was softer. More curious than antagonistic.

With a raised brow, Blade glanced straight at the man. "Because I'd just hired Morgan to investigate every aspect of my life. She'd mentioned going through my dirty laundry, and I washed the underwear." He shrugged. Threw up his hands. And sat there. As if daring any of the three of them to have a problem with his choice.

Morgan had a problem with him sharing it. Most particularly when the other two detectives' gazes turned, simultaneously, to her.

What could she say to defuse the situation? That she'd used the dirty-laundry analogy figuratively? That he was on his own? That she'd had nothing to do with Blade's activities that day?

That she could vouch for him?

Tell them to leave?

With another dead body out there?

She threw up a hand, tilted her head and kept her mouth shut.

She held no keys to the truth.

But Blade might.

Blade heard the newest development from the two detectives, each taking turns, back and forth, with their details.

While he sat in stunned disbelief.

Mark Hampton was dead.

Dr. Mark Hampton. Camp therapist, and kayak coach. One of the few personnel who worked both girls' and boys' sides of camp.

He'd been found dead, slumped over an opened drawer of his desk in his office. Poisoned.

With a ripped Carmichael Construction business card just out of reach of his outstretched hand. As though he'd been reaching for it when he'd passed out. Had been trying to let law enforcement know who'd poisoned him.

A used syringe had been in the trash, with no fingerprints. And the angle at which it had gone in the man's neck ruled out suicide. Death had been almost instantaneous.

There'd been no sign of a struggle, leading authorities to believe that the doctor had likely known whoever had killed him.

"I've never purchased, nor used, a syringe in my life," he said quietly, when the two finally stopped talking.

"A twelve-pack box of the kind used, with one missing from the package, was found in a Carmichael Construction dumpster an hour ago," James Silver advised, his tone somber. Blade knew the older man. Had built a shed for the guy with his own hands when he'd first been starting out.

"That's a little convenient, don't you think?" he asked, refusing to look in Morgan's direction. Unwilling to see those vivid blue eyes sparking with accusation again. Been there done that. And the memory of the first time, the vision he'd never been able to wipe from his mind, was enough to last a dozen lifetimes.

Put that in a syringe and shoot it.

"Sierra's Web thinks so." Morgan's voice, not tentative, but not filled with determination, either, sounded off to his right. "We've got Blade's home security camera feed on tape, as well," she added, surprising the hell out of him. Not regarding the camera feed; he'd willingly turned it over to her firm of experts. But that she sounded as though she was defending him…

"We see him arriving home this morning, as stated, and then no movement from the garage camera until he left for work late this afternoon, also as stated. I also, um, just checked the laundry as you two were speaking. Several days of dirty clothes in the basket. No underwear."

If it were possible for Blade to feel any more humiliated,

he didn't want to know about it. But wasn't going to cower. Or make any mistakes, either.

Life was exploding out of control. Two deaths in two days? Both pointing at him?

Both connected to that godawful summer camp?

Panic sluiced through him, but he tamped it down.

He knew how to play the game. Stay calm. Pay attention. Show them as little as possible and get as much information as he could. All of which would be carried straight to his dining room as soon as he was alone.

"Blade could have left this afternoon, on foot, through a window not covered on camera," Detective Blakenship was pointing out. The fact had been hanging there. Had to be said. "The cameras are his. He'd know exactly where and how to escape."

Blade continued to watch the detectives, as he'd been doing since they'd started talking. Morgan had left the room…had been going through his laundry basket…while he'd been put on notice that yet a third murder was being planted on his shoulders. The fact stung. All parts of it.

But she'd returned. To point to the possibility of his innocence.

Nice. Still, no reason to rejoice.

He was paying her firm a hefty sum. And they had a team of expert lawyers. They were doing their jobs. He couldn't let himself believe Morgan's words were anything more than that.

He'd broken her trust. She'd as much as told him so, earlier, right after apologizing for breaking his.

"Am I under arrest?" he asked, when the detectives glanced in his direction. They didn't have enough to charge him, but they had enough circumstantial evidence to hold him for a day or two.

Blakenship looked at James, who shook his head and stood. "I agree with Ms. Davis, for now," he said. "There's evidence that you're telling the truth. And while other evidence points at you, it doesn't necessarily touch you. But I have to ask you, for your own sake, please don't leave town."

He had no intention of going anywhere.

Not unless he had to, to find Madison's, Shane's and Dr. Hampton's killer.

Morgan left soon after the detectives did. Blade's suggestion, and one she felt she had to honor. He'd closed himself off.

A move she understood.

If he remained uncommunicative, she'd take herself off the job. There was no point in working with him if he wasn't going to be open with her.

But the third death—and pointing at him—it just didn't make sense that he'd done it.

He could be some kind of mentally disturbed individual who was playing them all, but she didn't think so. There were no signs at all of erratic behavior.

And no absences in his daily routine. Sierra's Web had been through his finances. His credit card usage was conservative, predictable and regular. The man hadn't taken a trip in years.

He owned a boat, docked at the marina in town. That had been news to her. Something that lightened her load for a second as she'd heard Glen rattle off, with no inflection in his voice at all, the information the firm had gleaned that day. Right after he'd told her about Hampton's murder—the purpose for his call.

Blade had always wanted a boat. His father, who'd had enough money to buy him ten, had chosen to rent vessels on the few occasions they'd been out on Lake Michigan. He'd preferred flying, traveling to far-off places. Just as Maddie had always talked about wanting to do.

While Morgan and Blade...hadn't.

The cabin cruiser was a decent size and had been searched that morning by the Rocky Springs police. Glen had forwarded all reports to her, another reason she'd left Blade as soon as he'd asked that she do so. She needed to get back to the hotel, to assess everything Glen had sent, without Blade looking over her shoulder. Filling in any blanks, filling her mind, before she had time to assess for herself.

She'd draw her own conclusions, come up with her own theories—and then listen to his. Put them in the mix.

Something very clearly wasn't adding up. Why, after seventeen years, had there suddenly been two new murders? Were they connected by the killer?

Or something else?

Were they looking at only one killer? Detective Silver hadn't seemed any more sure of that than Morgan was. Even if Blade had killed Madison, why would he suddenly start killing again?

And do so in such a way that put him in the spotlight?

Unless he wanted to get caught? Couldn't live any longer with the guilt?

But then, why not just turn himself in?

He could be playing them all. The possibility was there. The man was quiet. Somewhat of a loner, other than his work. His employees, his crews, all spoke highly of him, she'd been told. He paid better than average wages. Ran a tight ship, but was clear in his expectations, and fair. According to what Glen had told her, he had an army of supporters at Carmichael Construction.

A revelation that she'd been pleased to hear. For the case, yes, but for him as well.

So…was she softening toward her sister's killer?

The thought had Morgan on the car's audio system halfway through town, instructing the female voice to dial Jasmine. If they were looking at a serial killer, her ex-partner should be on the case. Could take over jurisdiction.

Morgan didn't trust easily, if at all, but Jasmine was someone she'd learned to rely on more than anyone else when something wasn't clear to her.

Her friend picked up on the first ring. Was relieved to hear from Morgan. Agreed that, at least with the two recent kills, they could have a spree on their hands, said she'd look into the case and get back to Morgan in the morning.

Her tension easing, though she hadn't mentioned that she might be swaying on the idea that Blade Carmichael was her sister's killer, Morgan pulled into the hotel parking lot. There'd been no sign of a black, tan or any other color vehicle following her. Relieved, hoping that Blade had been right and the local police had been keeping an eye on her, she pushed the button to turn off her car, and gathered her satchel, putting it over her shoulder before getting out.

If the police had suspected her in Shane's killing, Hampton's death should have eased their minds on that one. She'd been east, in Detroit, and then at her hotel during the time frame she'd have been needing to drive an hour straight north to kill the doctor. As they'd know if they'd been following her.

The satchel was heavy, but Morgan, while mourning for the doctor she'd barely known, felt lighter, walking toward the hotel, glancing off at the marina lights in the distance, curious about Blade's boat.

He'd wanted three of them. A pontoon, for larger gatherings. A speedboat. And a cabin cruiser. According to Glen, he'd ended up with just the last choice. Which, considering how his life had changed so drastically that last morning she'd seen him, made sense. Blade in his current state didn't seem the type to need high-speed thrills or do much par...oomph.

A grasp out of the darkness, the back of her arm...

Morgan spun on instinct, ducked, grabbed body parts and swung. Only realizing what she'd done when she had a dark-clothed body on the ground, her low-heeled dress shoe planted in the middle of the guy's stomach, right between the ribs, and her gun pointed at his head.

"Move and you're dead," she said, letting her anger spew through her tone, as, adrenaline pumping through her, she grabbed her phone with her free hand and dialed 911.

Her pulse was jumping as Morgan ended the call, but she didn't budge a muscle from her stance. Wouldn't hesitate to use her weapon if the guy dared to move.

Seventeen years of training, of being on guard...of waiting.

Could it really be as easy as a single flip to the ground to catch the guy? The young kid staring up at her with wide eyes and a bit of a nervous look about him wasn't the killer. He couldn't be more than eighteen or nineteen, if that. Certainly not old enough to have been at camp or killed Madison.

But he could be someone hired by the killer. Whether the guy's job had been to warn Morgan off, kill her or kidnap her, she didn't know. But as she stared silently at that face, her foot rising and falling with the guy's frantic breathing, she knew she wasn't going anywhere until she found out.

Chapter 9

Blade was still sitting at his dining room table when he saw James Silver's name pop up on his caller ID. He considered hitting End Call. Sending the summons to voicemail.

He could be in bed. Could turn his phone off, or sleep through a call.

But he didn't. Avoidance was not the answer.

"Yeah," he answered, bracing himself for whatever new evidence had shown up in the Hampton case, pointing at him. Reminding himself that every piece of bad news was really a clue that would lead him closer to the true killer.

Or killers. He couldn't get it out of his head that there might be two of them. That someone from the past was, for some unknown reason, resurrecting Blade's nightmare, for some completely unrelated reason.

Maybe a predisposed killer who preyed on those who'd seemingly gotten away with murder? So that *he* could? Do the deed with deflected blame…

His mind had been in high gear since he'd seen the detectives at his door, processing even as he'd drawn inside himself, but the second he heard what Silver had to say, that Morgan had been jumped in the hotel parking lot, Blade was grabbing his keys and heading for the door.

"I'm on my way," he said.

"She's fine...just..." Silver's voice grew faint and then abruptly disappeared as Blade ended the call.

He had Morgan on the line before he was in his truck. Heard for himself that she was fine—in her hotel room without a scratch—and told her that he was on his way.

He didn't wait for her to tell him not to come. Didn't give her the chance. He hung up as he started the truck and took every ounce of self-control he had in him to keep to the speed limit as he made it across town. If her life had been at stake, he'd have justification for speeding.

Knowing that she was fine, he had no excuse.

Adrenaline and a lifetime of suppressed emotions pushing to the core were not reasons to break the law.

But as soon as he'd parked his truck in the first spot he came to on the hotel lot, he was out and running for the entrance. Taking the stairs up to her floor two at a time. No way he was waiting for an elevator.

But as he opened the stairwell door to enter her floor, and his mind's eye got sight of himself, he stopped, took a couple of deep breaths, before walking more calmly to Morgan's door.

He rapped twice. She opened the door almost immediately. Let him in and quickly closed it behind him. Still in the beige pants and white top she'd had on, same beige pumps, too. He had to agree with James Silver—she looked none the worse for her ordeal.

Blade smiled.

"What?"

"Whoever would have thought you'd grow up to take down grown men like it was a walk in the park?"

Her gaze darkened and he realized the mistake of his words too late to take them back. She hadn't simply grown up to be a superhero. She'd been changed and completely shaped by her sister's death.

Which hung there between them, again.

Always.

Didn't diminish how much he was impressed by her abilities, though.

Two steps farther into the room, he recognized his second mistake. The place was small. Minuscule. A mouse house. While he was standing there at any rate.

For hotel rooms, it was pretty standard.

The bed. A love seat. A desk and large counter with re-frigerator and microwave. A closet and bathroom. A big mirror on the side wall that pretty much showed the whole place and everyone in it.

He'd hung up on her before she'd been able to tell him not to come.

"I picked up some beer downstairs," she told him, grab-bing the handle of the refrigerator door. "I don't know about you, but I could use one after this day." She took a can, held one out to him.

No way he could stay in that room and drink a beer with Morgan Davis. Even the can of light stuff she was hold-ing out to him.

He apparently didn't have it in him to refuse her, either. He took the can. And before he could do anything further to misstep, she walked away, toward the wall of curtains, throwing the sheer open to reveal a door handle. She pulled, and when he realized there was a balcony out there, Blade practically ran to accompany her outside.

Not really. He maintained his outward decorum. Man-aged his stride.

But he figured that door as his get-out-of-jail-free card.

The Morgan Davis jail he'd have been in had he attempted to sit on that bed and drink a beer with her.

He wouldn't have touched her.

But he didn't trust himself not to have blurted out something inappropriate. Like how he'd never found anyone even remotely like her...

Or how glad he was that she was working with him to find the truth.

How having her there was bringing him new hope— even as whoever was committing the current murders was squeezing the breath out of him.

He'd escaped charges in the past. There was no guarantee he would again.

The balcony was more spacious than he'd expected. And the sound of the waves, racing up on the beach and receding...he couldn't have scripted a better next step.

Dropping to the seat Morgan had left remaining when she sat on one side of the square table, he opened the beer. Took a drink. And held the can in both hands at his belt as he looked out into the night, letting the breeze, the night, wash away some of his tension.

But only some of it. They'd "discussed" their good news. She was fine.

They had a lot more business to discuss. None of it good.

"So who is he?" he asked, after just one more sip.

"You don't know? Silver said he was calling you."

Yeah, well... "As soon as I'd heard you were attacked, were okay and in your hotel room, I hung up and called you."

His words were revealing. He said them anyway. He'd promised her the truth.

"He's a homeless kid," Morgan said, her tone professional. Acknowledging nothing off about his proclamation.

"Said some guy approached him on the beach just before I got out of my car, said he'd heard that the kid was a pick-pocket, purse snatcher, and let him know that there was a woman staying at the hotel with a lot of cash. Said he described me and my satchel…"

"What?" Blade sat forward, looking over at her. Morgan was looking at him, too. Her eyes glistening pricks of light in the darkness.

"I know."

"Why would someone do that? Did he make a deal for half the money?"

"You'd think so, but no. The kid was clearly in need of some cash, new to the beach, and the guy said he wanted to help him out."

"Did he get a description, I hope?"

He should have expected Morgan's headshake. Her entire demeanor had already told him what he'd needed to know. He just hadn't been on the right page.

He'd been thinking she didn't want him there.

He'd been making it personal.

"He said it was dark, the guy was dressed in dark clothes, wearing a hoodie. Had a blanket around his shoulders so he couldn't tell much. Figured he was homeless, too, because he was barefoot, though he didn't know if he'd seen him around before. Didn't recognize his voice or think he'd talked to him. The kid had been lying down behind the public restroom, and didn't stand up until after the guy was gone. His parents are in Chicago, have been looking for him and are already on their way here," she finished.

He got the feeling she was ready for the conversation on the subject to be over as well, though she wasn't rushing through her beer, or seeming in any hurry to get up from her chair. She'd kicked off her shoes, pulling her knees up to her chest. Was hugging her shins.

Something he'd teased her about doing in the past. Telling her that he was jealous of those appendages.

Why was he even having the thought?

He couldn't remember so many details of the night of her sister's murder. Of the party. Hadn't been able to tell police definitively who'd all been there. Or what exact time he'd returned to his cabin. But he could remember a sixteen-year-old Morgan hugging her shins?

Her legs had been bare. She'd had on shorts...

Glancing from her hands to her face, he said, "You know someone is warning you off," he said. "The text to me... being followed... Someone had to have known you were just arriving back at the hotel and had gone down to the beach to find this guy."

She nodded. Her face seeming tense as his eyes adjusted to the dark.

"Question is, did he want the kid to kill me, hurt me or kidnap me?" she asked, turning her head toward him. "Silver said the beach has a regular homeless population, though they do their best to get everyone places to sleep for the night. But early evening, there are always people out there. So this guy, our perp, he knows that. And just gets unlucky enough to approach a kid on the beach who was too far gone to follow direction?"

He shook his head. "Wait, didn't you say he told the kid he knew he was a pickpocket?"

"Yeah." Morgan's tone was as calm, as lacking in inflection, as he'd ever heard it. He noted the moment for later assessment. "And it turns out the kid has a few priors for just that. It's how he supports his drug addiction. He's been on the streets on and off for a couple of years. Give or take stints at home with his folks while they try to help him."

Blade sat forward. "You're telling me this guy *knew* he was a pickpocket?"

"Yeah," she said again. Took a sip of her beer, casually, as though watching the moon rise up over the lake was all that mattered. Like she had all night to do it, too. "Which means very little," she said after she'd put her can back down on the table. "People who frequent the streets figure out who's who and what's what pretty quickly…"

"Law enforcement, people who work in the system, the courts and jail…they'd know, too," he said, having lost every hint of relaxation. "Someone wants you off this case pretty badly," he said then, staring at her.

Daring her to see the danger chasing right behind her.

Her nod didn't ease his stress any. "Which is the only good news that's come out of tonight," she said.

"Come again?"

She glanced at him then, shrugged, and said, "I'm obviously making him nervous. Which means we're getting closer to finding him."

He didn't disagree.

But he wasn't willing to see her killed just to clear his own name.

"There's a killer out there, Blade." Her words fell softly on the night air. "It's my job to find him."

Didn't matter if he fired her or not. She wasn't going to quit looking.

"If he wanted me dead, he wouldn't have used a homeless guy on the beach to do it."

She had a good point.

"He's warning me off, but not hurting me."

"Yet."

She acknowledged the point with another sip of beer.

"There are two dead bodies to attest to this guy's threat, Morgie." The name slipped out. He heard it. Couldn't take it back.

"Yeah. This guy has killed at least two people in less than two days," she said. "So why not me? It has to have something to do with that summer at camp," she continued as though they were discussing a book they'd both read. "My sister's death. Your seeming culpability, coupled with a lack of charges. Then all these years later, Shane's dead at your feet, and the very next day, Dr. Hampton is poisoned with your business card near his hand when you don't have an alibi. And I'm merely being warned off."

She looked at him. "Why?" she asked.

"He doesn't blame you." The obvious answer came to Blade. One that rang true to him. Personally. Every time he thought about that summer, the one person he hurt for the most had been Morgan.

Even after she'd betrayed him.

The look on her face, the sheer panic, horror, heartbreak, all mingling into tears and screams and convulsions...

Sitting there with her on her balcony facing the beach, watching her in the darkness, the past came back to him, in a different way. With a clearer understanding.

One that changed no facts.

But altered him.

That morning, when they'd both been woken up to a nightmare that was about to steal their youth, and irrevocably rewrite their futures, he'd been in danger of losing his freedom.

But she'd just lost the other half of her soul.

* * *

Morgan was drinking faster than Blade was. She wasn't driving.

And needed a minute.

While she'd handled the situation well that evening, handled it exactly as she'd have expected, she still didn't relish being attacked from behind.

"He never should have gotten close enough to me to warrant a flip," she said as she emptied the last of her beer and, stepping around Blade, went inside for a second one.

She'd let down her guard, alone, at night, in a parking lot, while working a case. Having been followed throughout the day.

She'd known someone was watching her.

Back outside, she didn't stand at the balcony as she might have done had she been alone. She dropped down to her chair again, setting the beer on the table. She'd take the second one slower. There were hours left in the evening and she had work to do.

The day's reports from Sierra's Web to digest.

And should eat, too. Blade had insisted she bring back the salad and bread she'd hardly touched…

"You berate yourself for not having eyes in the back of your head?"

She looked over at him.

"Letting him get close." He tilted his head toward her as he spoke, his words seeming intimate in the night air they were sharing.

Forcing herself to stare outward, not at him, she said, "I was preoccupied. I never walk in the dark without paying attention to my surroundings. Front, back and sides."

There was so much they had to talk about. All vitally more important than her mental stumble in the parking lot.

She hadn't irreparably damaged the kid. Just knocked the wind out of him. And scared him half to death. All of which he'd deserved.

"You had another death on your mind, Morgan," he said, sounding as though he was trying to reason with someone who should have already gotten the message.

His tone rankled. For no good reason. "No, Blade," she said, looking over at him. "I had your boat on my mind. I was looking over at the marina, not minding my own business."

Whether it was her tone, or the fact that she'd mentally trespassed on his private property, she didn't know, but Blade shut up.

Which disappointed her.

His boat. He'd named it the *M & M*. People thought it was for the famous chocolate candies. Maybe because he always had a bag of them in the refrigerator aboard.

M & M. Morgan and Madison.

He'd let them both down.

And they'd let him down, too.

Maddie, refusing to listen to him about staying away from Shane Wilmington. Blade couldn't prove that the womanizing high schooler had left his cabin of boys again that night. That Shane and Maddie had met up again after the party was over.

But his gut told him that's what had happened.

And Morgan... Well, he understood more clearly how she hadn't had his fear, his possible incarceration, his innocence, on her mind that morning.

Her sister had been the other half of her.

He'd just thought...for a few hours there...that he'd become Morgan's other half. That she'd somehow just know that he'd never, in a million years, have done anything to hurt anyone. Least of all her or her twin.

From the first moment he'd set eyes on Morgan Davis earlier that summer, he'd been filled with a need to protect her happiness. Juvenile, probably. But there it was.

Whether she was interested in him or not. There'd just been something about her that had called to him.

Gaining her attention and affection for himself had been a great bonus. For a split second there, he'd believed her when she'd said that she'd felt the same instant connection to him as he had to her.

Truth was, they'd probably both just been hit by hormones brought on by an intense physical attraction.

"I lived on the boat for a year while I built my house," he told her, leaving the part of the past with her in it where it belonged. Gone forever. "It's got a queen-size berth, and thirty feet of living space down below."

He told her because she'd talked about wanting to have an extended stay on a boat on Lake Michigan. Had wanted to take time to explore her 1,638 miles of shoreline.

He'd told her they'd do it together.

The same night he'd told her he wasn't going to attend the unsanctioned counselor party.

"I went to the party because Shane was going and told me that he was meeting Maddie there." He repeated what he'd told her earlier. "It wasn't like I could run over to the girls' camp and warn you." And back then, cell phones hadn't been allowed at camp. Counselors all had radios that they were to have with them at all times, to communicate in case of emergency. "I threatened to report the party, but he pointed out that if I did so, a whole lot of counselors would be out of jobs. So many that they might have to shut camp down early for the summer. Which meant I wouldn't have had any more time with you." Which was exactly what *had* happened. After Madison's murder that summer, the camp closed, and to his knowledge, never reopened.

His words drifted in the breeze. He and Morgan...they'd been speaking at each other—not to each other—since she'd shown up at the crime scene early that morning.

Which was as it should be. They were clearing air so they could better work together. Period.

Chapter 10

Blade's words conjured up things Morgan couldn't deal with. For seventeen years she hadn't believed in her ability to discern where personal relationships were concerned. She'd lost her ability to trust.

And had grown comfortable with that part of herself.

She wanted to believe that the warmth flooding through her, mixed with a few degrees of relief, was due to the beer she was consuming on a mostly empty stomach.

Blade hadn't lied to her. When he'd told her he wasn't attending the party, he hadn't been. Circumstances had changed, but he didn't get the chance to tell her. He hadn't joined the other rogue counselors to party. He'd attended as a chaperone. Her sister's chaperone.

The fact didn't change what ultimately happened. Nor did it change any of the facts of the three deaths she was investigating.

So she let it lie there, and said, "I'm convinced that you did not kill Dr. Hampton. You were exhausted when I left you at the restaurant this morning. This afternoon at your office, you weren't. No way you could have driven an hour each way, killed a man and been rested."

There was more. She just couldn't believe that Blade would deliberately take another life. She'd figured all along that Maddie's death had been an accident. A fit of rage, maybe, or jealousy. The result of overactive teenage hormones. Not a deliberate choice to take her life.

But Shane and the doctor? Those two acts had not only been deliberate, but clearly planned.

"You're frowning," Blade said, drawing her gaze to his. The moon had risen like a spotlight on the balcony. One that lit and left shadows at the same time.

"What if we're working with a team of killers?" She asked the question aloud as it occurred to her. "It's just not likely that one person would make a plan to pull off two murders, in separate towns, within twenty-four hours, with completely different methods of operation," she said, her FBI training coming to the fore. "At least, not feasible that he'd be able to execute the plan without a flaw. You don't just decide to murder someone and go do it perfectly… and to manage it twice without time for rest, or to glory in the spoils…"

Blade's gaze stayed with hers, as though they were thinking the same thoughts. "But if you were a team, had taken time to plan, with the goal of not only killing, but framing someone else for the murders, you'd each have taken your kill method of choice, would have researched, bounced ideas off each other, probably done trial runs, timing everything perfectly. And working together you'd feed off each other's adrenaline. You wouldn't want to let your partner down…"

"Maybe they're siblings!" The thought only occurred as she opened herself up fully to the scenario he was painting. "We've got to go over that list of campers again." Morgan jumped up. Went to the desk, to her computer, had it on and was typing before she sat down.

Carrying in a chair from outside, Blade sat down beside

and slightly behind her, leaning forward, his elbows on his jean-clad knees as he watched her screen.

"There," he said, reaching forward an arm, almost brushing her cheek, as he pointed.

"Alex and Josh Donnelly," she read aloud. Pulled out her phone and sent a text to Glen Rivers Thomas. Then looked back at the list. "I don't remember them," she said.

Sitting back, Blade shook his head. "I don't, either. They were twelve and thirteen, in with the younger kids..."

Morgan turned, felt Blade's closeness too acutely and stared back at the computer. "If you didn't have any interaction with them, why would they have it in for you to the point of framing you for murders you didn't commit?"

"What if something happened that summer? Something Hampton knew about, or something Shane did to them? What if it's affected them ever since? Maybe one of them took it harder than the other..."

"...and the dominant one," Morgan took over, "fearing for his younger brother's mental health, his ability to ever have a normal healthy life, concocted the idea to get rid of the people involved—thus empowering them both. Taking back the self-esteem they'd lost..."

"And they're framing me maybe because I was technically in charge of Shane, and also because they would have seen what happened the morning after Maddie was killed. I was clearly ostracized. I'm the obvious scapegoat... It's twisted, but clearly whoever is doing this is working with a skewed mental outlook." Blade stood, pacing the room.

With him putting feet between them, Morgan could turn to face him. Looked up at him, her mind flowing at its best. "For all we know, these aren't the first two deaths," she said. "It's possible that they started out smaller, an animal maybe. They could have preyed on someone vulnerable." Picking up her phone, she called Jasmine. Giving her friend a rundown on the theory, including the fact that Sierra's Web was already looking into the Donnellys in all ways they legally could. She needed Jasmine to check out arrest records, databases the FBI had access to. Looking for any unsolved missing persons, or homicides in the cities where either of the brothers had been over the past seventeen years.

"I'll get on it immediately," Jasmine said, her tone warm. Engaged. Just like always. She sounded glad that Morgan had called. "Approval just came through for the FBI to take jurisdiction of the case," she continued. "James Silver will be assisting us."

Relieved to have her ex-partner and friend fully involved, Morgan stared at the computer, not the man behind her, and said, "I'm happy to hear that." Wishing she was free to tell her friend how much she needed her on this one.

"I'm just getting started, but the one thing I can tell you for sure is that you need to steer clear of Blade Carmichael," Jasmine said, her tone carrying more friendship than professionalism. Talking to her as they'd spoken to each other over drinks after hours when they were on the job together.

Morgan's heart thudded. She trusted her friend. And… the man right behind her…she couldn't walk away from him right then. Not in the room, but in that moment in time, either. "I'll do my best," she said, keeping her tone on a squad room level. Suddenly needing the call she'd instigated to end.

"I'm dead serious, Morgan." Jasmine's words held definite warning. "Your reputation, your entire career, is at risk if you associate with, work for, the number-one suspect in a serial killer case and he turns out to be guilty."

Chest tight, Morgan took a breath, looking for the right

words to reassure her friend and end the conversation, too. But before she came up with anything, Jasmine added, "I'm worried about your emotional state, Morg. Worried that you're too intimately involved in both the murder and your past feelings for this man to be objective..."

The woman was most definitely trespassing where she had not been invited.

Had Morgan been alone, she'd have told her ex-partner right then that her mental and emotional health was always on her radar, on every case, and if she thought, for one second, she couldn't do the job, she'd pull herself off from it.

She'd have used her quick instincts in taking down her attacker that evening as proof of her ability to be focused when she had to be.

And then she'd have told Jasmine that she knew Blade hadn't committed at least one of the current murders, and believed he was innocent of both.

As it stood, with Blade pacing by the opened sheers on the French doors of her hotel room, she said, "You've got absolutely nothing to worry about there. Call me when you have something and I'll do the same." She wished her friend well and hung up.

She'd just given her loyalty to Blade, over her ten-year FBI partner and friend.

Neither of them knew that.

But she did.

Just as she knew that while she and Blade were both most definitely too involved in the murders to be completely objective, they were also the two people with the best chance of solving the case. Because they had both spent seventeen years working on it.

That case was the life they'd inadvertently shared, rather

than getting married, making babies and starting a family as they'd both once dreamed they'd do.

Blade couldn't help but notice Morgan's energy drain as she spoke with her ex-partner. Obviously, the conversation hadn't gone as she'd expected it to go.

"She didn't buy our theory, huh?" he asked, wondering how much impact Agent Jasmine Flaherty would have on Morgan's take on the case.

Her shrug didn't seem too threatening. "She's going to look into the Donnelly brothers, but she didn't seem to find as much merit in the idea as we did." She paused, glanced up at him and then said, "And I get it. We find a pair of siblings, know absolutely nothing about them and concoct an entire scenario around their names, making them guilty of two murders."

He nodded. "Yes, but isn't that how this works?" he asked. "You didn't call to have them arrested. Or to alarm anyone. We're just following through on a theory." He couldn't lose her. Not when they were finally working together.

The Donnelly theory could be completely bogus, but it was a starting place. A logical one, with everything fitting into place. The first one of its kind he'd had in seventeen years.

That still didn't explain Madison's death. And if Shane had killed her, as Blade believed, he might have just lost his chance of ever living free from suspicion.

A fact he'd take on when he had to. Not before.

"If the Donnellys killed Shane, they might have information regarding Madison's death," he said aloud, forgetting just for that instant that he and Morgan weren't a team on the same page.

"What if it wasn't siblings?" she asked, frowning, as she went back to her computer and started typing.

Noting that she'd ignored his statement about her sister's death, Blade went out to gather their beers. He sipped his tepid one, set hers on the desk beside her and took his own seat.

Rome hadn't been built in a day. Nor had it crumbled in one.

"Alex and Josh Donnelly might lead successful, law-abiding lives," she continued, "but the theory best explains what's going on. At least as far as we see it right now. Two different cars were allegedly following me today. Partners, taking different jurisdictions. One in town. One outside of town. Maybe one of them lives here, one doesn't…"

"The one who lives here would be familiar with the homeless people hanging out at the beach." Blade leaned in further, looking at names. Trying to remember faces, and more importantly personalities.

"Mark Hampton's death puts a whole different spin on this," Morgan said. "It makes sense that we'd be looking for someone who'd gone to him for counseling…"

Blade's excitement ramped up again. "Or someone who should have but didn't. Maybe blaming Hampton for not noticing. Or trying to help."

Morgan's glance over her shoulder at him put their faces within inches of each other. He noticed. His gaze dropped to her lips. When he realized he was lingering there, he quickly pulled his eyes back up to focus on hers. She was looking toward his lips.

Remembering? As he'd just done.

Their first kiss that summer had been her first. She'd been tentative in the beginning, to the point that Blade pulled back, fearing he'd made a mistake, read her wrong, that she wasn't wanting to make out with him.

She'd quickly righted his thinking on that one. He started to get hard in real time, and immediately brought Shane Wilmington's dead body to mind.

He would not disrespect Morgan, himself or the search for Maddie's killer by falling back into memories built on a fantasy.

Life had quickly shown him just how difficult, how real, it was going to be.

"There has to be something to this theory." Morgan's words threw him for a second. Sometime during his mental blip she'd turned back to the computer. Glancing at the screen, he didn't see anything new there.

Just the same list of camp attendees they'd been scrolling through.

"How do we know that the partners are even from the same year we are? Dr. Hampton was there for years, and Shane had been attending as a camper since he was twelve," she continued. "Say this duo attended during the previous year, and because of what happened they didn't come back the year we were there? The news of Maddie's death was all over…"

"As was the fact that I was the only suspect," he added, underscoring the part that he'd lived with ever since.

"So, they didn't have to be there when we were, just had to have attended at some point." She pulled out her phone, sent a couple of texts.

He didn't ask where those instant missives were going. She was doing the job she'd been hired to do. He was there because she'd demanded access into his entire life. Including his mind.

They weren't partners, a team working together.

"I'd like to run something by you," she said then, taking a sip from her beer, holding the can between their faces, as she turned to look at him.

Scooting his chair back a few feet, he nodded. Instinctively prepared to hear something he wasn't going to like. Ready to find a way to work with it. He'd put up with whatever hell was necessary to get to the truth.

"You remember Remy Barton? He was a camper, a couple of years younger than us." The question startled him. He hadn't been expecting a trip down memory lane. At least not one that carried a smile.

"Of course. He'd been afraid of his own shadow when he came to camp, but was determined not to let his fear stop him. He learned to swim. To kayak. Rope climb..."

"Did you know his mother had passed away just a few weeks before camp?"

He sat up straight. "Hell, no! He never said anything, never." But when he thought about it, he'd seen the kid go mellow a few times. Had put it down to homesickness. Something a fourteen-year-old boy would rather die than admit.

"I knew only because I caught him crying late one afternoon. He'd been down at the stream that divided the girls' camp from the boys' camp, and I'd just been coming back from my weekly evaluation with Maggie."

The camp manager. Blade hadn't thought much of her in years, either. Other than to resent how quickly the woman had believed what she was being told, that Blade was guilty of murdering a sixteen-year-old girl...

"Anyway, after Maddie's death..." Her pause was minute, but Blade felt it to his core. "Remy stayed with me that morning until my parents came. He didn't say much. Just hung around, making sure everyone else left me alone. We ended up staying in touch…"

If she was about to tell him that the kid had grown up to be her lover, he didn't need to know. Not unless it had to do with the case.

"He's married now. Has three kids, a daughter and a set of twin sons. He's also a psychiatrist who specializes in troubled youths. He's helped Jasmine and I on a couple of our cases. Since he was at camp more years than we were, I was thinking maybe we have him take a look at the camper rosters, and Sierra's Web's further investigation in the lives of the campers, and see if he has any insights for us. I already talked to Kelly Chase about him…"

The Sierra's Web psychiatric partner, he knew from the research he'd done that afternoon. "Kelly thought it was a good idea, and I'd like to ask Remy for input on your behalf," she said then. "I'm asking because he'd be officially brought into the case by Sierra's Web, which means you'd be paying for his time."

That was it? She wanted the grown version of a kid he'd admired to help them? "Do it," he told her, reaching for his beer. Hiding his relief in a swallow.

And maybe drowning a bit of hope there, too.

Morgan was going all-out—bringing in the best of her best to help. To find her sister's killer, he knew. But she was also sitting alone with Blade, giving him beer, in her hotel room.

Was it possible she was finally starting to believe that he wasn't the one who'd murdered her sister?

That he wasn't a killer at all?

As much as she was eager to get as many balls rolling at once as she could, Morgan did not text or call Remy yet that night. A family man, he cherished his home time with his wife and kids. And until Sierra's Web and Jasmine's FBI team did their legwork on the lists of camp attendees, Morgan didn't have enough to give Remy to warrant the evening call.

Buzzing with a need to delve deeply into the reports Sierra's Web had already sent, and to continue going through the seventeen years of information Blade had made available to her that day, she didn't say so.

Out of character for her.

She'd be up a good part of the night getting through it all and taking a fresh look at her own files in light of the new death—the possible connections, the floating theories.

And she'd been jumped in the parking lot less than two hours before. By a person who'd been manipulated by someone who was organized. Intelligent. Someone who was executing, or helping to execute, a meticulous, intricate, well-thought-out plan.

Someone who could be right there in the hotel with her.

Or just outside watching.

It wasn't that she was scared. She'd lived through far worse situations. And didn't spend time worrying about death.

She just wasn't ready to be alone with her jumble of facts and missing truths.

Not when Blade was showing no signs of leaving. He had to know something, even if he didn't know he knew.

And if he did?

Maybe she was the one to figure out what it was. If not directly than in other ways. As soon as she figured out what those ways were.

Drinking beer had not been the best idea. She'd been up since four the previous morning. The clock was heading toward nine. And the day, all that it had held…she felt like she'd lived months, not hours.

She wasn't at her sharpest. Most particularly not to face the culmination of seventeen years of searching. She'd come face-to-face with her obsession and couldn't turn away.

He was sitting back in his chair again, his brow furrowed, as he stared toward her computer screen. If he was deep in thought on the case, following some kind of memory, she didn't want to interrupt.

And almost as though he'd read her mind, he looked at her. Caught her watching him.

She couldn't look away. He didn't. The moment escalated, sending her places she couldn't go. Just like in the parking lot that evening, she had to act.

To do.

To save and protect.

To question.

To know.

"What if you were out that night, checking up on something, making sure Shane was still in his cabin, sleepwalking…" She stopped. Waited for his rejection.

He hadn't moved. Not his body. Or his gaze.

"What if you saw Maddie, thought she was me, grabbed me up to kiss me…"

He started. His eyes seemed to blaze with emotion. But he stayed right there, holding her gaze. And she sat there, tongue-tied. The moment, or the picture she'd painted, hanging there.

Encapsulating them.

She'd had the thought so many times. Needed to know.

And couldn't go any further with it. Because what came next was Maddie, thinking she was being accosted, striking out at him, kicking him maybe, and him, reacting, hitting out in defense. Or even trying to grab her arms, to calm her down, maybe stop her from screaming. She could have moved, his strong grip could have slipped.

Her twin had died from one blow to the side of her head. There'd been bark in the wound, but she'd been left in the dirt and leaves to bleed out. Had been found lying on a branch, a partial mark from which had been embedded in her head. The medical examiner had thought the indentation could have come from the fall, but that the initial blow would have had to have been much more powerful than a mere fall.

Blade wasn't talking. Leaving. Or even looking away.

She couldn't find words. Or turn around and get to work. He was her worst enemy. The face she'd carried, hated, for seventeen years.

And after the day they'd had—the things they'd said, being in his presence—he was more than that, too. She just didn't know what. Couldn't unravel all the messages her senses were sending her.

"Earlier, when we talked about the Donnelly brothers, it was just a theory." Blade's words were a lifesaver. And, somehow, a death knell, too.

"Right." Was he about to tell her the words she'd just uttered were more than that? Not just one theory, but fact? Had she inadvertently hit on the truth?

"The Donnelly theory was based on our reasonable assumption of what could be probable fact."

Why did she suddenly feel as though she was in a courtroom? She had experience in the venue. Training. Knew to respond with truth and utmost brevity. "Right."

"By what probable fact do you base the theory you just proposed?" He was frowning. Sounding more confused than accusatory—as a defense attorney might have done.

Unless he was playing nice to lead her into some kind of
hole that she'd fall into, never get out of, and he'd walk free.

Shaking her head, Morgan recognized the absurdity of
her thoughts. At the same time, every instinct in her body
warned her not to fall prey to emotions where Blade Carmichael was concerned. She'd trusted him with her life,
her sister's life, telling him concerns—worries—she'd had
where Maddie's wild streak was concerned. And her sister
had ended up dead with all proof pointing to him.

She needed the truth. And had sworn to speak it.

If a theory she'd carried through the years was correct,
she had to know. "I base it on the fact that I almost suggested that, while the party was going on, after all our kids
were asleep, we meet, at the river. I laid in bed that night
imagining what it would be like…"

Her standing there. Him running up, grabbing her off
her feet. Passion doing what it so desperately compelled
them to do…

He'd glanced away. Toward the still-open sheers.

She couldn't take her gaze off him. The tension biting in
his jaw. The vein in his neck, looking ready to pop.

That wave at the back of his hair, recognizable even with
him wearing it shorter.

"I base it on an assumption that you were feeling the
same way I was, thinking like I was. I figured, lying in
bed that night, that I could get to the boys' camp via the
river, could approach your cabin from the back, and then
push the radio button for a call, and just not speak. I knew
the static sound would wake you up…"

She'd been an idiot. Hearing the words aloud, the con-
voluted intricacies involved…

His jaw clenched again. Telling her that what she was

saying was affecting him more deeply than any other thing they'd shared with each other that day.

Spurring her on…filling her with horror…

"If you'd had the same kind of thought, were out looking for me, and Maddie had been sneaking back from the party alone, since everyone testified that Shane had left before her…if you came upon her at our meeting place…"

It could have been an accident. He'd still most likely go to prison, but for much less time. Involuntary manslaughter, or even straight manslaughter…

With a nod, he turned in his seat, facing her again. His gaze holding hers as though he had it imprisoned. It felt to her as though he did. "This is what you've thought all these years?"

She shrugged. Needing to search her mind. To stay truthful, in order to have any hope that he'd end almost two decades of a struggle for the answers that might free her. So she could have a future filled with a personal life to balance her professional one.

Wanting, instead of answering him, to promise to visit him in prison, if he ended up there. Which made her uncomfortable.

"At first, I thought I'd completely misjudged you. That you were some kind of evil being," she told him honestly, swallowing hard as she maintained eye contact with him. "But as I matured, studied criminology and let myself remember the young man I'd known…this is the only theory, or a rendition thereof, that seemed plausible to me."

"You didn't stop to wonder why on earth I'd hit her, leave her lying there to die, put the cross you'd given me in her hand, and then put her class ring in my pocket and go home to bed?"

Her eyes stung. She could feel a surge of moisture.

Forced herself to hold his gaze. "I figured you got scared and ran. Maybe didn't know she was even badly hurt. The class ring..." She shrugged. "Classically, it would be considered a trophy, but then you'd have to have known you'd done something for which you'd want a celebratory memorial...or...it flew out of her hand as you hit her, you saw it in your path as you ran, grabbed it up intending to give it back to her. Or maybe you found it as you were leaving the party, pocketed it for the same reason. Could be you saw Shane with it, told him it was against the rules, because you knew what I'd told you about my sister's weakness, and maybe you forced him to give it to you, to give back to her. Or to me to give to her. And the cross...when she struck out at you, if you still thought she was me, that one was simple. You figured I wasn't the girl you thought I'd been and gave it back."

There were holes in the idea. Things only he could fill in. Happenings of which she was unaware that had led to actual outcomes...

She'd begun to hope, at some point during the day, that it wouldn't come down to Blade being the doer. Her heart had apparently come back to life so quietly, she hadn't realized what was happening in time to prevent the rebirth.

But they still had two deaths to solve. And if they could have the past resolved, open on the table, the rest would...

Fall into place.

Leaving her young girlish hormonal heart forever cracked, but maybe not completely, irreparably broken.

Chapter 11

Hope was a curious thing. Blade sat there with Morgan, finding immense relief in her story regarding his supposed guilt.

A small tendril of belief sprouted from his barren surface, refusing to be trampled by seventeen years of disappointment and experience.

When they'd been teenagers, he'd wanted her to just know he hadn't done it. If they'd been the soulmates she'd claimed, she would have known.

Or at least stood by him long enough to reason things through.

And with his new insight into how that morning had gone for her, what it had done to her, ripped from her...how could she access a soul that had just been destroyed by unimaginable loss?

But over the years... Morgan—the woman who he'd taken to be a soulmate when he'd never before even believed in such things—had had to revise the base judgments she'd made that morning. Factoring in the person he really was.

She still thought him possibly culpable, but only accidentally so. So much of what she'd just said...him making Shane give back her sister's ring...could so easily have happened. She'd seen that in him.

And was sitting there studying him, looking as though her world had just ended.

While he felt like his might just be beginning again.

Leaning forward, his elbows on his knees, he glanced slightly up to meet her gaze. "I didn't do it, Morgan," he said quietly, his eyes as steady as they'd ever been.

Moisture filled her eyes. She blinked, but her gaze was brimmed full. No tears fell. Nor did she offer any words.

She studied him intently. She nodded. And she turned her back to him.

Giving her focus to the case on the screen in front of her.

Blade stood, poured the remainder of his beer down the drain by the refrigerator and quietly let himself out.

She watched him go. Staring at his back, needing to be there, waiting, if he looked back. He didn't. Morgan knew a sense of relief as she heard the lock click automatically into place behind him.

There was more. A boatload of emotions that defied all tides, coming or going, that just remained there, filling the room. And spaces inside her where she never went.

Ignoring it all, she closed and locked the balcony doors, pulled the shades, poured out her mostly full second beer. Opened a third, cold one, and brought out the salad and bread she'd barely touched at dinner.

Carrying the sustenance to the desk, she sat down at her computer, starting at the beginning of the files Sierra's Web had sent—research and backgrounds, life events and current status of key players. Police reports. Forensic evidence would come later. The next day, hopefully, as things from the construction crime scene, as well as all evidence from Madison's murder, had been flown to the firm's state-of-the-art lab in Phoenix for a quicker turnaround.

A man had died that day, and she was mostly numb about it. She'd known who Mark Hampton was. Had sat on the shore while some of the girls in her charge had taken kayak lessons from him. She'd seen him approach the morning she'd found out Maddie had been killed, but she'd twisted around so she couldn't see him. Had tearfully begged the female camp counselor coordinator who'd been sitting with her to make him go away.

It hadn't been anything against the therapist. She hadn't wanted to talk to any man at that point. If Blade could fool her, any guy could.

Still, she'd respected him. Had thought, throughout the summer, that he was patient and kind. She had no reason whatsoever to think that he'd deserved to die.

But what did she know, really know, about what had happened that summer at camp? She'd been so lost in her own little reality—having her soulmate appear before her. Falling in love.

Going through Blade's financials felt wrong, but she pulled them up as she tore off bread and dug into the salad. She'd had an oral report on them.

She had to see it all for herself. Mentally catalog things in the way she did that would allow them to spill back at her in just the right moment, with just the right catalyst to bring them forth. It was like an art form, the way her mind took in details and then gave them back to her in full picture forms that she'd used time and again to solve cases.

She'd barely made it through the list of accounts, hadn't opened any detail pages, even the summaries for each account, which would give her totals. Incoming. Outgoing. Remaining. And was interrupted by her phone's text message tone.

Figuring it for Blade, letting her know he was home—

though she had no reason to think he'd let her know that—
she picked up the device. Pressed to open the app.

And saw five digits instead of a full number. Pressed for
the conversation. The screen was blank, other than a terse
sentence.

Get out of town, and off the case, before something really
bad happens to you.

Where the sixteen-year-old Morgan who'd been trying to
push her way in would have panicked, dropped the phone,
Morgan texted back, Who is this?

And then, with a few presses of her thumb, sent the text
on to Hudson Warner at Sierra's Web, and then, in a separate text, to Jasmine.

If she could keep the sender engaged, either of the two
agencies would have a better chance of at least pinging the
tower from which the text came.

Adrenaline pumped through in healthy spurts as she
waited. The killer was right there. Reaching out to her.
Closer than he'd ever been before.

At least the current killer was. Which was closer than
she'd been to anything dealing with her sister's case since
the morning she'd ceased being a twin.

Not only was he close, watching her, but he wanted her
gone. Which meant that she was posing some kind of threat
to him. She was poking her nose where he didn't want it.

She was learning things.

After a minute passed, with only thumbs-up responses
from both of the people whom she'd just texted, she started
eating again. The salad was delicious. As was the bread.

Beer was her wind down. She'd relax. Take in as much

information as she could reasonably expect to process, and then, lie down and get some sleep.

With her loaded gun right beside her. A split-second hand grab.

She wasn't ignoring the very real threats coming her way. Nor the fact that they were escalating. She just wasn't letting them have the desired effect. Rather than letting them unnerve her, she'd use them to her benefit.

Cowards bullied. Good investigators found ways to use their perps fear to get them to make mistakes.

Three and a half minutes after the warning had come through, her phone pinged again. Jasmine, or Sierra's Web, were her immediate thought, letting her know the message had come from a burner phone. That one was a given.

It was Blade.

Home. Breakfast in the morning? To exchange notes.

He'd be spending the next few hours doing what she was doing. She didn't have to be told to know that.

Fine. She hit Send.

My office? Your hotel?

Not his home, she noticed. Though she still hadn't searched the place, as he'd agreed to let her do.

Here. And pay attention to the road. We need to know, am I the only one being followed?

She took another bite. A sip of beer. Scrolled on the computer.

Feeling a new burst of energy.

She was working late, on the same case she always took to bed with her.

But for the first time in her life, she wasn't working alone.

Something thudded on the balcony.

Instantly awake, alone in her room, Morgan moved her hand a couple of inches, wrapping her fingers around the grip of her pistol. Using her thumb to release the safety and positioning her finger on the trigger.

In one motion, she swung up, pointing her pistol, and saw the small blaze of red, within a haze of smoke.

Keeping her gun pointed, she reached for the hotel phone with her other hand. Dialed for security and reported a fire on her balcony, and then, setting her gun down right beside her, keeping an eye on the balcony, on a red blaze that wasn't growing, she quickly grabbed the top pair of pants from her opened roller bag, snapped on a clean bra, throwing in the dirties she'd changed out of before her shower... was it only three hours before? She ran to the closet and pulled a shirt off the hanger. Kept the balcony in sight, watched more and more smoke furl into the air. Fastening one button to keep the short-sleeved shirt on, she rushed for the desk. Grabbed up files and computer, cords, charger and her notepad, stacking them on top of each other and cramming them into her satchel.

Since the fire hadn't yet noticeably grown, she left her suitcase open as she pulled it toward the room's outer door, stopping at the closet to grab the rest of her shirts, and at the bathroom for her toiletry bag, and, just as she heard the first sirens—less than two minutes from the time she'd awoken—she was out the door.

Heading for the stairs.

* * *

Blade was asleep in his recliner—a place he spent the night more often than he should—when his phone awoke him.

Morgan? At four in the morning?

"Are you okay?" he answered, pushing down the foot-rest to head to his bedroom for jeans and a shirt.

"Yeah. You feel like a drive to Detroit?"

At four in the morning? "Of course, but are you okay?" he said, heart thumping as he moved his phone from one hand to the other, sliding his arms into a dress shirt he'd just yanked off the hanger, grabbing for jeans off the shelf and holding the phone with his shoulder and chin as he stepped into them.

"I'm fine. Someone threw a flare up on my balcony," she told him. "It exploded, caught fire, but only the chairs burned. If it had been a couple of inches further in, the glass in the door would have exploded and my carpet would have gone up in instant flames."

She sounded like she was discussing a breakfast menu. He stepped into his work boots.

"I need you to pack up your dining room table, bring everything along," she told him. "And get good pictures of every inch of the walls." She went on to describe particular shots she wanted him to take.

He stopped only long enough to throw a change of clothes into the duffel he kept on the floor of his closet, scooping toiletries into it, and was on his way to the dining room as he said, "Where are you?" She lived in Detroit. The FBI office was there, too.

"The police station."

And it hit him...she thought he'd tried to catch her room on fire? The flame of fear shot through him, but only for the second it took him to process and dismiss it. "I've been here, working, most of the night. I have time-stamped documents, emails I sent to staff members, to verify that."

"No one's asking." He had her on speakerphone as he gathered up his files and loaded them into one of the four boxes he had on the case. "The flare came from the beach," she continued, sounding completely professional. "No distinguishable footprints. No fingerprints."

"The make of the flare? Was it sold in town?"

"The local police, headed by Silver, are getting to work on that. Silver was at the crime scene." He thought he might have detected a slight catch in her voice with those last two words—the crime scene which had been her hotel room—but he wasn't sure.

"His warnings to you are escalating," he said, stating what she had to already know. "You didn't heed them. He's getting angrier." It didn't take a profiler to figure that one out. A simple understanding of human nature led to that conclusion.

"Right. Which is why I'm leaving town. Hoping to fool him into thinking he was successful, to buy a little time while teams get to work on the attack earlier tonight, the phone threat and the flare."

She delivered the last like they were a grocery list. Morgan, who'd been the most softhearted girl he'd ever met. He brushed past the change to say, "You want him to follow you home."

"No. We're going to leave my car at the hotel. And your truck at the police station. If he concludes that you're in custody, great. He'll figure out, quickly enough, that I'm not in town, but the plan is for us to take a rental to Detroit, back roads, now while it's dark. We'll have an escort until we're certain we aren't being followed. Hopefully, by the time we're at my place, we'll have come up with our next steps."

He'd finished packing boxes, was using his phone to snap photos while they spoke. "I'm actually part of a law enforcement plan to accompany you to Detroit?" he asked, deadpan. While consciously trying to contain the sense of freedom, of victory the knowledge gave him. To not only be off the radar, but to be a legitimate part of the investigation...

He got no further before she said, "You're my client. Part of the deal, on my side, is my access to you. I'm not leaving without you."

Reality hit again. In raw places. Harder due to his momentary letting down of his guard.

"We're too close, Blade." Her voice fell into the silence left by his lack of response, while he accepted that he was only a part of things because she didn't fully trust him. Was he also imagining that her tone was softer than he'd heard since they'd reconnected? "We're on the verge of getting him. We can't back off now, and we both know the way to do this is together. We were the ones most affected by what happened that night at camp."

He was out the door before she'd finished speaking and kept her on the line during his short drive to the police station.

Even if no one was ready to unequivocally believe, yet, that he hadn't killed Madison Davis, he was being given a second chance.

No way he was going to miss one second of it.

Or mess it up, either.

He was going to be right there, facing whatever he had to face, to bring the killer, or killers, to justice.

Blade offered to drive. Morgan refused the offer. She was trained for surveillance, trusted herself to be better able to tell if they were being followed. And needed her rearview mirror to best do that.

And she'd had more sleep than he'd had. As soon as they'd headed out of town in the blue rental sedan, and she'd heard he'd only been out about an hour before she'd called, having spent much of the night doing his own internet research on the lives of others who'd been at camp with them that horrible summer, she suggested that he use the driving time to get some rest. They could count on a full, taxing day ahead of them. She needed him in top form.

Mostly, now that he was back with her, she needed time to gather herself. To relax into who she was, what she knew, and do what she did.

To tune in and find herself while her entire life's work was exploding around her, to catch as many pieces as she could, and put them together into their final, rightful, resting place.

The fact that Blade's presence helped *her* was not good news. But recognizing the truth, she didn't fight it. Not when it meant she was getting closer to proving who'd killed her sister.

While she drove, remaining on edge with facts and impressions, with replays of the near escapes she'd had over the past twenty-four hours, coming to terms with the fact that she was the target of a smart, organized and determined but elusive killer…Blade Carmichael almost immediately went to sleep.

His relaxed form and even breathing might have made her smile in another lifetime.

Funny, most definitely not in a smiling way, she never in a million years would have figured his first time sleeping with her to play out quite like that.

A thought that brought a swell of emotion that had nothing to do with the case and put her on guard. To the point that she spent the entire rest of the almost-three-hour drive with all the route switches not only watching everything around her, but watching herself, too.

No more lapses into the past.

Even if it turned out that Blade Carmichael was not her sister's killer, he wasn't the man he'd been when she'd known him. And more importantly, she was most definitely not the girl he'd thought he'd fallen in love with.

Finding Maddie's killer would settle a huge load of tension inside her. It would allow her to keep her promise to her identical twin to not let a day go by without working on finding Maddie's killer and seeing him brought to justice. But it wouldn't bring Maddie back.

And living without the other half of her identity, being in the world without the one person who was so connected to her she could sense Morgan's moods, read her thoughts...

She'd do it. Had been doing it for seventeen years.

And doing so had changed her. Period.

It had robbed her of her deepest sense of self. Of her ability to love openly, freely. Of her ability to trust. Of her belief in happily-ever-after.

Forever.

Chapter 12

Blade was wide awake when Morgan signaled a turn before the intersection she'd indicated they'd be driving through to reach her condo on the next block up. He looked in his side mirror, out his window, hers, as she turned again, and then a third time, taking them out to the expressway.

"I'm assuming we were being followed?" he asked, surprised at the calm with which he approached the news.

Living seventeen years with the feeling of being hunted, he'd have expected a bit more distress. With every muscle tense, prepared to spring into whatever action presented itself, he wasn't afraid.

He was ready.

Had his legally registered gun clipped to his belt.

With another couple of glances in her rearview mirror, and both side mirrors, Morgan shook her head. "No, not that I can see, but that tan car…it was parked three driveways down from mine. Opposite side of the street."

"He's got someone planted there, to notify him if you go home."

She nodded. And he was confused. "I thought the idea was for him to think you'd quit and gone home."

"With you in the vehicle with me?"

"I'd duck down until you pulled into your garage."

Morgan shook her head, signaling and moving over into

the exit lane. "My plan was not to let him know I'd quit," she said then, and thinking back, he realized that she'd only mentioned the killer thinking Blade was in custody, nothing about her. He'd assumed...

"My quitting gives him a sense of victory," she said, exiting the freeway, taking the far lane, signaling a right turn as though she knew exactly where she was going.

"Mind telling me what we're doing now?" He could put a little more strength in his tone. He wasn't her prisoner. Could speak up for his right to be an equal partner with her. Clued in at all times. Remind her who was paying the bill.

But it wouldn't serve any good purpose. While he didn't appreciate being kept in the dark, at all, for any part of Morgan's investigation, he was getting exactly what he wanted.

Her giving her all, working diligently, to find the truth.

And only a fool put his foot in his mouth when there was good stuff cooking.

"We're heading to FBI headquarters," she told him. "Jasmine's giving us a conference room to go over any new developments. She wants to interview both of us, and has agreed to keep me apprised of anything she finds. With Sierra's Web officially on the case, we're all working together..."

A conference room at FBI headquarters. Not exactly what he'd have chosen for himself, personally, but for Morgan...to know that she would be out of harm's way, fully protected, for the next few hours at least, relaxed him a smidge.

"Mind if we get some breakfast before we head in?" he asked, his tone congenial. While his mind played over what he'd learned since Morgan's phone call had awoken him that morning. Putting it together with things he'd gleaned the night before. There'd been a girl at camp...

He hadn't thought anything of Emily. Not until the night before, when he'd come across her name and had looked her up...

If he didn't have to answer to Morgan, he'd have already been heading in the other woman's direction. To follow up on a bad feeling.

Instead, he was going to have to cough up some more difficult facts.

In search of the truth.

She didn't want to sit openly in a restaurant. Since she couldn't be absolutely positive the killer didn't have a way of tracking her, Morgan didn't want to put any more people in danger than absolutely necessary. She'd planned to leave her cell phone at her apartment. Had turned it off as soon as she'd hung up from Blade at the Rocky Springs police station. Was already using one of the burners she'd brought with her, just in case.

Instead, she'd be leaving her cell with Jasmine. Having it monitored. And if it was clean, returned to her. "I'm going to need your cell," she said as she pulled up to the newly installed drive-through window to collect their food order from a restaurant that, until a few years before, had been dine-in only.

And one of her favorite breakfast places.

Blade's instant frown, his clear tension, relieved her some. He'd been so...agreeable, to the point almost of docility, that she'd been on edge with him. Because he hadn't been giving her his true self. "My cell?" His challenging tone matched his body language.

"In case it's being traced," she told him. Pulling out her own burner phone. And her dead cell. "I'm leaving mine, too. We'll get them back after they've been analyzed."

With a nod, he mentioned the pictures he'd taken that morning, at her request.

And in between chatting with the woman at the window, paying, asking for extra syrup, she let him know the burner had a memory card and he'd have time to move over anything he needed.

Not because it was the truth and right to let him know what was ahead.

But because she wanted to keep him happy.

And that was most definitely not a good development in the case.

Blade knew the second he met Morgan's ex-partner that Agent Jasmine Flaherty did not like him. The woman was polite. He couldn't find any real fault with her treatment of him.

But as he left the room she'd invited him into for a one-on-one chat, he could feel the chill emanating from the other woman.

He made a mental note to himself of the less than positive reception, along with a footnote to keep his impression to himself. Agent Flaherty had worked alongside Morgan for more than a decade. It didn't take a genius to figure out that the FBI agent-in-charge's opinion of him had been influenced by that partnership. And had been years in the making.

Another reminder of, and insight into, the grown-up version of a young girl he'd once known. Every time he told himself he was seeing a resemblance between the two versions of Morgan Davis, he was being foolish.

A luxury he most definitely could not afford.

But the whole come-to-truth moment made it a bit easier

to sit down in the conference room, alone with Morgan, and take charge of the conversation.

"Regarding our next plans," he said as he held two cups, one at a time, to an in-room coffee portal, then slid the first toward her. "If I was working alone, I'd be heading upstate right now. To a little town just east of Reed City."

His own cup filled, he sat down a couple of seats away from her spot at the head of the table. His stuff was there.

Hers wasn't. Her satchel currently hung over the back of her chair, as though she hadn't been planning to stay long.

Which was just fine with him.

As though she'd read his mind, she turned, reaching behind her into her satchel, pulling out a stack of folders, along with her laptop, as she said, "Why Reed City area?"

And he opened the smallest of his four boxes. The one he'd packed from his table hours before. Taking out the folder he'd put in last.

Opening it, he grabbed the photo on top. That of a seventeen-year-old girl. Pushed it across the table, within Morgan's reach. "You remember her?"

With a frown, she studied the grainy, computer-generated-and-printed photo. Then nodded. "Yeah, that's Emily Kingsley, right? The kids' camp music director."

He nodded. Waited for her to look up at him.

"I came across her name last night and remembered something."

Her gaze sharp, her jaw taut, she asked, "What?"

"She was seated next to me in orientation," he relayed without hesitation. There would be no secrets between them. Not until they found the person who'd murdered her sister. "She was friendly," he continued, remembering back, trying to give her as clear a picture as he could. Checking to make certain he wasn't sparing himself.

"Knowing no one else there, I was friendly back," he continued, looking Morgan right in the eye. If her blink right then had been any more than a natural physical happening, he chose not to deem it as such.

"You two were flirting," she said, in that professional tone he was beginning to dislike. A lot.

He shrugged. "Maybe. But I honestly didn't put any stock in it," he told her. He'd done his soul-searching the night before. "It was before camp started. I'd read the rules. No fraternizing between boy and girl camp counselors. Before I knew that, behind the scenes, it happened all the time."

"It wasn't her first year there," Morgan said, glancing at the photo again. "She'd have known."

"Right, which is part of what came to me last night..."

"Did you date her?"

Morgan's tone had changed. Reminding him of one other sentence she'd said to him the day before. *You told me you weren't going, but you did.*

"I did not," he got out there with full confidence. And then followed his strong words with, "I helped her move music equipment, though. On move-in day. She said something about us hooking up later, and I nodded. Thinking we'd see each other at the first-night barbecue."

Which was when he'd met Morgan and Madison Davis.

"Not that we'd be hooking up in any kind of real-world sense." He continued speaking, as though he could dissuade her thoughts from traveling down channels that wouldn't be good for him.

For them.

"Since I worked with the older kids, I didn't see her much after that." He moved right along with his story. "But last night, when I first got a look at her face, I remembered something."

He paused, taking stock of Morgan's countenance. Finding nothing there but a detective in a cream-colored button-down cotton dress shirt with her long blond hair clipped up in some kind of do at the back of her head.

"Ice cream social night," he said then. A function for camp counselors and teenage personnel that took place during family night at camp.

"We were together that night." Morgan's tone, lacking any emotion at all, didn't bode well.

"Yes, we were, and even walked back to the river together, waving goodbye as we each went to our own respective areas." He found himself painting a part of the picture that wasn't necessary to the case.

Hearing his words, he quickly reverted back. "But when we were waiting in line for the hot fudge…she was across from us, in line for the topping table. I was just glancing around, seeing who all was there, and I caught her looking at me. Her gaze… She looked…mad."

Morgan sat forward. "Mad?"

"Yeah," he said, meeting her gaze head-on. "But it was weird because when she saw me looking at her, she gave me that flirty smile, and raised her eyebrows, as though letting me know that—"

"I know what she'd been letting you know," Morgan interrupted, her tone brisk. "You're sure she looked mad?"

"Yeah. At the time I figured she hadn't really been looking our way, hadn't seen me, but, rather, had been off somewhere in her head. I figured she'd had a fight with someone. Or was in trouble for something. When she saw me, and immediately changed, I figured it wasn't about me and completely forgot…"

Morgan had her computer plugged in and on in seconds.

Was typing. And scrolling. "I've got it all here," he told her, pushing the printed file in her direction.

She reached for the file, opened it to the first page, an incidences listing. In chronological order.

Domestic violence occurrences. With Emily as the perpetrator, every single time.

"The fifth charge down, it was dropped, but was against a roommate she claimed had been hitting on her boyfriend. She claimed the woman came at her and it was self-defense."

Her chin tightened as she read, but when she looked up at Blade, he saw something mixed in with the anger and determination gleaming from her eyes.

He saw what looked liked despair.

Bile rose inside Morgan. Her stomach knotted so tight she almost doubled over with it. So many times…from that very first day…most particularly with Blade as the suspect…there'd been the dreaded fear that her identical twin sister had died because of her.

And, oh God, was she finally on the cusp? Would this day—out of thousands of them that had passed between then and now—be the one that brought Maddie justice?

"I need to talk to Jasmine." She spoke aloud, not consciously, but just doing so, as she stood, heading toward the door. "She can do a deeper dive, possibly get a warrant to look at financials. We have to find out if she's been anywhere near Rocky Springs, or contacted Dr. Hampton. We need to know if she's withdrawn sums of money from her accounts and get her photo around the beach at Rocky Springs. See if anyone who hangs out there has seen her…" She broke off as Jasmine, seeing Morgan in the open doorway, came toward her.

And ten minutes later, she and Blade were on their way up north to the little town of Everson. Law enforcement needed warrants, had to go through specific channels, but as a private detective, she was free to knock on doors and ask people to speak with her. She couldn't legally compel them, but there were other ways of getting people to talk.

While Jasmine and Sierra's Web did the deep diving, she could do what they could not. And Blade… Bringing him along could be a catalyst, if they actually ran into Emily.

"If we're correct in our theory, seeing us together might set her off," she warned as they drove out of town just after nine that morning. "We could be heading into a minefield." As she said the words, Morgan pulled off to the shoulder of the road.

"I can't do this, Blade. I can't take you." The investigation would go better with him there. He knew more about his summer with Emily than anyone. Might remember something more. And the rest…of course he knew more. But… "If something happens to you… I can't take that on, too."

The weight of her sister's death was weighing her down so heavily she wasn't sure anymore that justice was going to free her from anything. How did you build a future if you'd been responsible for the death of your other half?

Blade's gaze, as he looked at her, was not at all congenial. Or cooperative. Instead, he was clearly a man who was going to do what he was going to do. But his tone wasn't combative as he said, "You can drive up on your own, but you can't stop me from also visiting Everson today."

No. She couldn't. But…

"My life, my choice," he said.

She didn't want him going out on his own. Possibly even

going rogue. They'd be safer together. She'd have more chance to protect him if she was with him.

And...he'd have her back, too. She was strong. Capable. Trained. And only human. Not invincible.

Not that she'd cared all that much, either way, since Maddie's death. If she died, she'd be whole again.

She wasn't living with a death wish. She just hadn't feared her own death. Hadn't given it much thought. Hadn't cared a lot.

So why, sitting on the side of the highway with a man who was still a suspect in her sister's murder, was she suddenly wanting to stay alive?

With one last glance at him, but not another word, she pulled back onto the highway.

I can't take that on, too. Morgan's words continued to reverberate with Blade. His perspective of the occurrences that had robbed him of his future shifted again. Being with Morgan, he wasn't just experiencing things through his own life. It was as though he could feel her, sense her, something. At the very least, he was gaining new understanding—outside himself.

I can't take that on, too.

Too. As though in addition to what she'd already taken on. And while she could have been referring to her sister's cold case, combined with the two new murders, he didn't think so.

She couldn't be responsible for his death. Too.

Meaning she felt responsible for Madison's. The thought hit him harder than a ton of bricks. Hit him in a real way. All those years...she'd been blaming herself?

And why wouldn't she, since she believed her boyfriend had been the one to kill her sister? And with the scenario she'd given him the day before—her thinking he'd mistaken Madison for her—he'd been so busy digesting the fact that she'd had serious thoughts about meeting him after hours, down by the river...

Because, yeah, he'd had those thoughts, too.

But the key point was, the two of them...they'd known better than to trade one night for their integrity. They'd been given a set of counselor rules for good reason. And other than the one instance of following Shane to the party, and staying until the guy had left, he'd never broken one of them. The one he had broken had also been for good reason. Looking out for the safety of others. Not for his own personal gratification.

And while he had no desire to point fingers at the dead, neither could he sit in the silence that had pervaded the car since she'd left the shoulder of the road.

"No matter what we find, if it *was* Emily, Maddie's death was not your fault, Morgan." He'd been vacillating between present and past so much he'd almost said Morgie. Caught himself.

She didn't even look his way. Just kept driving. Her face schooled into the professional expression he was growing to dislike a lot. He was fine with her keeping walls up between them—mostly fine, at any rate. He understood that. But to cement even her normal daily expressions...

They weren't strangers. And the circumstances that had brought them together...

"Madison chose to break the rules," he said then, whether it made her mad or not. If she'd been living in a torturous hell of her own making, with no one to help her see her way out...if that was the only good thing having him back in her life did for her then it would be worth her anger. "She chose to attend the unsanctioned party. To meet Shane there.

And she chose to be in those woods late at night. There was no sign of a struggle at the scene. No sign of anyone being dragged or trying to get away. No signs of restraint or defense wounds on her body. She was there because she chose to break the rules that were in place to keep her safe. And she chose not to tell you, to even give you a chance to watch out for her."

There. Whether she allowed him to help her or not, at least the words were in her brain. She'd have to play them through. And knowing her as he was beginning to believe he still did, believing that the Morgie he'd known hadn't been completely obliterated by that summer's events, he'd bet money that every time she blamed herself, she'd at least think about what he'd said.

Not because he was that important. Or that smart. But because she was a person who considered all sides of a situation.

When she had access to them.

He'd merely given her access.

And had one more thing to say about it. "Just like today. If something happens to me up there…it's on whoever does the damage. And would only be a really unfortunate result, a consequence, of my choice to visit Everson."

Because Madison Davis had most certainly not deserved to die that night. Her death hadn't been her fault. At all.

She'd paid horrible consequences for a choice she'd made.

And that was that.

Morgan instinctively rejected Blade's attempt to absolve her of any guilt in her sister's death. If Morgan had befriended someone, brought them into Madison's life, and then Madison died as a result, there was culpability.

But for a second there, her chest had lightened. She'd felt a flutter in her stomach. Had felt like a cupcake with buttercream icing. And it was nice.

She'd thought all deep, good personal sensations had died right along with her sister. They'd shared feelings. An ability to feel what the other was feeling. People had scoffed at the possibility. People who weren't identical twins and hadn't ever felt that sense of being an intricate part of another.

It's on whoever does the damage. Madison had made the choice to break the rules that were designed to keep her safe.

The thoughts presented a second time as they left rush hour city traffic behind, and she upped her speed. And again…that lightening in her chest…a fresh clear breath… came. And went.

When she needed to be focused completely on Emily Kingsley. "Tell me what you know about Emily's current daily life," she began, breaking the silence that had been trying to hold her in a world where Maddie's death wasn't on her.

"She's…" Blade's words were cut off by the ringing of Morgan's burner cell. Only people on the case had the number. She'd paired the phone with the car's audio system. Recognizing Kelly Chase's number, she let the psychiatry expert know that she was on speakerphone as she answered.

"Remy Barton has agreed to advise us in any way he can," Kelly reported. "I've looked over his portfolio, and after speaking with him, I think you made a good call, bringing him to our attention," she told Morgan. "I brought him up to speed on everything, sent over reports. He said he'll be back to me later this afternoon, and I'll let you know as soon as I hear anything from him."

Morgan would have liked to be in touch with Remy herself. Just to connect with her good friend, to hear what he had to say to her, personally, regarding the drastic turns her life had taken in the past two days. But for that reason, she hadn't texted him. She wasn't ready to talk about it.

Not even to Remy, or Carrie, his wife. Or Jasmine, either. Her friend had tried to get her alone, had managed to issue a small reminder warning in the hallway, stating she should think about stepping back and allowing the FBI to bring the killer in, but Morgan had managed to sidestep any response and then they'd been joined by Blade and any further chance for conversation on the subject had been forfeited.

On some level she knew that Blade was the reason she was distancing herself from the people who'd been her support group over the past many years.

She couldn't let herself dwell on that, either. Not until the work was done.

As soon as they hung up from Kelly, she asked again about Emily. Heard the rundown of what he'd found the night before. The woman had a degree in marketing. Had bounced from firm to firm, mostly worked from home, but had never seemingly been out of work. She'd been married three times, had no kids, was currently going through a divorce, and her home was on the market. From what he'd been able to find in public records, she didn't appear to have any family in town.

"Maybe the third divorce, especially if she's being forced to sell her home because of it, is her stressor and she went back to what she might think started it all," Morgan said, looking for the rationale behind what they were thinking the woman might have done. "She's blaming you for not wanting her, me for taking you away from her. Framing you. Trying to get me out of the picture...that part makes sense."

"But why Shane? And Hampton?"

"Maybe the who doesn't matter as much as they were at camp. For all we know she had sessions with Hampton over something at camp, or in her home life. And Shane? Maybe she went after him, too. Or, more likely, he went after her, and then moved on..."

Blade shook his head. "I don't remember Shane ever chatting her up, or even making booty call remarks about her..."

Still didn't mean it hadn't happened. It wasn't like the two guys had been buds. They'd just been counselors, in adjacent cabins, and so involved in a lot of the same activities with the same people.

"It's possible that she has nothing to do with the current murders," Blade said as the miles whizzed by in the shapes of Michigan wilderness in the summertime. Woods thick with green leaves, farmers' fields filled with corn, soybeans and asparagus. Small towns sparsely spaced around them.

Morgan glanced over at him. "You think she's the one who killed Madison, though?"

His shrug didn't tell her enough. And it occurred to her it could be because he might really and truly be as much in the dark as she was.

With as great a need to know.

His being there with her, having spent much of the night following up on a flash memory...felt more like compulsion than deflection.

He wasn't deliberately trying to steer her wrong.

She had no proof of that. And could already hear Jasmine telling her that thought right there was why she needed to pull back.

And maybe, if she was the agent in charge on the case, a member of law enforcement being entrusted to solve three murders, she would consider having someone appointed in her place.

As it was, she was helping those officially assigned to find the killer. And being paid to do so. Blade had legally and officially hired Sierra's Web, and in particular her. She was doing the job she'd signed on to do, with everyone involved fully aware of her personal attachment to the case.

It was that exact attachment that made her the one for the job.

And… "It seems a bit too coincidental that these murders happened, after all these years, within twenty-four hours of each other, involving you, if they aren't connected," she put out there.

"Any word on the Donnelly brothers?" Blade asked then.

And she shook her head. "Sierra's Web was still working up full profiles when I talked to Glen after the flare hit my room this morning. He said I should have the report by noon. But as far as he'd seen, there was nothing that stood out. Neither of them have police records. Alex had a speeding ticket, which he paid, four years ago. Last known address for both was Grand Rapids. Hopefully with techs sending current images of them through security camera footage, we'll be able to see if they've been in Rocky Springs recently."

Nothing that had turned up so far had definitively ruled them out, but there was nothing that made them suspicious, either.

And truthfully, the Donnellys had been a crapshoot. Names culled merely because they'd been siblings at camp. The rest had all been theory.

Good storytelling.

Like her relationship with Blade Carmichael had been all those years ago? A fairy tale she'd created in her mind?

And if so, what did that make him in the moment, in her car?

A suspect? A man she was keeping a close eye on? Her closest tie to what happened in the woods that night?

A co-sufferer? Someone in her same boat who needed what she needed nearly as badly as she did?

The man who'd hired her to find the truth so that he could not just be free but be exonerated in the murder that had been pinned on him seventeen years before? And the ones currently framing him?

He could be any or all those things.

As long as she didn't start creating fiction in her head again and cast him as a friend.

Chapter 13

Unless Emily Kingsley was some kind of supervillain, there was no way she could have killed Shane Wilmington, let alone Mark Hampton. She'd have to have been able to teleport from a divorce court hearing the day before to Hampton's office or create funds out of frozen assets in order to hire anyone.

The woman wasn't happy to see Blade and Morgan together. He got that loud and clear. Her sarcasm about how nice it was to see them together again couldn't be missed. And she'd been pretty much heartless in response to that week's killings. She was not what Blade would consider a nice person, in any way.

But she wasn't their killer.

He and Morgan were out of Everson less than half an hour after they'd arrived. And, at Morgan's suggestion, were heading to Lavenport, to talk to people who'd last seen Mark Hampton. It was what a private investigator did, she said, as though reminding herself as much educating him.

"You want to see if anyone recognizes me?" he asked, not in an unfriendly way, but serious just the same. The more he came to understand her position, what she had to have been through mentally and emotionally, the less he blamed her for doubting everyone and everything.

She glanced over at him as she pulled out onto a side road that would, in an hour's time, lead them straight into Lavenport. "No."

He believed her. The denial felt good.

"And for the record," she continued, "I already told you I don't believe you murdered Shane or Dr. Hampton. I'd appreciate it if you'd keep our relationship professional and quit baiting me."

"I wasn't baiting you," he heard himself say where he would normally have kept his own counsel. "I've lived under suspicion for the past seventeen years," he found himself explaining for the very first time. Would like to have wondered why, in the midst of a double homicide investigation and quest for a seventeen-year-old killer, he decided to open up. But he didn't have to wonder. He knew.

Morgan had that effect on him. In the past, when he'd been falling in love with her, and apparently in the current day, too, as his private investigator.

So be it.

He'd learned a long time before not to fight that which you had no power to change.

Might have shared that insight with her, too, if she hadn't just reprimanded him. The chastisement he could take all day long. For himself. But her uttering it meant that she was bothered. And that was something for which he did not want to be responsible.

The woman had suffered enough.

There'd been no sign of them being followed to Everson. No sign that anyone was following them out of town, either. And nothing new to learn in Lavenport. Everyone Morgan spoke to was shocked at Mark's death. Saying he was well loved. Had no enemies. He'd been divorced for years. His wife had moved away shortly after the split. They'd had no children. He'd never remarried. He didn't drink or hang around in bars as far as anyone knew. No one had seen who'd been in the psychologist's office. He'd had no appointment on his calendar for the time of his death. And no one had gone through reception.

Which meant the doctor had to have known his killer, and let him or her in.

The building, and Mark's office, had no security cameras, as patient confidentiality was a big concern for them.

Pulling over as they headed out of town, Morgan asked Blade if he minded driving. She'd still keep her attention on their surroundings, but she needed some time on her phone. Needed to read reports that had been coming in. She was missing something.

It had to be there.

Once they were back on the road, she read half a page of information from Sierra's Web, regarding campers from that summer, organized by those who had circumstances that stood out as possible homicidal tendencies or stressors, and, after another quick check of their surroundings, glanced over at Blade.

"You know Kyle Brennan, or Tammy Phillips?" Both at the top of the list. She'd known them both by sight and name. Had thought they were nice.

"Kyle was in charge of all the counselors," Blade said. "He was great most of the time, but he had a temper on him. I once saw him trying to hammer a stake in the ground. The stake broke and he threw the hammer so hard it flew into a tree several yards away and stuck."

Shocked, she looked at him. "Did you report it?"

Blade shook his head. "I didn't have to. Mark Hampton

was there. I saw the doctor look over at Kyle and figured he'd get a talking-to."

Tense, Morgan looked back at her page. "Says here that he's been in and out of jail over the past couple of years. He'd had a drinking problem, and anger issues, though apparently had both under control until his son died a couple of years ago."

Blade's gaze swung toward her before quickly returning to the road. The glance had been enough for her to see his shock. "None of that came up in my searches last night."

"It's from police and court records," she told him. "And there's more. He recently lost his father in a boating accident... Kyle was driving the boat. And had an alcohol level above the legal limit."

"Mark Hampton," Blade said then, sending her another urgent glance. "The way I saw him looking at Kyle that day with the hammer. Stands to reason he'd counseled Kyle at least once..."

"What about Shane? Do you know of any interaction between the two of them?"

Blade pulled over then. Abruptly. Stopping the car. Staring at her hard. "Kyle had a thing for Madison." He bit out each word. "It didn't occur to me to... Every guy at camp except for me seemed to have a thing for her—" His words cut off abruptly, as though he'd just realized who he was talking to.

Morgan shook her head, couldn't be bothered with supposed hurt feelings. "You know I was fine being the introverted twin," she reminded him impatiently. "And I knew full well how the guys all gravitated toward Maddie, and how much she loved being the belle of the ball..." Her mouth dropped open as horror surged through her.

"Kyle?" she asked. "You think he followed Maddie from the party after Shane left without her? That he…"

Her words broke off as pieces fell more solidly into place than they had since the entire nightmare had begun…making sense in a way nothing ever had…

Reaching behind them, Blade pulled a file from one of his boxes that he'd put back in the car when they'd left Detroit. "That's a recent picture of him," he told her. The image was printed in black and white on copier paper. Didn't matter. She saw what he wanted her to see.

The man had been at the beach, and the social media caption read, "Just chilling with my homies."

Heart pumping, breath coming in gulps, Morgan was about to ask Blade if he knew where Kyle was living, thinking he'd be the quickest way to the answer, when her burner phone pealed, startling her so badly she jumped.

Expecting the call to be from Jasmine, or Sierra's Web, she was startled to see Detective Silver's number on the screen. Recognizing it from the area code and the last three digits being zero.

Putting the call on speaker without hesitation, she looked at Blade and said, "Hello?"

"There was a bomb in your car." Silver's voice was urgent. "Kaycee went out to move it, and just happened to notice the device because the sun caught the black plastic…"

Blood drained from her face. She looked at the floor of the car. Caught in a sense of unreality as she said, "Tell me she's okay…" And then, eyes wide, looked at Blade.

Kept her eyes pinned on the depth of his as she heard, "She's fine. She made a run for it and got far enough away before it went off, but if she'd sat in the driver's seat…"

She got the picture. If that had been her, if she'd gone

out at night, or on a cloudy day, or just plain hadn't been looking in the right place as the sun shone in...

"He's escalating." Blade's words were sharp. Filled with very clear anger. "This was more than a warning."

She calmed herself as best she could. *Think*, she ordered herself. *Think!* "There's got to be something there that will lead us to him," she said then. "Call Jasmine, get FBI's bomb experts there..."

"Already done." Silver's voice had a tone of compassion in it that time. Something she didn't need. "They want you two in protective custody," he added. "I think..."

Her phone beeped another call. Jasmine's number. With Silver still talking, she showed Blade her screen, her brows raised. He shook his head.

"You'll be getting a call from the protection detail—" Silver was saying.

Ignoring the FBI agent's call, Morgan interrupted Silver to say, "I *am* protective custody. Blade and I are safer on the move, and we'll be in touch," she finished and rung off.

They could trace her call. They had the number. Could even show up wherever she and Blade went next, but they couldn't make her cower and hide.

If someone had to die bringing in Maddie's killer, it might as well be her. She couldn't sit back and let others die when she could be partially to blame. Or, for that matter, ever.

But this time...it was personal.

She was not stopping until the job was done.

Blade had spent seventeen years relying only on himself, fighting to build a life within a wall of suspicion, learning to live with the weight he carried, being on guard for mistrust from others and working to prove he wasn't the man the world had judged him to be.

In the space of one phrase, "if she'd sat in the driver's seat," everything had changed. His reputation didn't mean a whit when weighed against Morgan Davis's life.

Nor did his future. He'd been all in on their investigation from the beginning. His reasons for being so had changed in a blip. As had the urgency of his time frame. He had a lifetime to prove his innocence.

She might not have another day if they didn't get the fiend who was murdering people, framing him, and who was now after her. Seemingly for not heeding warnings to quit helping him.

As soon as she'd hung up from Silver, Morgan dialed Sierra's Web. Blade wasn't pulling back onto the freeway until he knew what the experts had to say.

"I'm putting you on speaker," he heard her say, just after her greeting to whoever had answered. "Blade's here with me."

She hadn't heard what the firm had to tell her yet, but was including him. He was their client.

"I just got off the phone with Silver," she started in. "I need to know what you have on Kyle Brennan."

"Enough to know we're concerned about him," the male voice responded. "Hudson here," the voice then said. "Glen's in the room as well."

Both partners in the firm. IT and forensic experts. Blade recognized the names from the research he'd done.

"And we need to talk about the bomb, Morgan. I know this case is important to you, but it might be better served by one of our other expert investigators. Carmichael, you're there?"

"I am," he answered before meeting Morgan's gaze. He

knew what he'd see there. And while his senses were all pushing him to accept the firm's suggestion, to run with it, to save Morgan from any more danger, his mind knew differently.

With one more glance at Morgan's emotionless, hard-rock stare, he glanced out the front windshield. "And I disagree that someone other than Morgan would be better for the job." The words were like death in his throat. But he continued, "Not only does she know the case better than anyone, but she's going to work, by herself, or with all of us, and she's safer with all of us than she would be alone."

He glanced at her as he finished, saw the firm set of her chin, the tightness in her jaw—denoting her anger.

But he saw something more there, too. The softening in her eyes.

And guessed she didn't have any clue it was there, as she looked at her phone and said, "What do you have on Kyle Brennan?"

"I had my team start on him as soon as we had the compiled list we sent you, Morgan," the man continued. "He has a home in St. Joseph..."

A beach town only ten miles from Rocky Springs. Blade's gut grew tight.

"Local police were there this morning. No one answered the door. Nor is he answering his last known number."

Morgan glanced at Blade, and he nodded. Pulled out onto the freeway, looking for the next exit so he could head back the way they'd come. They had to get to St. Joseph. Unlike local police, Morgan could talk to anyone, and ask anything. They just didn't have to answer. He'd already learned that sometimes the questions she asked gave them information simply by the nonanswers.

"We don't have a warrant for financials yet," Hudson

continued. "We need something more to compel that. But we've been obtaining footage from many surveillance cameras since early this morning. Some going back more than a week. Our people have been going through them and were able to get his license plate number from one of them. From there, they've been scouring the footage for other hits on the plate…"

His mind boggling a bit at the amount of work being done, Blade still grew impatient to hear the bottom line. He had to know what he was up against in his determination to keep Morgan safe.

The only way he had a hope in hell of doing that was to help her catch the murderer who wanted her out of the picture.

Because there was no way she was ever going to agree to quit looking for Madison's killer…

His mind tuned all focus to Hudson Warner's voice as the expert said, "We have him on camera at a gas station at the edge of town, heading toward Rocky Springs, the day of Shane Wilmington's killing. And passing through an intersection yesterday morning, in the direction of Lavenport. In itself, this means nothing, but if we could similarly place him in those towns near the times of the murders…"

"We were just in Lavenport," Morgan told the expert. "No one saw anyone or anything suspicious, which makes me think that Hampton knew his killer and let him in his office. It's either the doctor letting someone in—there's a back entrance for personnel to come and go through—or someone having to go through reception to get to the private offices. Hampton was the only one back there during the time of his murder."

"We've got calls going out right now for any surveillance footage we can get in the town," Hudson said, making Blade extremely thankful for having hired the firm. It would have taken him weeks, probably with no results, to get that information on his own.

"In the meantime, we've got him on camera, not today, but several times over the past week driving by a corner convenience store half a mile from his home..."

"I'm on it," Morgan told the man. "Send me the address..."

The two talked more. Details about Kyle's father's death. Impending charges that were likely going to hit the man within the next week or two.

Which would be why the killings had taken place so soon, one after the other. Kyle was on a mission to complete business before his time was up.

Blade knew how it felt to be driven to finish a job he couldn't leave undone. But Kyle's mission? Killing others?

That was something he prayed he never had cause to understand.

And was more determined than ever to help Morgan find the guy, to stop him, before anyone else got hurt.

They made it to St. Joseph with no sign of anyone following them. The black car and the tan one seemed to have disappeared to the point that Morgan had to consider that she hadn't been followed at all. That she'd been mistaken.

She didn't believe it, though.

"Why would he suddenly stop having us followed?" she asked Blade as they made their way to the convenience store by Kyle Brennan's house.

Barely taking his gaze off the road, Blade threw her a glance, and shook his head. "There are so many pieces in all of this that have never made sense to me," he said. "Until today. Kyle killing Maddie..."

His words dropped off and she glanced around them,

thinking at first that he'd noticed a car behind them after all, recognized one in front of them, saw Kyle...

But her quick, professional scan gave her nothing. And she figured that he'd stopped talking for more personal reasons.

"We're here to find out the truth, Blade," she said, softly. Her gaze on him. The stiff shoulders, that muscle in his neck, the tenseness of his jaw. "I've never been out to prove you guilty. All I've ever wanted, what I need, is the truth."

He pulled to a stop at a red light and his glance her way lasted uncomfortably longer than the previous one. "But those two points, proving me guilty and finding the truth, they're one and the same to you."

His words tugged at a piece of her heart she'd thought dead and gone. Forcing her to look deep before she answered him. And when she had her answer, she met his gaze. "No," she told him. "I believed that the truth would point me to you, but I wasn't looking for it to. Or in any way wanting it to."

The admission cost a lot. Inside her. Where she'd stopped living.

It scared her.

Left her uneasy. Unsure what it meant. What it changed. If it changed anything.

The light had changed. Completely silent, Blade was focusing on the road again. She did the same. There was nothing else *to* do. He was a client.

Someone had just tried to blow her up.

And they weren't just on individual quests to solve a seventeen-year-old crime. They were on the hunt for a current killer. Or two.

The convenience store was deserted when she and Blade walked in. A woman behind the counter, brown skinned, fortyish looking, named Bonita according to her badge, studied the photo that Morgan handed to her, leaving Morgan to wonder, as the perusal went on far longer than a glance or two, if the woman knew something. And was trying to figure out what to do or how much to say if anything.

"Who did you say you were?" Bonita finally asked, looking from her to Blade and back.

Morgan pulled out her creds, held them clearly for the clerk to see.

She was ready to pull her gun as well when the woman said, "I know him, yeah. He comes in here fairly regularly for his morning coffee. He's the guy who's under investigation for the boating accident that killed his dad. It's been all over local news…"

Morgan nodded.

"Someone from the family hire you to check into it all?" the clerk asked, sliding a hand into her short-sleeved, pocketed work jacket. Blade's step closer, putting his thigh against Morgan's, was no mistake. She was glad for his support.

"No, I'm actually…" She stopped, nodded toward Blade. "We…" she corrected, hating that she was happier not working alone after the bomb episode that morning, "we knew him, years ago. At camp. We're looking up people who were there that summer, talking about stuff that happened and wanted to see Kyle."

True. And yet…unless the woman knew more than she was saying, Morgan was mostly nonthreatening. She'd shown her credentials.

"I haven't seen him in the past couple of days," Bonita said then, her gaze clear, as she handed back the grainy photo. "I don't think he was in for coffee yesterday, and I know he wasn't in this morning."

Morgan looked around for surveillance cameras. Saw none. Suggested to the woman that she speak to the owner of the store about getting some in. For their own safety from theft, if nothing else, and was heading out the door behind Blade when the clerk called out.

"You might ask Jessica," she said. "His ex-wife. They split after their boy died, so I don't know if she can help, but they grew up together, so she might know who'd know."

Bonita's knowledge of Kyle Brennan went back a lot further than the few months since his father's death. Making a mental note, Morgan got Jessica's information, thanked Bonita and headed out the door. Feeling heat on her back as she did so.

As though every step she took was being watched.

Out of curiosity? It probably wasn't every day that the convenience store clerk had a visit from a nationally certified private investigative expert. Most particularly not one interested in a summer camp experience from her youth.

And Bonita could know a whole lot more about Kyle than she was letting on. Like the mission he was on—with little time to complete it. She'd clearly had sympathy in her tone when she'd talked about the man.

Because of his losses.

But surely the clerk didn't condone emotional pain as an excuse to run around the state murdering people. The fact that Morgan even considered the possibility gave her a clue as to how jaded her heart and mind had become over the years.

At some point, she'd begun to believe that anyone was capable of anything.

Which was the complete antithesis of what her exuberant twin would have wanted.

The realization sickened her.

Chapter 14

Jessica was an accountant for a small real estate firm housed in a three-story professional building in downtown St. Joseph. Blade pulled into a diagonal spot out front as Morgan finished a call with Sierra's Web over the car's audio system.

Kelly Chase had called to give them an update on Remy Barton's thoughts pertaining to the case. The child psychiatrist had gone over the case files and Kelly was keeping him apprised of new information as it came in. She'd reported that Remy felt certain, as they all did, that whoever had killed Shane had had something to do with Madison Davis's murder seventeen years before. He'd agreed that a recent stressor would have probably instigated the new string of murders. And had pulled Kyle and Tammy Phillips as the two most likely suspects from those at camp that year. He also strongly believed that the same person was responsible for all three murders.

His reasoning for thinking so had been sound enough that Kelly agreed with him.

Remy also felt that Morgan needed to leave town immediately, get herself as far from the case as possible, until law enforcement found the killer. The escalated threats against her were bothering him greatly.

As they were everyone—with the exception, apparently, of Morgan.

"He's a friend," Morgan reminded Blade as the call disconnected. "Of course he's worried. Same as Jasmine."

And her coworkers at Sierra's Web, too, though Blade didn't bother mentioning Kelly's reminder that if Morgan wanted to be removed from the case, they had other proven investigative experts who could step in.

He almost called the firm back and fired her, when she reached for her door handle, and turned, shaking her head, as he grabbed his. "This is an ex-wife, Blade. A woman who lost a son. The father of whom is likely going to be charged with some kind of negligent, DUI homicide in the death of his own father. She's not going to be receptive to opening up with an unknown man in her midst. And if she happens to know about what happened at camp seventeen years ago, which she might since she and Kyle grew up together, she'll probably freeze up completely with you there."

The sense the woman made pissed him off. Put him on edge. Because she was right. And because he did not, in any way, want her walking into that building alone.

He might not be a cop, but he was a licensed gun carrier and knew how to shoot.

"I'm a big girl, Blade. I'm really good at what I do, and know how to watch my back." Morgan's odd tone hit him in a very personal way. Was she attempting to…comfort…him?

Because she was a professional, and right, he nodded. "I'll stay right here," he told her, his tone firm. "And wait…"

He stopped her with a hand on her arm before she got out of the car. "Put me on speed dial," he told her. "And keep the screen on so you just have to press once."

The glance she gave him, like she wanted to smile, or was about to reach over and give him a quick, reassuring kiss, shook him far more than it should have done, as she slid from the car.

But before leaving him, she paused long enough to set up a speed dial icon for him on her phone's front screen. Held it up for him to see. And then bent down. "If I'm anywhere near as good at my job as I'm told I am, I'm probably going to be a bit," she told him. "Maybe you could use the time to visit a few of the bars near Kyle's house? Show his picture around? Ask if anyone has seen him?"

With a knot in his gut, Blade nodded.

While she'd escaped the explosive planted in her car that morning, they were clearly sitting on a time bomb that was ready to go off. They couldn't afford for Blade to sit around and play babysitter.

But he watched her safely into the building, saw her show her credentials to the security guard, saw the uniformed man check her gun and hand it back to her, before he drove off.

As soon as Jessica Brennan heard Morgan's name, her face changed from questioning to almost warm and she gently ushered Morgan down the hall to a small conference room.

Morgan turned as Jessica shut the door behind them. "I'm sorry just to show up like this, but…"

Jessica cut her off before she could finish. "Oh, don't apologize. I've wanted to meet you forever. I just have to say, I'm so, so sorry about what happened to your sister. I've thought about you so many times over the years. The way that summer changed Kyle…he was so much more aware…more vulnerable, maybe…letting people know he cared about them…and I can't even imagine how it changed your life. I just…please know that your pain is shared…"

Jessica's words broke off as tears filled her eyes, and Morgan, fighting her own rush of emotion, nodded. Took a deep breath. She was there to work. To focus.

Not to feel.

"I was sorry to hear about your son." The words slid forth because they were right. Not because she was working.

Blinking, Jessica nodded again, motioned to a couch along the back wall, took a seat at one end and when Morgan sat on the other said, "The day after he returned from camp that summer, Kyle asked me to take a hike in the woods with him. He told me all about that horrible morning, when Madison's body was found…"

Another force hit Jessica. Chin trembling, she kept her lips together and nodded.

"He told me how much he loved me and asked me to marry him. He said he didn't want to wait another second for me to be his wife and wanted to elope. And…we did…" The woman's smile was bittersweet. Completely lacking in anger or resentment.

And she hadn't yet asked why Morgan was there, suddenly showing up out of the blue.

Morgan took on the sweet woman's pain, pushing away her own, forcing her mind to kick into gear. Kyle's eloping as soon as he got back from camp, after having been clearly interested in Maddie, spelled one thing to her. Guilt.

"He was so angry that summer. He'd talk about everyone who hadn't protected your sister. The camp psychologist, Hampton he said his name was…he just kept going on and on about the man's incompetence, said he was serving his own self-interest and not watching over the kids in his care. Said Madison would still be alive if not for him…"

Morgan didn't tell the woman that the psychologist was dead.

"He's kind of been that way ever since," Jessica said then, her face shadowing. "Always taking it to heart when someone hurt someone else. Not long ago he risked his job as director of technology at Bloomington's." The woman named the national chain of clothing stores. "He actually went to the CEO and threatened to go public with workplace inequities over what he thought was poor treatment of a store manager."

Jessica sounded as proud of her ex-husband as she did worried about him. Maybe more so.

"Have you heard anything recently about the summer that started it all?" Morgan asked, willing herself to stay above water with the compassionate woman. She couldn't afford any sympathy for herself at the moment. Couldn't let the grief take hold. "I was hoping to talk to him, but haven't been able to reach him. The woman at the convenience story thought you might know where he is."

Jessica shook her head. "I've made a point to check in with him regularly since his father's death, and he hasn't said anything about that summer. Hasn't mentioned it in years. But he's in bad shape. I'm really worried about him. I haven't talked to him in a few days. I've been working long hours for a midyear close of books, and I'm worried that I haven't been there enough for him. I tried to call him last night and again this morning, but there was no answer."

Clearly, while the woman didn't want personal involvement with her ex-husband, she cared about him.

And Morgan knew what she had to do. Without telling the woman the ramifications, she suggested that Jessica call the police for a welfare check, and then, if they couldn't find him, place a missing person's report. And sat there beside her as Jessica made the call.

Well over an hour had passed by the time Morgan texted

Blade that she was on her way downstairs. And the first thing she told him, when she climbed into the car, was that she feared Kyle might be suicidal.

If he thought he'd finished his business...he had nothing left for which to live.

"If his last act was to kill me, and he didn't know I'd given my car keys to the police, he'd know that the bomb went off and might think me dead," she told him.

"I'm willing to hope for that," Blade said as he pulled out into traffic.

And then she told him her bigger news. As soon as a missing person's report was filed, they'd have access to Kyle's bank account and credit card statements. She'd already texted Sierra's Web and Jasmine to be on the watch for the report.

The quick look he gave her felt personal as he said, "You *are* impressively good at what you do."

When Morgan felt herself sliding into the warmth his words sent through her, she quickly forced her mind to the job at hand. Asking Blade if he'd found out anything new. And then paid attention, listening between the lines, as he told her he hadn't found out anything new during the hour. Listening for anything that might not seem important to him, but that clicked with her. He'd visited a couple of bars. Kyle hadn't frequented them. Someone from the grocery store closest to his house recognized him but didn't even know him by name. The manager of the bank in his neighborhood said they couldn't give out information to anyone without a warrant, even as to whether Kyle was a client or had been in recently. Blade had posed as an old friend as he'd approached the man's neighbors, but only a couple had been home, and no one had seen him in the last day or two.

In a way, the news was good. Kyle's seeming disappearance could mean that they were more likely on the right track.

But she was too aware of how the world worked, too seasoned at her job, to sit around and count on that. She called in a full report to both Jasmine and Sierra's Web, heard praise from Jasmine and Glen Rivers Thomas regarding the missing person's report—and then, with Blade's full buy-in, told both teams that she and Blade were going to head northeast, toward Flint, to see if they could get an interview with Tammy Phillips. The woman was older than she and Blade, so neither of them had known her well. She'd been in charge of camper special activities—drama and camp photos was all Morgan remembered—taking kids a group at a time, and the counselors had most often just dropped off their charges and come back later to get them.

She'd been someone Morgan had looked up to. Had never, to Morgan's knowledge, ever given anyone reason not to trust her.

But Tammy had been in and out of trouble ever since that summer. There'd been a pregnancy that next year, with the baby placed with child services, to eventually be adopted out. After that she'd done time for a number of things, including petty theft, prostitution and purposefully running her car into a male boss who'd fired her. The man's injuries hadn't been serious, and she'd been out of jail almost a year. But her family members had all refused to take her back in, so she was sharing an apartment with another former prostitute. She'd just, the week before, been fired for the third time since her release—a job stocking shelves at a discount store—for losing her temper with customers. From what Sierra's Web had found, there'd been talk on social media about her having threatened a customer, but no charges were filed. Tammy had claimed that the guy hadn't filed because he'd deserved what she'd given him.

It could all add up, the final stressor being the most recent job loss.

"But what would any of it have to do with Madison's murder?" Morgan asked herself as much as Blade, thinking aloud as they sped across highway miles. "Or Shane's or Hampton's? I don't remember her ever having any kind of crisis at camp."

"Shane never talked about her, either," Blade added.

So maybe they were on the wrong path. But she had to keep looking, anyway. Two expert teams of professionals were working the case. Morgan's job was to go underground and find out what they couldn't.

To find the one small crumb that could bring it all together.

Something for which she'd been searching, unsuccessfully, for close to two decades. But there were so many more pieces now. Which meant a lot more crumbs that could be languishing out there, never to be found if she didn't look all over. Overturn every single rock.

No matter how unlikely it might be to tell her the truth.

At Morgan's suggestion, they drove through a well-known high-quality sandwich shop on the way toward Flint. And at his own, ate while he drove. As unbelievably busy as Blade had been over the past few years, as his company reached heights of success he'd failed to dream of, he'd taken to using the time driving from construction site to construction site as his lunch hour. And lately, his dinner hour, too.

Whether by some kind of telepathic agreement, or just because they were both filled with thoughts and impressions pertaining to the past forty-eight hours, he and Morgan were silent for most of the way to the little town just before Flint, Tammy Phillips's last known address.

Unlike their attempts to locate Kyle Brennan, they had no trouble finding the woman. Though two minutes into the interview in the small living room of her rented apartment, Blade was beginning to wish they hadn't been so lucky.

"I wouldn't have thought it possible for you to get any sexier, Construction Man," the woman purred, taking a seat right next to him on the couch. With the whole couch stretching out bare beside them.

While Morgan sat in the armchair perpendicular to him. *Construction Man.* The woman had kept track of him?

"But look at you, you have," she finished, touching one finger to the top of his hand.

Blade didn't even chance a peek at Morgan. Didn't want to know, either way, if she was at all bothered by the camp activities director's familiarity.

As though they'd known each other far more personally than he'd told Morgan they had.

What he knew was that he was a distraction, getting in the way of the job.

He stood and asked if Tammy minded if he used her restroom. Even though she made a point of telling him that he could use the one attached to her bedroom down the hall and to the right, making a point to apologize for the little bits of lingerie she'd left out, he quickly excused himself as though he couldn't wait to find out for himself what was there.

And scoped out a different half bath, first door on the left.

To give Morgan time to do her job so they could get the hell out.

Since he was in the little lavatory, he actually took a

few seconds to pee, but then, second-guessing his choice to leave the room, hurriedly washed his hands and made a beeline back to the living room. Morgan was trained. Armed. And capable.

Blade still didn't like leaving her alone with a murder suspect.

Morgan was standing by the front door when he returned. Tammy, still on the couch where he'd left her, stood as soon as he appeared, and walked toward him. "You don't have to go so soon, do you?" she asked, touching her arm to his as she glanced up into his eyes.

He glanced over at Morgan, who didn't say a word.

"I can always drive you where you need to go afterward," Tammy said softly, her tone loaded with innuendo, at which point Blade's tolerance ran out.

"I'm with Morgan," he said, quite clearly, glancing at the investigator he'd hired as though there was a whole lot more between them than work.

Doing so convincingly enough that Tammy stepped back, a sullen look overtaking her lined and used-looking features. "Well, who'd have thought?" she said, her accommodating sexy tone suddenly filled with sarcasm—and bitterness. "He gets the girl, kills her twin and then gets the girl again?"

"Let's go." Morgan's tone was an order.

By the time she'd finished uttering it, he was at the door, pulling it open. Trusting that she'd managed to get all the information she'd needed during his minute down the hall.

Neither of them spoke until they were back in the car. He'd started the engine and was pulling away, trying to find a way to get Morgan to believe that he'd never had a single personal conversation with Tammy Phillips in the past, when Morgan said, "I sent a text to everyone while

I was waiting on you. Tammy's just joined Kyle at the top of our suspect list."

He'd been in the bathroom no more than a minute, two tops. Glancing at Morgan, seeing the tension in her jaw, he asked, "Why?" Praying it didn't have anything to do with him.

They were running out of time. He had to keep Morgan alive. And would be much better able to do so if she could trust him a little.

"That baby she had? The one that ended up being adopted out? It was Hampton's."

Blade pulled to a quick stop at the end of the street. Stared over at Morgan. Shook his head and looked again. "What?"

Throwing up her hands, she said, "According to her, at any rate. I've got everyone following up as we speak."

"How did that…? What did you…?" He'd known she was good, but, in less than a minute she'd managed to get so much information.

"I asked her how well she knew Mark Hampton," Morgan said. "She told me, 'Well enough to have his baby.' And then, when my mouth fell open, she told me that they'd had an affair all summer. She'd thought they had a future. But when Maddie was killed and summer camp came to an abrupt halt, she asked him about their next steps and he told her there weren't any. He was married. Apparently, she went to his wife, told her about the affair, about the baby. She took great delight in letting me know, without taking a breath, that the marriage ended less than two years after that."

"And the baby?"

"She claimed Mark signed off on the adoption. Oh, and…that the drugs in the baby's system were ones Mark gave her to help regulate her emotions."

"You believe her?" Blade asked, glancing in the mirror to make certain there was still no one behind him.

Morgan's shrug registered right about where he was landing. Turning the corner, heading toward the town's Main Street, he said, "We'll wait to hear what Sierra's Web reports back on that one."

And when Morgan said that she'd like to speak to Tammy's last employer, the manager of the discount store they'd passed on their way to the apartment complex, he headed in that direction. Trying like hell to tell himself that there was no change in Morgan.

No new doubts in her mind.

But with several glances in her direction, couldn't get a feel for where she was at. On anything.

And before he'd even decided to speak, he heard himself blurt, "I knew Tammy like you did in the past. Period. She was someone I dropped the boys off to. I swear to God, she didn't even seem to notice me, and even if she had, I sure as hell didn't notice her. Not in that way." He sounded like he was some kind of geeky high school kid trying to impress someone.

Rather than the wealthy, successful contractor he'd become.

Because he didn't see himself as successful. And didn't give a damn about the money. How could he when he lived under the shadow of an unsolved murder that had his name on it?

When he stopped at the next light, and turned to look at Morgan, she was studying him. He couldn't make out her expression but didn't feel arrows coming at him. "I swear to you, Morgan." The second he'd seen her, talking to her twin, trying to get Madison to listen to her about something while Maddie had been busy watching Shane, he hadn't looked at any other female without having the other come second.

Which was why he was still single.

That, and the shadow he lived under.

When it felt like Morgan was going to just sit there, not talking to him, forever, the light changed, and he pulled forward. Fully aware that he wasn't going to convince her of anything.

She needed the proof they didn't have.

Tammy's employer, and the bartender at a bar around the corner from her apartment, both painted the same picture. Tammy Phillips was a bitter woman with anger issues who blamed men for everything bad that had ever happened in her life.

And she was a woman who couldn't seem to live without men, too. She flirted with any guy she thought had money, and then, if he slept with her and ditched her, she targeted them. The bartender knew of two different times she'd told men's wives that she'd slept with them.

Both times, she'd been telling the truth.

The information by itself didn't make Tammy a killer. But the way she'd homed in on Blade when he'd made it clear he had no interest in Tammy—blurting out about killing one sister and still getting the other one...

She'd been reminded of things she'd heard the summer Maddie had died. Maybe not the exact words, but the tone of them, the content...

Her parents had tried to keep her away from all the publicity, but they hadn't been able to keep her off the internet. She'd read everything she could find.

Desperately searching for answers she still hadn't found.

And if Shane Wilmington's and Mark Hampton's deaths

remained unsolved, she would still be seeking. The quest had no end without the answers.

The bartender had brought up a self-defense instructor Tammy had mentioned, someone who could feasibly have taught the woman how to kill with pressure to the neck, among other things. She'd also said that Tammy, who was usually in every night, hadn't been at the bar the past couple of nights. The FBI team and Sierra's Web were already checking into Tammy's activities as much as they could without a warrant.

Any information Morgan and Blade could add would speed up the process. Until someone came up with enough for a warrant to bring the woman in for questioning.

She glanced over at Blade as he drove a few miles out of town toward the business address of the self-defense instructor. She couldn't talk to him about the confusing emotions roiling around inside her where he was concerned—couldn't let her focus be sidetracked right when she was on the cusp of something huge. But knew she had to get one thing out.

"I believe you," she said, only realizing it was a sentence hanging there out of the blue, when she came out of her own head enough to hear herself. She'd given that statement no modifier. Believed him about what?

But when he glanced over at her, his green eyes alive in a way she'd missed so much, giving her a nod before returning his attention to the road, she figured he understood.

And felt better.

Chapter 15

Donna Abigail, the self-defense instructor, hadn't been willing to speak with them and Morgan hadn't pushed.

"A hostile witness is likely to go straight to the suspect," she told Blade as he pulled out of the driveway and, taking Morgan's next suggestion, to try to see if Tammy's mother, who lived in Flint, would talk to them, he headed back to the highway.

She knew he was frustrated. Seemed to be seething with an overload of the tension that was consuming her, too, as her mind took her on yet another rundown of the case.

There'd been nothing from the coroner on either body that could tell them anything except how Shane and Hampton had died, and approximate times of death.

No fingerprints. Nothing even that tied Shane's and Hampton's deaths together.

The bomb in Morgan's car had been flown to Sierra's Web and was being analyzed. She was hoping that it would give them a clue. At least a place to search next.

"Unless something changes, I think we need to find an out-of-the-way place to spend the night tonight." She dropped the suggestion into the silence that had fallen in the car. Dinnertime was approaching. A couple of hours after that and darkness would be upon them.

The second night since Shane had landed at Blade's feet in the pit.

"Just in case whoever put that bomb in my car thinks it killed me, I'd like to stay out of sight of Rocky Springs, and Detroit."

It meant they'd be spending the night, if not in each other's direct company, at least very close.

"Agreed."

"Your duffel and my go bag are already in the trunk, and we can stop for anything else we might need."

He'd shown no reaction, no indication of any emotion at all attached to them being out overnight together. She should be thankful.

Ironically, his lack of care to something that, at one point in their lives, would have been the most major experience of a lifetime, left her a bit peeved.

Her response was so unacceptably unprofessional that she brushed it away. "I'd like to have Sierra's Web secure an overnight private rental for us so it can't be traced to either of us," she continued. "Small-town-getaway kind of thing. We'd be just another couple of strangers, and yet, in a place by ourselves in case Kyle, or whoever, discovers us. I don't want anyone else hurt, like they could have been with that fire on my balcony last night."

He didn't even glance over at her, his gaze trained on the road, as he said, "Fine. The safest place they can get where we can blend in undetected. Whatever it costs."

Ten minutes later, with the firm promising an overnight destination within the hour, Morgan was once again silently going over case information. She needed more space than her phone to see everything together. She needed Blade's dining room, his wall.

And until she could get out of the car and spread out to

get a more complete picture all at once, Morgan focused on the road, the woods and farmlands they were passing, every part of their surroundings, looking for anything that sparked her. She mentally reviewed the verbal report Sierra's Web had just delivered to her and Blade over the car's audio system.

The flare on her balcony the night before had been a dead end. Any identifying information had burned up. But based on size and what forensics had determined as content, the thing could have been purchased anywhere, most likely online. Silver's men had checked local places and had gotten nowhere.

Same with the bomb in her car that morning. Glen's team was still working on it, but from what they could determine, the thing could have been made in any kitchen. Hudson's team was checking internet searches for bomb creation tutorials made by Kyle, Tammy, the Donnelly brothers and Blade, and would then be doing the same search for the entire list of camp names starting with those their research led them to believe were most likely to commit a crime. Based on past criminal history—other than Kyle and Tammy, there were only some minor infractions—combined with any known life changes that could be stressors. From there, they'd go from oldest campers to youngest, as Maddie's death had been blunt force trauma and therefore more likely caused by someone big enough, strong enough, to deliver the blow. They'd also be doing searches of any of the common household chemicals contained in the bomb and comparing them to any possible flare purchases.

Local law enforcement would get warrants for financials where they could, which would allow Sierra's Web to pinpoint their searches more rapidly.

Shane's autopsy overview by Sierra's Web concurred

with the medical examiner's report. Cause of death had already been determined, and both examinations had concluded that the man's body had shown no defensive wounds, leading everyone on the case to believe that he'd known his attacker. His clothes had all been put through forensic testing and there'd been nothing on them to point to the identity of his attacker.

The pressure on his neck had been applied by some kind of smooth surface. The bottom of a shoe with an unmarked arch sole, or anything else that was smooth and four or so inches in width. The break had been smooth. Probably just one quick snap. With the gunshot wound being postmortem.

"Why would someone shoot Shane after he was dead?" She asked the question aloud. It bothered her. That bullet. Mostly because it made no sense.

Which meant she was missing a piece that would explain the action.

"I'd say to frame me, but that means whoever killed him would have to know that I have a license to carry, always have my gun on me, know at least the approximate caliber, know me well enough to know that, given the circumstances that night, I'd shoot. But you'd figure the killer would know that the coroner would be able to tell that the bullet didn't kill Shane, so it doesn't really make sense, does it?" His frown was half in shadow as the lowering sun cast a beam across him.

"The caliber of bullet does," she answered him honestly. "And if you did shoot him, knew he had a gunshot wound, shooting in the air that night could easily be explained as your attempt to make it look like self-defense. But...why? Why make up such a ruse, if you didn't need to shoot him at all because he was already dead, which you'd know if you'd killed him?"

"Unless I didn't know whatever I did to his neck had been fatal. What if he was still breathing?" Blade's tone held none of the fatigue she'd heard from him two days before. As though...he wasn't feeling the weight of suspicion on himself, but, rather, was putting himself in a killer's position.

He was right there with her. Committed to the truth, just as he'd told her he'd be. Her heart swelled, her admiration for him grew more than she'd ever have thought possible it could, as she looked over at him.

"From what the ME said, the break was in the upper cervical spine and resulted in instant death," she said slowly. "Breathing would have stopped instantly. There'd be no pulse. So why shoot at close enough range for the bullet to go completely through?" Depending on how long after death that shot had been made, there wouldn't have been any blood spatter. But, still, why shoot at all?

"If someone knew you carry a pistol, but wasn't sure of the exact details that would show up in forensics, and was trying to frame you..."

But that still didn't fit. Anyone who'd go to all that trouble, who knew that much, particularly someone who knew how to kill a person with quick pressure to the neck, would know that an ME would discover the shooting had happened after death...

"It has nothing to do with you," she said then, staring at Blade. Catching his gaze briefly as he glanced over at her and then back to the highway. "It's overkill. Whoever killed Shane already had the plan in place to frame you, by dumping the body with you alone on a locked site. The gunshot, that was just for himself..."

Silver and his people were already working with Jasmine to interrogate everyone who'd had access to Blade's schedule, who might have known that he'd be at the site late at night alone. But the killer could also just have been following him, like he'd had Morgan followed the day before...

And if the killer was Kyle, who lived just minutes away from Rocky Springs...who could make the kill, and the dump, and be home in bed within the hour...

"If I'm Kyle..." Blade's voice drew her gaze back to him, her mouth slightly open. It was like he'd read her mind, that he'd known what she was thinking...something that had happened in the past. The one thing that had convinced her that what she felt for him was real.

Because he'd been the only other person in her life, still was, other than her identical twin, who'd ever done that...

He was still talking, and she quickly focused, catching up with his description of how he'd feel as a senior camp counselor falling for the most beautiful, vivacious girl at camp. "And I think I had the girl first, I've made it clear she's the one for me, and Shane, the womanizer, who didn't really care for anyone but himself at that point, comes along and steals her away, just to play with her..."

She nodded, energized in a way she hadn't been in a very long time. Kept her eyes on Blade as she took over. "He has trouble controlling his temper," she said. "He's furious when Shane goes to the party to see Madison, waits around, thinking he'll charm some sense into her after you make Shane leave. But she's thinking she's in love with Shane at that point. She starts to scream, and he lashes out. Meaning just to quiet her down, but...the way you said he threw that hammer, an instant reaction that could have been deadly... he just used more force than he meant to on Maddie. She dies on him. He knows no one knew he'd been out there and takes off, leaving her there to die. The next day, when he gets away with it, it's like a new lease on life for him. He marries, keeps himself in check. Until his son dies..."

"He starts drinking heavily…his wife leaves him…he's out with his dad, the one person who probably stuck by him…"

The words caught at Morgan and she stared at Blade's profile. Needing to know…had his dad been there for him? After the suspicion in their small town had ruined the older man's business?

None of *her* business.

Blade's conversation was and she tuned in to hear "…and he goes after Hampton because the guy talked to him about his anger issue after the hammer incident, but didn't intervene? Didn't get him fired and into an anger management program? He's blaming everyone else for the hell his life has become?"

She drew air in sharply, unconsciously, as something else occurred to her. And drew Blade's gaze to her, too, before he quickly returned to the road.

"And he blames you for making Shane leave the party," she said. "And since you were already a suspect, he's hoping to make you pay as he expects to…with an indictment and long prison sentence."

"And you?" Blade asked, glancing at her one more time. "Why does he want you dead?"

She'd thought because she was getting too close to catching him, but that look in Blade's eye, as though he expected more from her…

"Because I'm not Maddie."

Blade's slow nod, that intense look in his green eyes, the grim set of his chin, told her, more than anything past or present, just how much the imminent threat against her life was affecting him.

They told her that he still cared.

Even if he didn't want to.

* * *

Blade had thought fate an enemy in the past. But the ironic twist of cruelty hitting him between the eyes as he drove was beyond the pale.

He'd grieved for Madison Davis. And for Morgan. He'd never recovered from that summer at camp. And not just because of his suspect status. He'd hurt because Morgan was hurting. Had never gotten over the loss of the future he'd thought they'd have together.

And he was now not only being framed for more murders, but he was also facing an unknown fiend trying to kill Morgan, too?

Kyle Brennan, Tammy Phillips or someone they didn't yet know. They could be sneaking up on them that exact second, on that very road. How could Blade possibly hope to beat what he didn't know? What he couldn't prepare for?

He couldn't let her die. There'd be no life left inside him.

When Morgan's phone rang, he felt the sound reverberate through every nerve in his body. Hoped to God they were about to hear that someone had caught Kyle. That he'd had definitive proof on him to nail him for all three murders.

And remembered that he'd given up on hope as soon as he heard Agent Jasmine Flaherty's voice come over the car's audio system. "Take me off speakerphone." The tone brooked no refusal.

With a glance at Blade, maybe with some apology in it, Morgan did so. And then signaled him to pull over.

Heart pounding with dread, he did so immediately, getting to the shoulder, and putting the vehicle in Park so that he could turn and glance all around them.

No, that didn't make sense. The FBI wouldn't be having them pull over if danger was coming up behind them.

Must mean it was in front of them…

Morgan's ashen face stopped his train of thought. She glanced at him, stared at him rather, her expression full of emotions he couldn't decipher, and then looked out the front windshield as she said, "We're on our way," and hung up.

Then, staring out the windshield said, "We have to head back to St. Joseph. You're wanted for questioning."

Blade's gut, his entire being, steeled into numbness as his mind took over. He stared at Morgan. "For what?" But he knew. Another body.

Who?

And how many more people had to die before...

Morgan was a talking statue. Sitting straight, staring straight. If not for the blinking of her eyes he...

"Gary Randolph was found an hour ago in the dumpster behind the office building where Jessica works."

He felt a prick of emotion. A flash of the man's face appeared and was gone. "He was our boss," he said slowly, sitting there in the driver's seat, going nowhere. But back. "He hired all the boys' camp counselors. Was the one who..." His words faltered as he slid back in time, felt the stab of panic, and then, forcing himself out, finished his sentence. "The one who hauled me out of bed that morning. The first person who asked me if I'd killed Maddie." Throat tight, he swallowed. Shook his head.

"He's dead, Blade. He died fifteen minutes after they found him. He'd been shot, had lost too much blood."

His brain started to catch up with the present. "In St. Joseph?" The city they'd just left. *He'd* just left. Behind the building where he'd dropped off Morgan, and, an hour later, had been texted to come pick her up.

"Time of dumping was within the last three hours. And based on when he was last seen..."

"...he was shot when you were with Jessica Brennan,"

he finished for her. While he'd been heading around town. Building an alibi of people, a few of whom would say they'd seen him, but none of whom could speak for what he might have done in between those short visits.

And Morgan wasn't looking at him.

Getting out of the car, he headed to her door.

She was out of the vehicle before he'd made it halfway around the hood, passed him by and was already behind the wheel before he got in.

He could make a run for it. She didn't know he wouldn't.

He'd pulled over beside a forest of pine trees. Something Michigan was famous for. A world within which, with his skills, he could survive, and keep hidden, until they quit looking for him.

A cornered man would run.

A guilty man would.

And Morgan wasn't doing anything to make sure he didn't. She just sat there, car running, waiting for him to get in with her.

She had to think like a professional. To remain fully on the job—mentally and physically. Morgan couldn't look at Blade. Couldn't bleed with him. Emotions would cloud her judgment. Make her weaker than either of them could afford.

When she felt him drop beside her, and her peripheral vision caught his hand closing the door, she put the car in Drive and took off. Looking for the first available turnaround.

Even as she did so, everything inside her tensed at the idea of getting anywhere near St. Joseph. Jasmine had told her that they wanted her there for her own safety. Thinking that Blade had been responsible for the warnings to her to back off. For the flare on her balcony that hit after he'd been in her room that night. Would know exactly where and how to aim. And a contractor would most definitely have access to flares.

The bomb…he'd been with her more than anyone. Could have planted the thing when he'd arrived at the police station that morning.

Her friend had had a supposition that fit. Made sense.

But it didn't ring true to Morgan. And she was done believing what other people told her.

She'd left the FBI so she could do what she had to, within the law, to follow her instincts and the clues to the truth. Not just to a confession. But to provable truth.

Jasmine didn't know Blade. Hadn't known him in the past. Didn't know about the careful way he watched, making sure everyone was okay, even as he joked and played around. Hadn't heard about his hopes and dreams for himself and his family. His love of Michigan.

And she hadn't spent any time with him in the present, either. Hadn't seen his reactions as each piece of evidence came in. Or witnessed him not jumping to his own defense, as a guilty person would have done.

Turning her back on the confidence her one-time partner had given her, she had to tell him, "I'm concerned that the killer is setting us up." From there, free thoughts just started pouring out. "I'm afraid because he had to know we were just in that town. Or had known we were heading to it. That he's been following us all along, and we just haven't caught his tail. Maybe he got close enough to put a tracker on something we carry with us…"

She swerved before the words were even fully out of her mouth. Pulled off, stopped so abruptly she and Blade were both projected forward against their seat belts.

And looked over to find him unhooking his belt. "I'll

take the trunk, and exterior, you handle inside," he said, already climbing out.

She checked the OBD II diagnostics port first. Under seats and floor mats. Glove box and console. Then dived for the items they'd carried into the car with them. They hadn't noticed anyone following them since before they'd changed vehicles.

After a search, she used her phone to run a manual tracker alert, came up with nothing, and exited the vehicle to run the scanner under the bumpers and hood.

"Check the wheel wells," Blade, who'd been going through their bags in the trunk, said as she passed by him.

She did so without comment. Conscious of everything around her, and on the journey ahead. As soon as they were back in the car, buckled in, she put the car in gear and sped off, spewing gravel behind her. "We have to show up," she told him, her gaze glued to the road, and the mirrors. Specifically, not running into Blade. "It's an official law enforcement request. But we need to be prepared that the killer is counting on that."

Her mind was in full gear. He'd paid for that service.

She'd give it to him for free.

The knowledge should have landed with a severe blow to her equilibrium. Taking her breath. Instead, it settled upon her with the peacefulness of truth.

"When I'm being questioned, he'll have a trap for you," Blade said, again sounding more like a work partner than any kind of suspect she'd ever interrogated. He hadn't even asked why he was wanted, what evidence they had against him.

Nor had he questioned their turning around.

Or made a noise about the fact that she had to drive.

It was when she realized that, that she glanced at him. "This has been your life...for seventeen years...you've lived with the doubt of others, the questions coming at you again and again, out of the blue…"

He shrugged. She only caught the move peripherally. Didn't think he'd even glanced her way.

"He had one of your business cards in his wallet. And a call, not from the number we have for you, but in a voice message that says this is Blade, on his phone…before the call was cut off. He also had a meeting scheduled with you on his calendar for this afternoon." All of which could have been done by the killer. Or, Blade could have used a burner to call the man as soon as Morgan had entered the office building that afternoon. Could have met up with him, shot him. Could have, as Jasmine speculated, been rushed when Morgan had called to say she was ready, and been forced to dump the body, still alive, in the dumpster.

"There's a record of him calling your number, Blade," she said then. "This morning." The statement should have been in question format. Or at least in challenge.

Instead, she felt the warning in her words. Her warning him to be careful. Not to say anything that could incriminate him.

He was being set up. She was certain of it. Would take the belief to her grave if it came to that.

But she had no reason to think he'd believe her.

He wasn't pulling out his phone to check incoming calls. "What time?" He'd asked the right question at least.

"Eight twenty."

"We were at the FBI office. I had it on silent." That's when he pulled out his phone. Pressed and scrolled. And then held it up.

She grabbed the phone. Glanced at the screen.

The incoming call was there. A missed call. It was the

only listed in recent calls by that number. "And you didn't wonder who'd called?"

"I get robocalls all the time, just like everyone else. I didn't recognize the number. There was no voicemail."

Good. The answer was a good one. No one could argue with it. If he kept that up, he'd be fine.

She couldn't check outgoing calls while she was driving. Blade pocketed his phone without doing so. Because he knew he hadn't made one. The thought came to her and was brushed aside for more important business.

They'd lost precious time searching for trackers that hadn't been there.

If she didn't get him in for interrogation soon, she could be thought to be compromising her working relationship with the FBI and making herself a suspect in collaboration with a killer.

Pressing a little harder on the gas, figuring if she got pulled over, she'd have an alibi proving they were trying to get there quickly, Morgan kept both hands tightly clenched to the steering wheel as she gave him the worst. "He muttered something as he was dying," she told Blade. "A bystander got it on video. Parts were indecipherable. Sierra's Web has the recording and is breaking down the decibels to see if they can get more. But…he clearly said your name, Blade."

That's when the man next to her turned his head, forcing her to make a quick glance over, and with that brief glimpse of emotion in his gaze—was slammed back into the past.

She'd seen the look before. Seventeen years past. The morning after Maddie's death. Blade had come toward her.

And she'd called him a killer.

Screamed at him to get away from her.

And there was no way she could take that back.

Ever.

Chapter 16

She wasn't screaming at him. Or trying to get away. Blade held tight to that thought as he repeated what she'd said. Something he'd already been thinking. "It's a setup. You have to turn back around, Morgan. We already know he wants me locked up, which is fine, but he needs you dead before he goes to prison. He's setting a trap to kill you and you're driving straight into it. He needs to know that no part of Maddie is still out here."

"If it's Kyle." She wasn't arguing the setup.

And if what she'd just put him through was her idea of an interrogation, she wasn't nearly the expert she'd been cracked up to be.

He knew that she was, though. Which meant...

"You know I didn't do it." The emotion that came up in him as he finished the sentence overwhelmed and shocked him.

"Yes."

He couldn't leave it at that. "You believe I didn't kill Maddie."

Her chin puckered, and her lips tightened. "Yes."

Blade blinked back the emotion welling behind his lids, gritted his teeth against it and focused on keeping Morgan alive. He couldn't afford to get weak.

Not even with relief.

There was no good news until he knew Morgan was safe.

"You have to turn around."

She shook her head. "I can't, Blade. If I do, you become a fugitive. And I'm one with you."

"Only until we find the truth."

"Without help?" She sent him a quick glance, a look in her eye he hadn't thought he'd ever see again. That look... it had carried a wealth of feeling.

Aimed at him.

That wasn't hate.

That was, in fact, the opposite of the grief-filled words she'd hurled at him during their last meeting so long ago.

"You and I have been working on this thing for almost two decades, Blade. We're both intelligent people. And more determined than anyone else will ever be. But alone, doing it ourselves, we've failed. With the new murders, we have the best chance here we're ever going to get. We have to do this the correct way."

He knew she was right. Didn't want to accept what that meant. "We haven't failed." He told her something he used to tell himself, when he got so tired he'd start to wonder why he bothered. "We just haven't succeeded yet."

As long as he kept trying, he was on his way to success.

Which meant they were going to have to head back to St. Joseph.

But not without a plan.

One that, even if it failed, ensured that Morgan Davis stayed alive.

"Take me to the beach, at the edge of town," he told her then. "There's a marina, a guy I know, a friend of mine. He'll get you across the water to my boat. It's not the one that's registered in my name. It's registered under an alias with a post office box. It's legal, can be traced back to me, but not without effort and probably warrants. You get on that, take it out and wait for me to call." He gave her the details as they came to him. Names. Where to find keys. Made sure she still knew how to drive a boat. "The boat was Michael's idea," he said, naming his friend. "Said I didn't have to use it but having it there would give me peace of mind if I ever felt the walls closing in on me. Did I mention that he's a retired therapist who counsels victims of various forms of PTSD?"

And before she could get a word in edgewise, he continued with, "I'll drive myself into the station. And when I'm done there, if Sierra's Web has done their job, we'll have a private rental with a dock for the night."

"They're not looking for a rental with a dock," she told him. But he noticed she was staring ahead, driving steadily. Not frowning at him. Or shaking her head.

"They will be," he told her, and pulled out his phone.

She couldn't leave Blade to drive himself to the police station. There were too many unexplained actions hanging over them. She couldn't desert him.

But she liked the boat idea a lot. And a rental with a dock. She heard Blade on speakerphone talking to Glen Rivers Thomas about having someone there get them one for the night. And she inserted, "When you get an address, call Blade or myself with it. Don't put it in writing. And don't tell anyone else about it."

Blade's gaze shot to her. And he continued to watch her after he hung up.

"I don't like that we didn't find a tracker," she told him.

"You think someone on the case is involved in this?"

"Do you have any other explanation for how someone knew we were in St. Joseph, at the exact time we were there, when we only decided to go on the spur of the moment, and only the teams working the case knew about our whereabouts? How could anyone have framed you without knowing exactly when we were there?" She ended with where she'd begun. Repeating the question that had been hanging there bothering her since she'd first heard about Randolph's death.

"The fact that we were only there for such a short time, and no one knew we were there, makes it look more like I did it."

Yeah. She got that. Had understood it since her phone call with Jasmine. And to that end…

"Jasmine…we were partners for years… We'd grown really close, like sisters, I thought. But when I quit…she was glad. Relieved. And at my shock, she explained that no longer being partners meant that we could pursue a personal relationship. I swear to you, I had no idea she had feelings for me. She'd never let on. And I let her down gently. Told her my heart was dead in that area, but… She's been adamant about wanting me off this case and every time I talk to her, she gets more and more uptight. This morning, she actually pulled me in for a hug before we left. Told me that she loved me. And what if she's lost sight of the case because, she's seen, with you back in my life…she knows that my heart wasn't dead? That it had been in your possession all along? Locked up with all the other truths I couldn't find?"

She continued to push the pedal nearly to the floor as she spoke. Her hands sweaty on the steering wheel. But…they were likely driving into some kind of trap. And if she wasn't good enough to get them out of it in time…he had to know.

And even if they made it through and went on with their separate lives, she owed him the truth. She loved him.

She wasn't telling him right out. They were working. But…

Blade hadn't said a word. Speeding along, she couldn't

spare but a glance at him. Didn't dare test herself with even that.

She hadn't been making an avowal to a potential hookup. She'd been speaking a long-overdue truth that a good man deserved to hear.

Working for her client so he had all the facts.

Because if Jasmine was the one who'd let the killer know that they'd be in St. Joseph… "Whoever leaked our location has to have figured out who the killer is," she said softly, into the silence that had fallen. "How else would they have known who to tell?"

Blade glanced at her then. She felt the intensity of his gaze, even before his face appeared peripherally. "It's not like someone who worked the case in the past could be in on it," he said slowly. "The detectives in Ludington…they're all retired. They just sent case files…"

Ludington. Or rather, the huge acreage of camp land just outside city limits, which had been the end of life as both of them had known it.

"I'm going to drive you to the station, Blade. Walk inside it with you. And wait there, surrounded by police officers, for you to finish your business there."

"No." His tone was as harsh as she'd ever heard it. "No. I refuse to go."

"Blade." She could be firm, too. "We have to see this through. He was rushed today with Randolph. Mistakes were made. And I say he, but it doesn't have to be Kyle. You notice how Tammy seemed to know you instantly? And even have information about your career? If she was tipped off, she could have driven to St. Joseph this morning and then have time to get back to her apartment before we did. We stopped to get sandwiches…"

"You're not driving into a trap for me," he said again.

She saw the headshake even from the corner of her eye. "I can't sit here and be a part of that."

"You're right, you're driving," she said. "They need you alive to be their scapegoat, so you'll be safe. I'll be down on the floor. When we get to the station, you pull up to the door, and I'll get out and hide in front of you as you walk in."

"No."

He'd developed a stubborn streak.

"I will not live to see you die, Morgan."

"And I won't live at the cost of your freedom."

"I'm the boss." His tone was sharp.

He was her official link to the case, yes. The one who'd hired her through a firm that was known to successfully assist the FBI in all kinds of cases.

Didn't matter anymore.

She hadn't stood behind him in the past. Perhaps if she had, her life would have turned out differently. Maybe she wouldn't have been alone all those years...

"You can fire me if you want to," she said right back. "I'm not leaving you to face things alone. Not again. You either take us there with me hidden on the floor, or I drive us there in plain sight."

And that was the last she was going to say about it.

Blade's instincts were screaming at him not to go to the police station in St. Joseph. More bodies turning up...the guy was escalating... Which meant to him that there was no way to catch the guy with logic.

Or the bodies were the result of years of planning, and the kills were being executed by more than one person. Perhaps murder for hire? With one person at the helm?

Remy Barton and Kelly Chase both thought they were

dealing with one killer, based on the way the bodies were being deliberately staged, but also the overkill. Though, with Randolph there'd been none. Because the killer had run out of time.

"If there's someone on the inside, and we head to the station, they might just lock me up," he said aloud, stating what was concerning him most at the moment. He didn't give a whit about spending a night in jail. Been there done that. "If that happens, I can't be out here, helping you."

He couldn't keep her safe.

When she didn't immediately respond, Blade pressed a little harder. They were only twenty minutes from town and he was already in the driver's seat. "What if I agree to show up for questioning in Rocky Springs?" he asked. He knew James Silver well enough to trust the guy to play by the book. And the idea was growing on him for other reasons as well. "If there's a trap in St. Joseph, we avoid it," he pressed. FBI Agent Jasmine Flaherty had traveled from Detroit to meet them in St. Joseph. And with Morgan's doubts about the agent…it seemed smarter to be in more of a protective custody when the agent came at him.

And they'd be closer to his boats, both the legitimate and the alias.

The boats were not only his haven; they were also his safe place. Both were built with bulletproof synthetic fiber in between sheets of fiberglass. And were fully stocked with enough supplies to last him for months, if need be, including fishing poles, burner phones and bullets. Dr. Michael Comer had suggested that when he felt panic coming on, he should go to work on something that brought him both strength and pleasure. When he'd run out of things to do on the first boat, he'd started on the second. There were state-of-the-art televisions, closets with clothes for all seasons, life vests and inflatable boats. He could sail if he had to preserve gas...

Morgan had picked up her phone. He saw the Sierra's Web number come up on the dash display. And glanced back at the road to be momentarily blinded by the nearly setting sun glinting off flashes of metal appearing directly in front of him.

"Down!" he hollered so harshly his throat stung as he threw the car into Reverse and floored the gas, backing at breakneck speeds as bullets sounded in front of them.

He heard the shots. Wasn't sure if they'd landed. Tires squealing, he was rounding a corner, and then backing onto an adjoining country road, to back onto another, and then another. Years of backing construction trailers and cranes into tight spaces were serving them well.

Would his efforts be good enough? With the speeds he was traveling, he couldn't look forward to check. Morgan was still in her seat. Had her gun.

"Morgan? Blade!" Glen Rivers Thomas's voice came over the phone.

"Shots fired!" Morgan's tone was sharp. Controlled. "The car's hit, once. We're not."

The succinct words, her tone, calmed Blade some and, as he reached his destination, he threw the vehicle in gear and shot down the beachfront road toward the marina.

"What the hell's going on?" another voice came over the phone. "Talk to me."

"Hudson, it was a trap. Two motorcycles. They appeared out of nowhere onto the road in front of us, a blockade." Morgan's response was immediate. "They had guns. Hesitated before they shot. Amateurs. Young guys. Peach fuzz. Smaller street bikes. One black. The other silver." She named a well-known brand and then said, "I think we have a mole. Maybe Jasmine. Or someone on the St. Joseph force. Someone knows who the killer is. Tipped him off."

"James Silver might help," Blade inserted then as he rounded the last bend before the marina. "I've got a boat. Will get us on it and wait to hear from you," he said then. Giving orders as though he was law enforcement himself. Or talking to his employees.

A contractor taking back control of his life.

A man determined to save the life of the woman he loved.

Chapter 17

Morgan wanted Madison's killer. Had been prepared to do whatever it took to find him. To die for the answers. She'd made it through seventeen years of failure by imagining what it would be like when she finally had the guy in her sights. Imagining the takedown. No way she'd ever seen herself out on the waters of the massive Lake Michigan, moored far enough out to be invisible from shore, in a thousand-square-foot living quarter beneath the deck, watching cameras for anything approaching—with Blade Carmichael.

In the dark.

He had a satellite phone. Of course. They were using it sparingly.

"All this stuff," she said, looking around, at the supplies she could see, and those he'd shown her, hidden away in cabinets and compartments. "Were you planning to go underground? Run? If they ever came after you again?"

The question seemed to dim the light in his eyes as he sat across from her at the small table that folded down into a double bed. But he held her gaze as he said, "It's a mental health project." And then he went back to the pages of evidence he had spread in front of him. Some of them from one of his boxes, others that he'd printed from an email they'd received from Sierra's Web before they left shore. Reports pertaining to people at camp when Madison was killed. Looks at social media, and other records they could access, one search pertaining to known associations between any of them.

She'd hurt him with her question, so she laid one hand over his. "I wouldn't have blamed you," she said softly. "You've been persecuted for seventeen years for something you didn't do. There had to be a way you could promise yourself that enough was enough."

His green eyes rose to hers slowly. And seemed to show her parts of his soul. As she'd been so certain they'd done in the past. "Living on the run would be worse than persecution," he told her. "I've always known that there was a killer out there who had to figure that I'd be looking for him. I think some part of me was always prepared for him to come finish me off, so the threat was no longer there. I just never thought...for one second...that he'd kill other people first."

She wanted to pull him to her. To hold him tight. And felt his hand turn in hers, his fingers threading through hers. She held on.

"They'll catch the kids on the motorcycles," she told him. "And the fact that they were there...tells me the killer is getting more out of control, which means more mistakes. He's desperate. Knows we're closing in on him."

His gaze holding hers steadily, seeming to burn with liquid fire, he said, "He's desperate, and determined. Willing to risk everything. Which makes him unpredictable. This person, if there is just one, has killed multiple people in less than three days. He wants you gone. He will try anything to make that happen as quickly as possible."

He wasn't telling her anything she didn't know. Was

just saying aloud that which neither one of them had talked about since they'd left the car at the Rocky Springs police station. With James Silver's and Sierra's Web's intervention, they had gotten into a local vacation rental van to drive back to the marina in St. Joseph, where Blade's friend Michael had boated them to the marina to get on Blade's alias cabin cruiser.

Only Sierra's Web, their sole contact, and James Silver knew that they were staying on the boat. The expert firm was still working the case with the FBI. And in light of the near ambush, and the fact that neither Blade nor Morgan were under arrest, it had been made clear to the FBI that Sierra's Web had them in protective custody.

Michael had been told that they'd be boating to a vacation rental with a dock. Not because Blade didn't trust him, but because they had to keep those in the know to the fewest number of people possible.

Blade had given a list of the people he'd seen in St. Joseph that afternoon, and Hudson Warner's tech experts had been able to find him on surveillance cameras. That, in light of the attempt on his life, had convinced the FBI to back off an immediate need to question him in the death of Gary Randolph. They didn't have enough evidence to hold him for anything.

Everyone who'd attended camp the summer of Madison's death, other than Kyle and Tammy, had been notified to be extra-vigilant, and get out of town if possible. Tammy was under twenty-four-hour surveillance. Law enforcement was still attempting to locate Kyle.

Darkness had fallen shortly after they'd anchored. They'd had dinner on the deck, take-out pasta and salads that Silver had had in the van for them. But they'd gone down under immediately afterward—with the windows covered with room-darkening shades that would conceal the light—to get to work.

Blade was still holding Morgan's hand as he said, "Something more had to have been going on at camp that summer." As his words ended, he pulled his hand away, shuffling through another set of papers, and grabbing for his phone.

She missed the warmth of his fingers, missed the sense of being held, but knew he was right to keep them firmly on track. They'd need to rest. Neither of them would be able to keep going at the top of their game on the little bit of sleep they'd had over the past couple of nights.

"What if whatever it is, Madison found out about it?" he continued, scrolling through his phone. He stopped at something. Turned his phone to show her a series of pictures he'd taken at camp that summer. She recognized them from ones she'd seen on his dining room wall. Had it only been the day before?

Seemed like they'd lived months since then.

The photo he'd enlarged, so that only parts of it were showing on the screen, caught her immediate attention. She homed in on what she knew he'd meant her to see.

A group photo, arranged by Tammy but taken by their camp photographer. A boys' camp memorial, with so many heads, they were mere dots until you enlarged them. But all three of the murdered bodies in the morgue were in it.

They would be—that had been the purpose of the photo. There was another one, which had been hanging right next to the first, on Blade's wall, filled with girls' likenesses, including all their counselors...

She looked at Blade. "The camp photographer."

Blade nodded. "He'd have hundreds of photos of activities from that summer. Pictures that might have caught something behind the scenes."

Getting energized again, Morgan continued, "Like Tammy and Mark Hampton in intimate conversation. Or Tammy looking at him as a woman looks at the man she loves."

Her words faltered, fell away, as she looked over at Blade. Like any photos taken of her and Blade might have done?

He held her gaze. Neither of them spoke.

And then they both started in at once. "What if...?"

"We need to..."

"You go," he said to her. "We need to what?"

"Call Hud and get them on those camp photos. Hope to God there are still at least negatives of them."

"We need to wait until ten. We agreed, signal off until then," he reminded her.

Fifteen minutes. "So, what do we think might have been going on at camp?" she asked, forcing herself to stay focused. She was tired. Had started the day very early with a fire on her hotel room balcony. Had been home, to her old office, across the state on interviews, had her car blown up, found out another person she'd known had died. Been shot at.

And had admitted that she was still in love with Blade Carmichael.

Shaking his head, Blade kept scrolling on his phone. Looking at pictures, she assumed. "I don't know," he said. "Maybe Madison stumbled on Hampton and Tammy together? And told Shane? Who told Randolph, who went to Hampton with it..."

The chain of people made sense. "Maddie tells Shane about something...whatever. He goes to the guy who's the boss of all counselors, Kyle Brennan, who goes to the next guy in line of command, Randolph. And if *he* went to Hampton, it either had to do with Hampton's affair, or something that Randolph thought the camp counselor should know. Should handle. Like maybe a phone call to parents of whoever was involved?"

Blade nodded. "Unless it had to do with staff. Tammy and Hampton…maybe…but what if there was something going on with the staff?"

"Like a poker game?" she asked.

"Or something worse. Drug trafficking, maybe?"

"Did you ever hear of anyone being high while you were there?" she asked him. She hadn't.

Blade's headshake was short, to the point. "Didn't mean it wasn't happening, though," he reasserted, looking over at her.

The look wasn't particularly personal. Wasn't at all sexual. But Morgan flooded with desire for the man. Sexual, but far more than that.

He was good for her.

Right for her.

Another part of her.

Sitting there with him, speculating, as she'd done with Jasmine and other coworkers over the years, felt like far more than work all of a sudden. She felt like…more.

More alive.

Fuller.

"What?" Blade asked, bringing to her attention that she was staring at him.

Shaking her head, Morgan meant to get back to work, to make a case-pertinent comment, but something deep inside her compelled her to say, "Back then, I felt like we were on the same mental wavelength." As a piece of information. Not a declaration.

He didn't speak. But didn't look away, either. "I still do."

She expected him to look down, to grab a file. To vacate

the conversation. Stayed present anyway, waiting for him to look away. He didn't.

And eventually said, "I do, too."

It wasn't any kind of proclamation.

But it made her heart soar anyway.

Blade had failed to calculate one very critical danger in his plan to get Morgan away from danger. His own libido.

He'd had lovers over the years—most for periods of time. Had enjoyed his time with all of them. And hadn't felt one iota of the burning need coursing through him as he sat in his haven, his refuge, with the one woman who'd taught him that sparks could actually fly between people.

And with her over there, making it pretty clear that she'd begun to feel things for him again, too—first in the car, which he'd managed to avoid and then...right there—how did a guy sit there on fire and not need to extinguish the burning? Even if only temporarily.

He had no experience with that one. *Excuse me while I pop into the tiny head right on other side of that cardboard wall you're sitting by and relieve myself.*

When his satellite phone rang, he knocked it over in his haste to grab up the lifeline it seemed to have just handed him.

If Morgan noticed his fumbling or was aware of his... physical...distress...she didn't let on. Instead, she answered the phone, turning up the volume on the speaker as she said, "Please tell me you have something substantial."

As though she was drowning and didn't know how much longer she could hold on.

Or maybe he was just reading his own state of mind into her tone.

"We've got something," Hudson Warner's voice came over the line as Blade looked at Morgan.

And he knew, by the quick light in her eyes, that he wasn't completely alone in his struggle to keep the two of them away from personal feelings that seemed to be as alive in the present as they had been in the past.

In spite of the age and experience both of them had gained.

"Good work on Jessica Brennan, Morgan," the tech expert said first, and Blade's gaze slid back over to her, right after he'd managed to pull himself away. Pride for her seeped through his skin, despite the fact that she was not his to take pride in. And the split second ended abruptly as the man continued to speak.

"We've got Kyle's phone and financial records, put everyone on them at once."

They'd located Kyle? Blade's mind flashed ahead, his attention all focused on the case again, as he listened with an ear to figuring out his own next move. How he could help. Whether anyone wanted his help or not.

"Whatever money he's spent, wherever he might be staying, he's paid for with cash he would have had to have on hand. There's no credit card activity. No withdrawals from his accounts…"

Blade's energy fell a level. Warner had said they had something…

"Are we starting to think he's a casualty, too?" Morgan's question drew his gaze, more to see her reaction to the possibility. She didn't seem fazed, one way or another. It bothered him a lot. If their best suspect was dead, were they back to square one again?

How many more times could they do this?

"No," Warner's response came slowly, drawn out as

though the man was in thought. "There was a call made from his cell phone this morning. To Gary Randolph."

Blade's enthusiasm dropped a notch.

"Before or after Randolph called Blade?" If she was looking at him, he didn't know. He wasn't raising his gaze from the paperwork in front of him to find out.

"Before."

Before. "That's interesting," Blade murmured aloud. And then, leaned in toward the phone. "He could have been calling to warn me." He could be trying to deflect suspicion from himself. He understood that. But was part of the conversation, had a valid thought, and was damned well going to be heard.

"That's our theory, as well," another male voice said. Glen Rivers Thomas. The forensic guy who'd actually taken Blade on as a client. The man sounded...more alive than he'd heard him in the past. Not just an automaton with a few words doing his job.

Blade sat up straighter, ready to pursue the matter further, when Hudson's voice came over the line again. Mentioning a name Blade thought sounded slightly familiar but couldn't place—Randy Thomaston. "He was the youngest kid in Shane's cabin," Hudson continued, filling in Blade's blanks. "Agent Flaherty's team was notifying everyone from camp to be vigilant and Randy, upon hearing that Shane Wilmington had been murdered, said that he'd seen something the night of Madison Davis's death. Had mentioned it to Kyle Brennan, but the man had said not to speak up. They knew who'd killed Madison and didn't need to cloud the waters any, or point suspicion at an innocent kid, no matter how much of a douchebag he was. A quote from Randy, not my words," Hudson inserted as, heart pounding blood through his veins, Blade's gaze connected with Morgan's and held on tight.

"Thomaston said that keeping quiet has been nagging at him ever since," Hudson continued, his voice seeming to blare throughout the small cabin inside the boat. Overwhelming it…and Blade. He wanted to end the call. Hang up the phone.

Had to know.

He glanced back down at his papers.

Detected no movement from Morgan's side of the table.

"The guy's a light sleeper. Said he woke up that night when Shane left for the party. Woke up again when he got back. Said it wasn't unusual for Shane to skip out after the guys were asleep. Happened a lot. But that night… Shane left a second time."

"Wait," Blade demanded, his tone fierce as he stared down the phone. "What? Shane left a second time?"

His gaze shot up to Morgan's then, stared into those striking blue eyes that were so wide he almost got lost in them.

"According to Randy Thomaston he did."

That was it. A one-sentence confirmation. And then nothing.

A sentence that could change everything, and no one was running with it? He stood up. They had to do something. Go somewhere. Make something happen.

He saw Morgan, still sitting at the table, and took a deep breath. Reminded himself they were still on the phone. Slid back into the booth.

"I assume you're all thinking, as I am, that this lends more weight to the theory that Shane killed Madison," Morgan said, her tone so void of emotion that Blade stared at her. And understood. She was a grieving twin, devastated by a loss she'd never recover.

And a professional seeking justice.

She couldn't be both at the same time.

The realization toughened him up. He'd messed up seventeen years ago, had clearly underestimated Shane Wilmington, should have reported the party. He would not let Morgan down a second time.

"We are," Hudson's voice was just as unemotional.

And Blade found that he shared that space as he heard himself say, "Which begs the question, if Shane killed Madison, why the recent murders? Who stands to gain from them?"

"Who do you know who'd want to see you suffer again?" Glen's voice came immediately. As though he'd been waiting to get the question out. "Someone who carried pain from that summer?"

"Kyle makes sense." He said the first name that came to mind. "Particularly if he told Thomaston to keep quiet about Shane's post-curfew antics." And as he spoke, pictures began to form in his mind. "He was in on it," he said. "I'll bet they covered for each other. They were both womanizers, always talking about who was hot, who'd be the best sex…"

He couldn't look at Morgan. What he'd heard then, what she thought about him, had ceased to matter.

"He knew, the bastard, and let me take the fall?" He stood again. Paced. Needed miles in front of him over which to jog…

"Our theory is that Shane, the killer, has been carrying the guilt all these years. And unlike Kyle, whose life fell apart, he needed to make amends. Starting with you. My guess is, out of respect, he told Kyle first. And that, after his father's death and his own impending charges, was his last straw."

"What if Kyle wasn't the only who called Hampton?" Morgan asked then. Blade couldn't look at her. He felt like he was coming out of his skin.

He checked the cameras that showed him the deck, and the waters around the boat. Felt certain that someone would be out there, ready to attack. To stop them before they all spoke the truth.

"You're thinking Wilmington called, to let the doctor know what he was about to do?" Hudson's voice sounded again.

"Makes sense, now that we know Hampton was also having an illicit affair that summer. It all happened after dark. When the rest of us were locked in at curfew."

"It does make sense," Glen said. "But we've checked both their records and found no calls between them. At least for the two years back we looked."

Yanking on a drawer handle, located by his head, Blade pulled out an unopened package. "They could have been using prepaids," he said. Then dropped the phone back in the drawer.

And sat down on the edge of the bench on his side of the table, too. He had to think. Not react.

"It could also be Tammy," he said then. Reiterating what he and Morgan had already revealed earlier that day. "I could see either one of them making me their scapegoat."

"I could, too," Morgan said, her voice a little softer, drawing his attention to her face. She wasn't mooning over him. But there was a look there.

As though she understood.

And in that look, for that moment, she'd given him everything he needed.

Chapter 18

Morgan's mind raced, searching for evidence within her years' full cache that would help them definitively prove who'd murdered her sister. And who was behind the current string of camp-related deaths.

What in the hell was she missing? One little thing that would help them find Kyle Brennan, and then get him to talk. Something from camp that summer. Remixed with what Jessica had told her that day…was there anything that made sense?

"We've got another theory on the table," Hudson said, bringing her mind back from her instinctive, all-consuming need to get it right, for Madison—and for Blade—to the auditory meeting in which she still sat. "Kelly's here to share it with the two of you," the tech expert finished.

"I just had a long call with Remy Barton," the psychology expert started right in. "He sees merit in the current theory but isn't convinced we're on the right track."

The woman's words caught Morgan's attention full force. She knew Remy. Trusted his judgment. And if they were falling for some kind of red herring, she wanted off the ride immediately. Could that be why she couldn't find the final pieces to close the case? Why she kept feeling as though she was missing something?

As Blade tensed across from her, she kept her focus on the phone, the words coming from it. And the images she had spread before her on the table, all depicting Blade's dining room walls. Giving her the most complete picture of what they knew.

"Dr. Barton believes we're looking for a younger person. He said someone who was sixteen or below, based on adolescent emotional development science. I'm inclined to agree with him. His reasoning, based on actions seeming to be driving a now adult, that appear to be coming out of a juvenile sense of injustice. This conclusion is not only sound, it's scientific."

Morgan felt her muscles tightening, as though she was aware of each one in her body, one by one. She wanted to reach out for Blade, find his hand, but knew she couldn't.

Couldn't afford the chance that she'd be distracted.

She had to keep herself 100 percent at attention. She focused on kids she'd known at camp as she heard the profile she knew was coming.

"We've already contacted the FBI team to get Hampton's patient records from camp and they're working on it. Barton doesn't think our perpetrator is escalating. We're looking for someone who's calculated, with well-thought-out moves. Partly to fulfill his sense of justice, and in part to throw us off course, to show us for fools, due to our previous inability to provide that justice. And, of course, to keep him or herself from getting caught. Different methods of murder could either be a part of this, or they could be about the perpetrator getting his murderer's feet wet, and then growing in power with each successful kill. The hiring of at-risk people to try to get Morgan removed from the case could all be part of the ruse to throw us off, but it could also indicate that the killer is on the fence about whether or not she has to die. Most likely, Morgan, this is someone who knew you. Whether you, as a counselor, knew him or her or not, this could be someone who looked up to you. Who, while he or she now struggles because they hold you partially accountable for so many years of injustice, but who also genuinely liked you. Or, at the very least, feels sorry for you. Probably someone who saw you the last morning at camp. Dr. Barton says that you were held apart, partially with his help. He's spent the past twenty-four hours trying to remember anyone he noticed hanging around, watching you, but said that he was so distraught himself, he can't think of anyone. He's hoping you'll be able to. Or you, Blade. You were there, and also, obviously similarly distressed, but we'd like for both of you to sit down with another long look at camp photos…take time for every face. Close your eyes. Try to remember."

Morgan was already reaching for the file. Blade handed it to her. She threw him a glance, nodded, but wouldn't let herself connect. She needed her mind in the past. Hating him. Because that's where she'd been that morning.

Before she'd even opened the file, Kelly's voice came over the wire again, forcing her to keep the folder closed a minute or two longer. Giving her a major panic-induced hot flash, as well.

"This perp has two teams of experts looking for him, and us appearing to be no closer to finding him is likely feeding his sense of power. Which means we can count on more bodies if we don't get this done fast," the expert said. "Dr. Barton and I both agree that we need to be looking at someone who's insinuated him- or herself into this investigation." Kelly coughed, more like a hard clearing of the throat, and then said, "Dr. Barton also pointed out, without actually pointing fingers or giving his own opinion on the matter, that Blade fits this entire profile. He and Shane were only sixteen. Their camp elders let them down."

The energy in the room shifted. As though it had gone stale. Something they could not afford at that point. Standing, she spun around to the other side of the table, the file of pictures in hand, pushing against Blade with her hip until he moved over so she could sit down.

And then she dropped her free hand to his thigh.

It wasn't the move of a lover.

But she couldn't deny, even to herself, that the touch was conceived in love.

The kind that supported, believed, even in the worst of times.

Blade hadn't been surprised that Remy had mentioned him as fitting the profile. The man wouldn't be doing his job if he hadn't done so. Blade had been counting off every detail as they'd been spoken, seeing himself in every one of them.

The age thing…he'd been sixteen when summer camp had started. Morgan had just turned sixteen. None of the campers had known that he'd had a birthday. He hadn't wanted a fuss.

All he'd wanted was some private time with Morgan, for them to have cupcakes, hold hands and talk about life. They'd made it happen.

He'd been wondering if she'd remembered that, and then there she was, in the moment, shoving him over and…putting her hand on his thigh.

As she'd done that long-ago afternoon.

And that, he hadn't expected.

By the time her hand was landing on his thigh, Kelly Chase's voice filled the room with, "I'm turning this over to Hudson again. You two...above all else, be careful," and Blade couldn't help but figure the message was a warning to him, in particular, to keep his hands, and physical needs, off the table. Literally.

The table they sat at was going to fold down and serve as Morgan's bed for the night.

"Okay," Hudson's voice boomed loudly. "My team is already looking at footage in and around every crime scene, to see if anyone shows up in multiple places, or even more than once, and run any repeat images through facial recognition software. If we find no multiple appearances, we'll run every single face on every single tape through the software. I've also got people working on age progression photos from the camp photos you two will be studying. If this guy or woman is out there, we'll find them."

Blade heard the words. Felt a little...strange...that Warner hadn't also mentioned that they knew already that Blade would appear on some of the cameras. He'd been at the crime scenes. After having insinuated himself into the investigation big-time.

At Morgan's request, of course, but only after he'd asked her for the initial interview.

And begged for her help.

The fact that he was paying the bill had not meant that he was to be overlooked. They'd all stipulated that from the beginning. Glen Rivers Thomas first and foremost.

He didn't like the idea that the firm could be fooled into being convinced of someone's innocence without the proof. Not only had he hired them for the sole purpose of getting that proof, but if he could manipulate them, someone else could, too. Jasmine, for instance?

"I'm turning this over to Glen," Hudson said, bringing

to Blade's attention that he had no idea what the man had said immediately before that statement.

"All right, we have one last report to make," Glen's voice came into the room. Again, sounding just that bit...different. As though the man's emotions had entered the picture. Which made no sense.

"Give it to me," Morgan said, her tone as professional as always, not seeming to notice any change in her boss's demeanor.

Because she knew him far better? Had seen different sides to him?

Made sense, but it didn't ease Blade's tension over the firm's lapse where he was concerned. Jasmine could have left some clue, in some conversation, that they'd missed because they'd been...personally occupied...

He had to tell them Morgan's concerns.

"Wait," he said, leaning over the table. "I think we need to discuss the fact that I fit the profile," he said, starting in slowly, before bringing the firm's possible lapse back to the FBI agent—who'd be a much harder sell than a contractor who'd been a prime suspect in a cold case for almost two decades.

"To that end," Glen started in. "As you both know, my team has been running tests on all the case evidence from Madison Davis's murder," the man continued. Blade's attention, while acute, was acutely split between what the man had to tell them, and the fingers digging into his thigh.

Here it comes, was his first thought. But he knew confusion, too. If they had more on him then why...?

"The class ring found in Blade's pocket..." He heard the words. Started to zone. The ring, the most key piece of evidence, along with the little ribbon cross that Morgan had given to him that had been found clutched in her sister's hand. There'd been no viable fingerprints. How was Morgan going to handle being trapped with him on a small boat too far out for her to swim back to shore…?

Glen was talking about new technologies in forensic testing. DNA advances in particular. Ways to tell male DNA from female DNA. They'd found only one sample of male DNA, and it had been found all over both the outside and inside of the ring. Blade couldn't inhale.

"Over the years, as investigators took a look at the case, mostly at Morgan's continued urgings, the one thing that no one had was Shane Wilmington's DNA. But with his corpse in the morgue, we were able to get a good sample. They prove that the only man who touched that ring found in Blade's pocket was Shane Wilmington."

Blade sat there. Waiting. The ball would drop. Another shoe would fall. He'd take it and keep pushing forward.

"Oh my God!" Morgan's squeal, the way she was suddenly up off the bench, had him staring at her. "They did it, Blade!" she screamed, sounding like the sixteen-year-old sweetie he'd once known. While voices came over the phone, in triplicate.

"Congratulations, you two," Kelly Chase's words came through most legibly.

And Blade sat there.

Morgan pushed her face right up to his. "You didn't do it, Blade!" she said, half kneeling on the bench as she reached her arms around his neck and hugged him.

He didn't do it.

He'd always known that.

But…he stared at her. At the phone. Listened to the voices all talking about the discovery, about who made the connection, running into the office, with the news.

He heard the excitement. But it was Morgan's eyes, gazing into his with the adoration to which he'd once been addicted, that brought the message home to a heart and mind that had been buried too deep to accept a release from the internal prison.

"I know," he said, and then, with tears in his eyes, matching the ones in hers, he pulled her down onto his lap and kissed her.

Long. And then hard.

Morgan half heard her team joking about what was going on in the boat. At the other end of their communication. And then heard an "oh." Followed by a quiet click.

She'd maybe pay later for her unprofessional behavior. But probably not. She didn't care one way or the other.

They had the proof that Blade didn't do it.

They'd found the truth.

He was fully exonerated.

And...he'd pulled back from a kiss that had her wanting to throw an arm across the table to rid it of debris and then climb up on it.

"What's wrong?" she asked as he slid them across the bench, stood and let her go.

Was there someone else in his life?

She hadn't asked. There'd been no reason to discuss their private, personal lives.

Or...he no longer wanted her...in that way.

He wanted her. She'd felt the evidence of that against her hip. But maybe as a sexual partner, not a lover.

Not like the couple they'd once promised each other they'd be.

"We're right where we were when we came on this boat," Blade said to her, breathing heavily, not meeting her gaze. His tone soft.

They weren't a couple just because he'd been exonerated.

"We knew I didn't do it, Morgie. And it looks like Shane did, and framed me, but we haven't proven that yet. Someone else could have murdered Maddie and convinced Shane—by bribe or threat—to put the ring in my pocket. We don't have your truth yet. And even if Shane killed Maddie, we can't prove who's out there now, murdering people from camp. And gunning for you." He glanced at her then, his green-eyed gaze filled with a fire she hadn't ever seen.

"I'm not stopping until you're safe," he told her. "My freedom from suspicion will be huge to me at some point. Right now, it doesn't matter when I think about your life in danger…"

He hadn't said *I love you*.

Maybe he never would.

But Morgan heard the declaration anyway. In what he *was* saying.

And doing. He'd slid back onto the bench on his side of the table. Opened the file of camp photos. "I'll sit here, you sit there," he said, nodding toward the bench she'd been occupying most of the night.

"We have to put ourselves back in the frame of mind we'd been in that morning…"

Morgan was already seated before he finished the sentence.

She'd go back. She'd feel the horror. The hell.

She had to.

But she would not forget, ever, that she'd just fallen in love all over again.

Kelly had told them to close their eyes and remember every aspect of that morning so long ago. The sun on their faces, the grass beneath their feet, anything that would take them back in time. He sat across from Morgan, watching her look at a picture and then close her eyes, again and again, watching expressions cross her face. All painful distortions of the joy she used to wear so naturally. Blade was resisting his own trip back.

He knew what the past held.

Could figure out the future later.

The present was everything. Because if they didn't keep Morgan safe, neither the past nor the future mattered to him.

And the only way to keep her safe was to figure out who in the hell wanted her dead and stop them.

They had to find the truth.

So he looked at photos, closed his eyes and slowly let himself drift away from the boat to a sunny summer morning that held nothing but horror. Darkness.

And a young face...looking at him with fear. Not the horror and shock that had shot his way from every other face he'd encountered that morning. No one had looked at him for more than a second. That he'd seen. He'd glance at someone, and they'd immediately turn away.

It had felt as though everyone had been staring at him.

And that one face...

He couldn't place it. It hung there, in the air. Just a flash. And then gone. There and not. From photo to photo, eyes opened, eyes closed, he couldn't match the face. The eyes.

That fear.

Was it a younger version of himself he was seeing? He'd gone into the bathroom to throw up. Had brushed his teeth and caught a sight of himself in the mirror.

Had started to cry.

And turned his back on his image—just like everyone else was turning their backs on him.

Was it his own face he was seeing?

Maybe it was.

He didn't think so.

And didn't trust himself to know, either. He'd been a young seventeen-year-old, distraught, terrified kid, who'd fallen asleep in love and woken up a murder suspect. Surrounded by enemies he'd thought were friends. Branded by those he'd trusted.

He'd been in shock.

Boom! Crack! The sounds reverberated outside, and then in. Blade was out of his seat before he fully comprehended what was happening. Morgan, her gun in hand, was right beside him.

Pulling his weapon out of his ankle holster, he stepped in front of her, peering at the screens depicting footage from his security cameras. Heard another blast. Glass breaking.

A screen went dark.

And Blade strode toward a bench a couple of feet away. Threw it open, and grabbed the life raft, along with two waterproof satchels.

"Take these," he told Morgan. "We have to vacate, now."

Morgan, putting the straps of both bags on her shoulders, grabbed for her phone, and said, "They know where we are."

"Leave the phones," Blade barked, as though he was the expert. In a sense, on his boat, and in his life, he was. And saw that Morgan had already put hers back on the table and was reaching for the drawer he'd pulled open earlier, grabbing two new phones, and unsealed one of the bags she was carrying to put them inside.

She started when another couple of shots were fired, ducking, and then moved toward the steps leading up to the deck, saying, "They're on the port side. And still a distance away. Long-range rifle."

Blade had determined the same, based on the faraway sound of the shot, followed a few seconds later by cracks as they hit the boat. He pulled out a couple of wet suits.

"It's going to be too big for you, but you'll need it on," he told her. "Booties first so the water doesn't inflate them." He was already stepping out of his pants as he talked. "Keep your underwear on." He kept an eye on her, only to make sure she got the suit on right, and then, in his own suit, grabbed handfuls of clothes from their go bags, and shoved them into one of the two waterproof satchels he'd pulled out of the bench. He added their guns and with a nod from Morgan, turned off the lights, but when he stepped toward the stairs, Morgan pushed by him.

"I go first," she insisted in the darkness.

There was no time to argue. He started the boat's inflation, pushing in front of her with it, and went up on deck. And then, hiding any glow of human movement behind the growing black raft, he waited for her to crawl to the starboard side of the boat. "Jump in, and hold on," he told her, handing her a rope tied to the boat. Heard the splash as she went over and, securing the life raft, threw it down as well, before rolling himself over the side.

Chapter 19

There were two sets of oars. Morgan's arms ached as she reached and pulled, reached and pulled in tandem with Blade. Fighting waves on the cloudy night.

Focusing on his back in front of her, she tuned out the darkness. No visible moon was good for them. Kept them hidden.

But it prevented her from seeing what was around them. Just ahead. Behind.

How did she protect anyone when she couldn't keep an up-to-the-second assessment of her surroundings? Her ability to take in, to file and hold on to details around her was one of her strong suits.

Blade had told her, before they'd boarded the boat earlier that evening, that both of his cabin cruisers were bulletproof. But the killer had already used a bomb once. If he realized that his gunfire was largely ineffective...

They had to get far enough away from the boat to not be caught by shrapnel if it exploded.

"He's portside," Blade said as they rowed in a line perpendicular to the boat. "As long as we stay starboard, we're safe from gunfire."

And as long as the killer thought they were still on the boat, they were even safer.

Morgan hoped to God that their escape had gone unnoticed.

If the killer knew that they were on an inflatable boat, they were as good as dead. He could already be headed their way.

Shivering, partially due to the sweat building up in her suit as she exerted herself in the seventy-degree summer night air, she forced herself to focus on the job. On the truth she'd promised herself she'd find before she left the earth.

They had their guns out and loaded. And had talked about diving into the water if need be, staying under as much as possible to avoid any bullets that could come their way at any moment. They hadn't talked about how much the relatively light raft would bounce around on the huge lake, even with relatively calm waters.

"We should be good, from here, if he bombs the boat," Blade said twenty minutes after they'd vacated their overnight lodging, leaving all the copies of evidence that it held.

A call to Sierra's Web could replace all of it.

Her mind continued to segue between past and present. The pictures she'd been studying when the gunfire had started. The memories she'd accessed—many she'd refused to allow to the surface due to the pain they caused.

And the man Blade had become. Everything she'd imagined he'd grow to be. And more. His awareness of the preciousness of life, his depth and, based on investigative research, his dedication to staying on the right side of the law, not missing a single inspection or failing to file a single form in the running of his business...she'd expected him to be a good man.

He'd turned out to be one of the best. At least by her standards.

And, he'd been exonerated. Not that there'd ever been an official charge against him. She still had no idea how the little ribbon cross she'd made in crafts and had given to Blade the evening before Maddie was killed had ended up in her dead sister's hand, but it was easy enough to follow the dots. Shane had taken it from Blade when he'd planted the ring in Blade's pocket.

Whether Shane had given it to her sister before her death or shoved it into her hand afterward might never be known.

But it could be. With Sierra's Web on the case.

Reach and pull. Reach and pull. She was with Blade Carmichael. They were alive. Alone on the lake that they'd both professed to love so much neither had ever wanted to live outside the state. If not for a string of murders and bullets flying, she could be living a dream come true.

Neither of them were speaking much. They had no plan, past getting away alive.

Pulling her oars through the frigid water, Morgan hoped for a bomb with every stroke.

It was their best option.

If the killer thought that their body parts were among pieces of an explosion…they'd have a spare minute to catch the fiend.

"We have to stay off the grid," she told Blade, her voice as soft as it could be to reach him almost a yard ahead of her in the lifeboat.

She'd expected a nod, at best. Instead, he put his oars straight down in the water, slowing them. She ceased rowing as well as he turned to face her.

"I know of an inlet," he said. "Used to be a popular pass-through for boats to the Applethorne River, but both sides were overgrown with cattails, which are protected in the state. For the past few years, it's no longer been wide enough for boat passage. A new passageway was cleared from the lake to the river about five miles downriver. There's a small, overgrown beach area on this inlet. And a two-man tent in the one duffel…" He nodded toward the two bags in between them on the floor of the raft. "I suggest we get there. Build the tent, pull the raft inside and get some sleep. We can use one of our phones to set an alarm to make certain we're up before dawn. From there, it's your call." He talked a little more about the inlet, about the plethora of trees and lack of human habitation.

Had they been in another time and place, the itinerary he was describing would have sounded like heaven to her. So many times that long-ago summer she'd dreamed about a night all alone in a tent with Blade. Doing things that lovers did.

Going through those old photos, closing her eyes with her heart and mind spread wide open, allowed to freely live the bottled-up memories from that summer, so much had come back to her. The way she'd tingled inside, and down below, every time Blade had held her hand. And when he'd kissed her, she'd been on fire there, flooding with warmth and wetness.

In her private moments, every night as she'd fallen asleep, she'd lain there imagining what it would be like when they could finally lie together and she'd know what it felt like to have him actually enter her…

Instead, her sister's life had been stolen away, taking all of Morgan's dreams with it.

Maybe the shots that night were a sign. Reminding her that she had to live every minute while she had it. Not hold off for a future that might not arrive.

Blade's voice had fallen silent. For how long, she wasn't sure.

Morgan nodded. "Let's go," she said.

Keeping the rest to herself.

* * *

As he rowed, steering them toward the inlet half a mile ahead, Blade kept getting hit with mental flashes of that face. Was it him? Showing him his own fear?

He didn't feel afraid. Not for himself, at any rate. His entire being was filled with a cold, hard, steel-like determination to find the man who'd stolen Morgan's future from her, and his, too. Find him and end his life.

Either through arrest, or something more permanent.

He wouldn't kill without provocation. Would not take a life unless it was self-defense. No way he was going to let the bastard make a murderer out of him. He would not let a killer make his own sick falsehoods into truth. Nor ever be the man he'd been living to show the world he was not.

But to protect Morgan from certain death? He was ready.

Would shoot to kill.

No doubt at all on that one.

Having Morgan remove her oars from the water, he took over propelling the boat as he steered them into the inlet, heading back the way they'd come, but on different waters. In the gulf, leading to the river, with land on both sides, there were no waves. But here in the overgrown remains of a gulf, going was slowed by the sludge and weeds that had risen from the ten-foot-deep bottom. Cattails scraped the sides of the raft. But he welcomed their presence. Was thankful for their cover.

Morgan, one oar in hand, had slid in front of him as they entered the gulf, moving from side to side of the raft as necessary, keeping them free from any growth that would impede their progress.

Neither of them spoke.

They didn't need words.

There wasn't enough to say, and too much left unsaid for far too long.

And yet, they worked together as one. Anticipating, delivering, without instruction or question.

She spotted the little cattail-gated beach just as he did, turning to point it out to him, a quarter of a mile from being parallel with the boat they'd abandoned. While he calculated the yards of cattails they were going to need to get through to access land, she used her oar to help pull them closer to shore. "The water used to be about five feet in through here," he told her. If they were lucky, it would be still. They could hike out, carrying the boat above their heads if need be.

As it turned out, with both of them in the water, walking side by side, Blade and Morgan were able to pull the boat behind them. The lightweight vessel slid across the cattails almost easily, leaving Blade's mind to wander over how they must look—maybe to her sister from above— traipsing in their look-alike suits, an hour or so before midnight, side by side.

With a processional behind them.

The horror version of the wedding that never was?

He was shaking the dark thought away, hoping if Maddie was up there, she was helping to keep Morgan safe, when the world seemed to rumble around him.

Not an answer from Maddie Davis.

Jumping, he made it to the small piece of sand-covered shore, and reached to help Morgan climb up behind him, as another, larger rumble hit.

"Thunder?" Morgan asked, but she didn't sound as though she expected to be right.

Blade had a guess. Couldn't be sure. Until he looked in the direction where he knew his boat had been and saw the reddish sky.

An era had just ended.

His refuge had been bombed.

Tears filled Morgan's eyes as she watched Blade stand tall in the darkened wilderness, watching a part of his life going up into a red flare in the night sky. The moon, still mostly hidden, cast enough of a glow for the bomb's rising smoke to seem like curling snakes in the air.

She wanted to wrap her arms around him, hold him to her and never let go. Neither of them knew how long forever would be. Could end that night.

Such maudlin thoughts were not the way she'd become an expert in her field.

Focus on what she could control did that.

Setting up camp was a welcome diversion. Walking a foot into the woods, she stripped off the wet suit and equally damp underwear beneath, donning the clothes Blade had thrown in the waterproof duffel. Underwear. Jeans. A dark button-down shirt. And nothing else. The bra she'd packed with the small bundle was nowhere to be found. Hanging her wet bra on a branch so it would be dry by morning, she stepped back out to see Blade similarly dressed. Jeans. Short-sleeved button-down shirt. Dark color.

He looked...too good to be true.

And she quit looking.

The tent went up easily, and was large enough to fit the entire boat, with the tent's front zippered doors still able to close.

Of course it had, she thought, as she crawled inside and settled back against an inflated side as a backrest. Wishing she had a glass of wine.

Or a beer.

And settled for the bottled water she found in the bag,

along with a supply of dehydrated packaged meals. And a small, battery-powered lantern.

Turning it on, she set it at the head of the boat.

If nothing else, the past had taught Blade to be prepared for anything.

Her go bag was stocked with her own brand of dehydrated food, and other packaged things that didn't have to be cooked.

They might not have spent their lives together as they'd planned, but they seemed to have traveled a lot of the same paths anyway. The realization saddened her.

And warmed her, too.

For the first time in seventeen years, she didn't feel completely alone on her journey.

Her heart jumped, and her belly quivered a bit when the tent flap moved and Blade appeared, taking up what was the rest of the space in the boat-laden tent.

Taking her air, too.

He was...everything.

And she'd existed on nothing for so long. Staring up at him, her gaze glued to him in the dim light, she didn't even try to hide how she was feeling.

He wasn't looking away.

Until he did. "Get some sleep," he told her. "I'm going to sit up awhile..." He'd seemed about to say more, but Morgan didn't wait to hear what it was.

He'd said enough to remind her who she was in the real world.

And who he was.

A client.

A man she used to know.

All that remembering, putting herself back in those moments, she couldn't let them get to her.

Scooting down in the boat, she turned her back to him, tucked herself up into a ball and tried to pretend to herself that she was thankful that Blade was keeping them on the right track.

Only...she wasn't. "What if we don't make it through this?" Her voice sounded small, even to her, as she lay there hunched, listening to crickets and cicadas chirping outside the tent.

"Don't talk like that."

Not the direction she was taking. "It's a viable possibility."

"You giving up?" His voice sounded a bit less...calm. He'd wanted her earlier, at the table. The evidence had been rock hard and impossible to miss.

"The opposite, actually," she said, not moving. "I want to feel fully alive."

There. She'd put it out there. And as the silence continued in the darkness, she knew she'd done what she could. Technically, she was his employee, but it wasn't about that. For either of them.

She'd turned her back on him when he'd needed her most. Had professed undying love and then hadn't even given a scared kid the benefit of the doubt. She'd screamed at him in front of everyone...

"I'm sorry," she said softly enough that she shouldn't wake him if he'd fallen asleep.

"For what?" He didn't sound the least bit sleepy.

"Not opening my arms for you to run into them that morning. I'll regret that for the rest of my life."

"You'd lost your identical twin, Morgan. Your other half. You were in shock, with a shattered heart..."

His words sent her back there again, alone. Frightened. Desperate. "Please hold me, Blade," she said, a young girl and a grown woman on the run for her life, too. "Just hold me? Just for tonight?"

Turning, half sitting, she saw him still upright in the back of the raft, just as she'd left him.

"I can't just hold you."

Oh. *Oh!*

"That's okay, too," she told him. "It doesn't have to mean anything." She heard herself justifying, and didn't give a fig about it. She and Blade...honesty was all that mattered.

"That's just it, Morgie, it would mean something. Too much."

He wasn't ready. Might never be ready. Lying back down, Morgan thought about his words. Knew there was truth in them. And willed herself to go to sleep for the few hours they might get.

Was just drifting off, when she felt his body sliding down beside her, spooning her. And kept herself still, concentrated on breathing evenly, as she waited for whatever came next.

And, minutes later, heard his deep, even breathing.

Satisfied in a way she couldn't understand, Morgan drifted off as well.

His body was hard, on fire, moving instinctively, back and forth, and not getting anywhere. Not going in. The body next to him wasn't open to him.

But her softness...her nipple under his fingers was hard, not soft.

And she moaned.

The sound woke Blade from his semisleeping, half-dreaming state, to find himself riding Morgan's butt like some brainless jerk. He tried to stop, to freeze, his first thought being not to wake her. But her fingers slid up over his hand on her breast, guiding his fingers to the naked flesh.

While his groin shot an immediate message of urgency, she rolled over and planted her mouth on his.

He couldn't stop her. Couldn't tell her no.

Wasn't sure he'd be able to tell himself in any way that would have any effect.

Instead, he rolled her to her back, pulling both of his hands up to cup her face, to open his mouth over her lips and let his tongue dance with hers as it had done in the past.

But with a whole lot more finesse.

He moved. She moved. Clothes disappeared. At a fever pitch, blood pumping through his veins, and his breathing ragged, Blade wasn't sure he'd be able to hold off long enough to bring her all the pleasure he wanted her to have. If they only had one night, it had to be...

Her fingers curved around him. Squeezing lightly. Holding him. He felt himself let go a little bit, but managed to hang on when he remembered... "I don't have protection."

Morgan continued to hold him. And to smile up at him as she lay, naked and spread beside and half beneath him. "For a guy who's more prepared than an entire country of Boy Scouts I find that hard to believe," she told him. Her smile slow, and so sexy he had to kiss it away.

But he found words, too. A minute or so later. If she wanted to play, he could do that, too. Except that he was completely serious when he said, "I don't ever have unplanned sex."

So no need to carry anything extra in his wallet. A reminder to him that he was not a man who was going to meet a woman and get carried away.

And yet, there he was...doing just that.

Except that he hadn't just met Morgan Davis. She'd carried his heart away with her years before. "So, you just… what…stop and buy condoms? Because—" she licked his lower lip "—I know you aren't a guy who expects her to take care of things."

"I have condoms in my bathroom at home," he told her, licking her right back. "And always take one with me for planned sex."

That stopped her. With her arms draped behind his neck, her expression serious, she said, "So you've never had sex, even once, without a condom?"

He shook his head. "Nope."

The look on her face, a mixture of awe and something else, a little sad-looking, she said, "Neither have I. So I guess that means, in a way, we're going to have virginal sex, just like we planned." Her words fell to a whisper before she was through, and Blade caught the last one with his lips. Kissing her long and hard.

But held back when every muscle in his body was urging him to climb on top of her. "You're sure you want to do this?" he asked her.

"My cycle's regular and based on what just ended, I'm not at risk for pregnancy," she told him.

And he felt like a fool, but had to tell her the truth. "I wasn't thinking about that. It's just…not too late to stop."

"Maybe not for you," she said, turning to her side, with her legs open, guiding the engorged muscle in her hand to her private spot.

But he pulled back. Separated them long enough to look her in the eye. "I'm serious, Morgie. If this isn't what you want to look back on…"

She sat up, those glorious breasts right there, his for the taking, except that he couldn't look away from the light in her eyes.

It showed him more emotion than he could decipher. Sadness, need, confidence, warmth…maybe love…whatever it was, he took it in. She grinned and said, "If I'm going to be seeing my sister in heaven in the next day or two, I at least have to be armed with the answer to the one question Maddie will have first. Since sex was always on her mind and she never got to do it. Was Blade Carmichael any good?" Her attempt at levity failed, but the words told him how very much she wanted to finish what they'd started.

Because Maddie had known her innermost heart. Could feel it. Morgan had just given him her sister's blessing to quit thinking and put them both out of their misery.

Without wasting another second, he moved, and so did she, and he slid inside her as she pushed herself onto him. He froze the second he was fully home. To savor. But also to hold on. Seeming to sense his need, she kept her lower body still. And kissed him. Softly.

"Heavenly meeting or no, there's no way I'm ever telling anyone about this," she said, squeezing him.

Her words spurred him too strongly to hold back. Out of control, he pulled, and plunged, their bodies meeting, separating and coming back together with the force of seventeen years of waiting. Of longing. And when her convulsions started around him, he emptied himself of every longing he'd ever had.

Found a satiation he'd never experienced.

Reached heights of pleasure he hadn't known existed.

And was healed.

Chapter 20

Lying in Blade's arms, Morgan drifted, knowing that she'd just touched heaven. That she'd lived a perfect moment. She had to sleep. Wanted to stay conscious, to savor. But she was so tired…

Dark hours of the morning were looming. They were on their own, on the run from a killer they knew, but didn't know who. She didn't want to go forward.

Couldn't go back.

And held herself in a state of dozing as long as she could, half dreaming, but aware of the arms that held her.

Of Blade's even breathing, soothing her, like a mother's womb. Or a sound machine. Waves coming in on the beach…

The beach.

Water.

A river.

Sweating a river…

Morgan sprang upright, hot, rivulets running between her breasts, not sure where she was in that first second.

Eyes wide, adjusting to the darkness. Walls close enough to touch and…Blade.

"What is it?" He was up, pulling on his pants by the time she fully realized where she was. He'd flipped on the little lantern. The night came flooding back.

The bullets. The raft. Fighting waves on the lake. Rumbling earth. A red sky.

The profile. Pictures. Sitting on a bench, waiting for her parents. Stares.

"I don't know," she said, shaking her head, and reaching for her clothes. "What time is it?" Had the alarm gone off? Startled her awake?

He touched his watch and the face lit up. Waterproof, of course. "Three thirty."

Half an hour before they'd agreed to rise.

Three hours, maybe, of sleep.

He was staring at her again. "I think we should get back out to the lake and try to make it to Michael's marina," he said, still watching her as he started to button his shirt.

Her bra was outside hanging from a tree. He was heading out. She asked him to get it. Stood after he left. Put on her underwear. Stepped into her jeans.

The river.

Jeans.

Shaking, feeling sick to her stomach, Morgan dropped down to her knees. Shaking her head. She'd been dreaming. But...

It hadn't been a dream. Her head hurt.

Shivering, chilled, she pulled on her shirt. Buttoned it. Wrapped her arms around herself.

And glanced up, eyes wide, horror filling her as Blade came back in, holding her bra.

She shook her head. Left her bra hanging there from his fingers. "I know," she said.

Sliding down to his haunches, beside her, he was close enough to touch, but didn't reach out to her. "Know what?" His tone was gentle. Soft.

And as filled with concern as his gaze was.

"I know who the killer is. At least… I think I do. I might know. Someone from camp. A younger kid. Intelligent. Controlled. Able to gain the confidence of people at risk, to discern how to play with individual minds and influence them to do things. Definitely involved in the investigation. Something happening at camp. Knew me and Maddie. And you and Shane and Kyle, too."

She tried to swallow. Couldn't. Fought back a wave of nausea. She was wrong. Had to be wrong.

But it all made sick, horrifying sense.

Except, he wasn't sick. She would have known, wouldn't she?

Staring up at Blade, she felt so foolish. And so guilty, too. How could she not have known? It was her business to see, to notice, to figure it out.

"He's been playing us," she said, "and I fell right into his trap…" As much as she needed it all to end, she prayed she was wrong.

"Who?" Blade's tone was sharper. He still didn't touch her. She needed him to touch her. To convince her she was…

"Remy." The word fell off her lips and she almost felt foolish for her thoughts. Except… "I found him down by the river, crying…grief for his mother… He made me promise not to tell… The guys would all make fun of him… I told him to go see Dr. Hampton…he wouldn't laugh. That day, at the river, I hugged him, Blade."

The words felt like a death knell. In a way they were.

The dream hadn't been a dream. It had been long-buried memories, awakened by opening herself up to memories the night before…

"I felt…hardness against my thigh. He was turned on. Attracted to me. I knew what it was, but convinced myself I was wrong. I had no experience, and maybe it was just how a penis felt, I thought…but I knew. He was just four-teen. A kid. Probably couldn't help the instinctive reaction. I didn't want to embarrass him. And I was so in love with you. I didn't want to know that I'd turned him on. Didn't want to deal with it. I pretended it didn't happen…didn't even tell Maddie…"

She'd forgotten all about it. With Maddie's death. Blade being named as the only suspect. The end of life as she'd known it. She'd forgotten the moment by the river. Not the hug she'd initiated. But the boy's reaction. It had been a second in time.

"Oh my God, oh my God."

She was rambling. Blade wasn't stopping her.

He wasn't leaving her, either. She'd expected him to.

At least to turn his back on her drama.

She stared over at him, let herself drown in the intensity in his gaze in that so small space. "The profile he gave us… it fits completely," she told him. Naming everything Kelly had relayed. Seeing the pieces sliding concisely into place. And then, as more lucidity came to her, her mouth dropped open. Until she said, "Oh my God," as more facts dropped into place. More recent occurrences. "And the stressor," she started, looking up. "Blade, he lost a patient, about four months ago. A *sixteen*-year-old girl. Maddie's age. She died by suicide. His first patient loss. I knew he took it hard, but…"

Blade's gaze continued to bore into her. Didn't seem as focused.

"You think I'm losing it, don't you?" She didn't blame him. She was doubting herself. First thinking Blade had killed her sister. Then figuring Jasmine was helping the killer—and she still wasn't sure the agent wasn't doing so.

Except…if it was Remy…he knew where they were every single second, because he was getting all the reports.

Blade still didn't speak. But was all intent and deliberate action as he stood, started putting things back into the satchel. "We have to go," he said. And then, just as abruptly, stopped. Turned to her, dropped to his knees in front of her. "I've been trying to place a face," he said urgently. "Since last night. Studying those photos. I remembered a face looking at me that morning. Not so much the face, but the look of fear in someone's eyes. I was thinking it was me. I'd been sick. Was looking at my face in the mirror in the boys' bathroom… It wasn't me, Morgan. It was Remy. When he was guarding you. Everyone else avoided looking at me. And Remy…he was confident and oddly in control as he kept people away from you. But me…he looked over and he looked scared. Like, right then and there, scared out of his wits. Like I might do something to him in front of everyone, I thought. But now…he was scared because he somehow knew I didn't do it. He thought I knew something, and that it was going to come out. It was that kind of look."

The words hit her hard. She knew pieces were flying into place. Didn't want to see them get there. "And Shane was the first person he killed," she said slowly, watching it fall.

Blade was throwing things out of the tent. She carried out what she could. And when he joined her outside, said, "He knew Shane killed Maddie."

Blade's nod broke something inside Morgan. All those years…she'd been searching for the truth…the proof…that the man she'd thought she loved had killed her sister. Remy had been her strength. Her life preserver. Grieving with her, sharing his own grief of his completely changed life with his mother gone. And later, always telling her there was nothing wrong with her for having loved Blade. Tell-

ing her there'd been two sides to him, and there's no way
she could have seen that other side.

He'd held her when she was sobbing, had listened to her
on the phone so many times over the years, promising her
that she'd find the proof she needed someday.

Letting her think that when she did, the man she'd loved
would be in prison, where he belonged. Feeding her beliefs,
her hatred for Blade Carmichael.

But for herself, as well. Because she'd fallen in love
with a murderer.

He'd let her live in hell, let Blade live in hell, for seventeen years.

Telling her again and again that she'd find her proof.

When he'd had it all along.

Blade had thought, over the past few days, that knowing
who they were after was going to make their quest easier. A
manhunt would be underway. They'd get the guy. Instead,
the nightmare got worse.

In part because the woman on the run with him had
just become a permanent part of his soul. He never should
have let it happen.

Not until they had all the answers to their pasts, the killer
was behind bars and they had a chance to meet in more
normal circumstances.

He knew his feelings weren't going to change. But Morgan's could. Did she even want a relationship? The family
he wanted with her?

She traveled all over the country. While he worked with
wood and concrete in the dirt in small-town Michigan.

None of which mattered in the moment, but distracted
him from the shock of Remy Barton likely being responsi-

ble for his own seventeen years of hell. Distracted him long enough to get the tent rolled back up and into the satchel.

He and Morgan worked together, silently. There just weren't any words. They were after someone they'd both trusted. That Morgan cared about. A friend.

Until she stopped, staring up at him. "Kyle," she said. "He's been missing for a couple of days. Because no one has found his body yet?"

The rock in Blade's gut cemented over. "Remy may have killed him, but when he heard that Kyle was our main suspect, he hid his body, rather than framing me for the death," he said, aware of how much he'd begun to think like a killer over the years of trying to find one.

And went back to work when Morgan nodded.

They didn't know they were right. It was all just theory.

But it was the only one, ever, that filled in every single gap.

Before they left camp, they put a call from Blade's new prepaid phone into Hudson Warner's private line. A signal to not automatically be put on speakerphone.

Not that Remy would be there. But he could be on a call, even at four in the morning. A cabin cruiser had exploded on the lake. Blade and Morgan had no proof of that. Yet. But the conclusion was inevitable. And if the boat had exploded, there'd have been crews working it…people reporting in. Evidence flown to Sierra's Web by private jet. Morgan had told him how it all worked.

And if there was a chance no one knew he and Morgan were still alive, they needed to keep it that way. At least until they'd all talked. And he and Morgan had decided their next moves.

The call picked up in the middle of the first ring. "You're

okay." Warner's urgent tones sounded before they'd even identified themselves.

"Yes," they answered in unison. Blade staring out toward the lake. He had no idea where Morgan's attention lay.

"Thank God. I've been waiting for the area code to come up."

Blade left it for Morgan to explain the hours without contact. She said, "We thought it best to be presumed dead, just until we could get some rest."

"We just got word a few minutes ago that, so far, there's no evidence at all of human flesh, blood or remains…"

Blade had assumed as much, but still didn't like hearing the news. "Who knows?"

"So far, Jasmine Flaherty, Glen and I. Kelly got called to another case, a child's life in immediate jeopardy in Missouri. Silver is waiting to hear the preliminary results. Jasmine's orders were to have everything flown here. One chain of command. We got the first shipment, interior of the cabin, mostly, an hour ago. Half a dozen experts were in the lab waiting. Had everyone local on deck. Checked first for signs of life."

The longer they talked, the more Blade's blood was pumping. They had to get moving.

He had to do something. Anything that would bring them closer to ending the horror.

"We know who killed Shane, Morgan." Hudson's tone had changed. Almost hesitant, not in his findings, but in their delivery.

Blade held his breath, needing the truth, not wanting it to be Remy Barton.

"We tested his clothes for DNA," Glen's voice came over the line, sounding…tired. Really tired. Blade felt Morgan's hand slide into his and he curled his fingers around it. "There were tears." Glen took a discernible breath. "We matched them to Dr. Barton, Morgan. He and his wife had registered with a national database."

Her fingers clenched Blade's as her knees buckled. She recovered almost instantly, but for that second, as he'd held her weight, Blade grew stronger, being there for her. And knew he would stand by Morgan Davis, in whatever capacity she needed, for the rest of their lives.

Tears on the clothing worn by a dead body didn't make a man a murderer. But it definitely made him a suspect. Most particularly considering the short time frame in which Shane Wilmington's body had been deposited in the Carmichael Construction pit. And knowing what they were looking for, a Sierra's Web expert traveled to the morgue to test the other two corpses and found matching DNA there as well. Skin cells those times. No sign of remorse for the other two kills.

Jasmine had been notified around midnight and had immediately been issued an arrest warrant for the child psychiatrist. Only to find that the man wasn't at his home. And hadn't been for over a week. Prior to that, for the past couple of months, he'd been staying in the spare bedroom. Telling his wife that with the suicide of his patient, he wasn't sleeping well and didn't want to keep her up.

He hadn't been to a single one of his son's Little League baseball games that summer, when, in years past, he'd coached and never missed a game. He didn't eat dinner with the family anymore. Was always obsessed with work. His wife thought that he'd been afraid to take his thoughts out of his cases for fear of missing something that could ultimately save a life.

And…he'd been talking, constantly, about inviting Morgan to dinner. Had even mentioned that he was thinking about offering her a partnership in his private practice.

She'd keep a watch over kids for him, to make certain that he always had all the facts.

Morgan's heart squeezed, anguish seeping through her, as, moving away from Blade, she listened to Hudson and Glen fill her in on Jasmine's overnight report. She was a trained agent. Had a job to do. Gave the words her entire focus.

Tammy Phillips had been formally cleared of all three murders. With the help of surveillance tape, she had solid alibis. Wouldn't have had time to leave where she was seen to make a kill and dump a body where they'd been dumped.

And Kyle...was still missing.

A full-out manhunt was underway for both Kyle and Remy, with warnings that Remy Barton, while seemingly harmless, should be considered armed and extremely dangerous.

And, standing there on that small patch of beach, everything became clear to Morgan. Painfully, glisteningly clear. "I know where he is," she said, her tone deadpan, as emotion voided from her system.

Remy was at camp. At the river. She'd been his endgame all along.

The man was diabolically smart. Far more than she'd even realized. The fact that he'd been playing her—along with his wife, his kids, his patients, his community—for almost two decades was proof of that.

He'd manipulated them all. The FBI. Sierra's Web. Had managed to pull off perfect crimes one right after another.

To pull off a perfect life while others languished from the secrets he'd held.

And would continue to do so until he got what he wanted. Her.

"He told me over and over through the years that I'd find the truth. Get my proof," she said, as though in a daze.

In reality, she was finally on the path she'd been stumbling around looking for all those years.

"And the profile," she said, "he told us what we had to know. He was, in his own way, confessing. He knew I'd figure it out. He wants it over." And wasn't able to stop himself.

"That's why his last kill, the way he framed Blade, was easily put into doubt. He wants to be done."

Remy might also have known that the Sierra's Web forensics team had been closing in on him. He'd have heard detailed reports of the testing being done.

Just as he'd known that Blade and Morgan would leave the boat when he shot at it. He gave them time to get away before bombing the vessel.

Because he had to see Morgan.

Somehow, a grieving, pubescent adolescent had found something in Morgan that had eased his pain to the extent that he'd been convinced that she was, and always would be, his permanent panacea.

Until an innocent girl had killed herself. She'd bet Remy had been thinking about Morgan, instead of his patient, during his last session with the girl.

He'd reached out to Morgan after the girl died, but she'd been on a case and hadn't responded right away. And had been sent out on another immediately afterward. Had figured he would need time alone with his wife and kids.

Either way, didn't matter.

If Kyle wasn't dead yet, he would be. Others from camp would follow.

Morgan couldn't have that on her shoulders.

"He's waiting for me. I have to go to him."

"No." Blade's single harsh word came first. Followed immediately by Hudson and Glen in unison.

But in the end, none of the three had a say. She was a free woman. And she was going. They could help her or not, as they saw fit.

Blade had figured he'd already been living in hell, but he hadn't even scraped the surface. Watching Morgan, in full tactical gear, getting out of the vehicle, preparing to take on a serial killer single-handedly, he learned just how painfully hopeless life could feel.

Morgan was certain that Remy would be waiting for her by the river. Figured that he'd been staying somewhere at the deserted camp. That was where he'd been going every day, in between his kills, making calls from there, waiting for her to figure it all out.

Things he'd said to her over the years came back to her. Asking if she ever thought about visiting camp again…one time reminiscing about the river, and another suggesting that a cognitive interview on-site might help her think of something. She'd rejected that idea outright.

She'd said, on the drive to camp in the back seat of Jasmine's agency-issued vehicle, that it was as though those moments by the river with her, the day before Maddie was killed, were his last healthy memories.

The goal was to bring Barton in alive. There'd been no proof of a weapon in his hand. Nothing definitive enough to prove his absolute guilt. And authorities needed to question him about Kyle Brennan. To be able to locate his body if nothing else.

And when Jasmine heard that Morgan was going in regardless, the agent had agreed that Morgan had the training to make a live arrest. She'd have people ready to move in, but Morgan insisted that Remy not be spooked before she had a chance to approach him. Talk to him.

It was clear to everyone that the man had been asking to be caught.

Morgan believed she could bring him in peacefully.

And Blade? He got to be on the premises. A witness. Or so everyone, at his and Morgan's insistence, had determined. He had his own plan. He'd made a promise to himself—he would not let Morgan die avenging her sister's death—and it was a promise he had to keep.

So as agents gathered around Morgan, checking that her wire was emitting good sound, that her gear was all it could be, Blade quietly excused himself to the men's room.

And simply didn't return.

Chapter 21

Remy wasn't at the river when Morgan, hand on her gun, approached the log dam where she'd met up with him that long-ago summer. Keeping her back to a tree big enough to cover her, with the river in front of her, she sat on the same log she'd seen Remy on back then.

Just yards from where she'd been told her sister was murdered. The bend in the river behind them had had a big fallen tree across it, which had been used by campers and counselors, both boys and girls, to secretly access the other side.

She didn't look back. Hadn't been to the site since they'd told her her sister was dead. She wasn't there to reminisce. To relive. She was there to finish.

She listened for the sound of a killer's approach. Heard only the soothing sounds of the river's flow.

Being Remy's sitting duck, trying to be prepared for anything horrible that was coming her way, was excruciating. But no more so than her twin's death had been.

It had to be done.

Her mind didn't wander. Her focus was on Remy Barton. On remembering every conversation they'd ever had as much as was humanly possible. Asking for the impossible as well. She had to be ready for him. No matter what play he lobbed her way.

She had to know what he was alluding to, associate it as he did. Stay up with him.

She was hoping to walk with him out to meet Jasmine. To stand with him while he was taken into custody.

A cracking twig just to her right alerted her to his presence. While her heart jumped, her body remained completely still. The river's flow had prevented her from hearing his approach. And that, she was sure, had been part of the plan.

And then he was standing there on the bank. A step from her seat on the log. In his usual cotton pants and short-sleeved polo pullover, with expensive leather slip-on shoes, he sat down beside her. Close enough that their arms were touching. A test, she was sure.

She didn't scoot away.

Nor did he seem to move at all as he said, "It took you long enough."

"You know my weak point, Remy," she said, ready for him. "My heart sees what it sees."

She had to let him know he mattered to her. That he'd been an important part of her life. And as much as she hated to do it, she was going to have to promise to continue to be there for him. To testify on his behalf as to all the good he'd done in the world.

It was the only way to bring him in peacefully.

And because she was who she was, she'd do her best to keep those promises.

The sun hot on her forearms, her jean-clad legs, she tried not to let him see her sweating. And found the calm that she'd been seeking within herself.

The job would get done. One way or the other, it was ending.

She was getting what she most needed.

Remy, sitting on her left side, took her hand. Held it between both of his. Because she still had her gun hand free, she let him do so. "There are things you don't know," he told her.

"I know that you killed Shane." She'd talked to Kelly Chase on the way to the camp. Knew that it was better to get the worst out as quickly as she could. Get things on the table and let him see that she was still there for him. That she'd known, and she'd still come.

He nodded. Didn't commit one way or the other. Which meant still no confession for the wire she was wearing.

"We can plead temporary insanity, Remy. You were a kid when you saw him kill a sixteen-year-old girl. And having just lost another one…" She had no idea if such a plea would stick.

"I couldn't sleep that night. Had come down to the river. Saw him with her right back there." He nodded behind them. "Except, I didn't know it was him. Or her. I thought it was you and Blade. I'd seen Blade follow him back to camp and warn him not to leave again."

It took everything she had not to pull her hand away. To keep her features schooled into an expression of understanding.

Trying to fool one who was trained to figure out what people were thinking when they didn't even know themselves.

And one who'd been a close friend for almost two decades.

"She was holding the cross that I'd seen you wearing around your neck earlier," he said. "He'd just given it to her. I figured you'd given it to Blade, and he'd given it back to you."

Shane had had the cross she'd given Blade after dinner

that night? She had no idea how he'd come to be in possession of it, but they just had proof, on tape, that Blade hadn't been responsible for that piece of evidence against him, either. Was glad that she'd lived to know he'd heard that. His being permitted to listen to the wire feed as everything went down had been part of her bargain with Jasmine.

"So when he kissed her and left... I was thinking Blade just broke things off with you and I walked up to her." Turning, he put his face close to hers, forcing her to look him in the eye. Intimately. "You were my own personal angel that summer, Morgie. You were the only one who could ease the painful grief..."

She swallowed. Felt moisture in her eyes. Hoped he was far enough gone to think the tears were for him.

When all she could think about was her poor, sweet, outgoing sister.

And the rage sweeping through her. Because she knew what was coming. What he was about to tell her. Putting her free hand down near the butt of her gun, she nodded at the dangerous man. She could have the gun in hand in two seconds. Less than another to pull the trigger...

As she had the thought, Remy was the one who moved.

And suddenly, there was a barrel of a gun on his thigh. Pointed at the ground.

She'd expected him to come armed. They all had. But she was better trained. Was counting on her ability to aim and fire first.

"I wouldn't do that," he said to her.

And she nodded. "You're the boss, Remy. You've always been the boss. You've made that perfectly clear."

He'd killed Madison. There was no question now. And she had to sit there with him. Play his game. Or die.

"You want to know what happened or not?" he asked,

his tone resigned, either way. "You said you had to have the truth. I'm giving what you need more than anything else."

How many times had she told him, when he'd encouraged her to open her heart to the idea of a love interest, that she didn't have enough of a heart to give a man? That more than any relationship or family, she needed to find justice for her sister?

Maddie had been her heart and soul. Her other half. There was no love, no marriage, no family for her.

Or so she'd thought.

Blade had taught her differently. And she might sit there and die without him knowing that. What could she say, so he could hear over the wire, what he meant to her?

"And I'm here for you," she said, thinking of Blade. "You've been in my heart since that summer, Remy. You have to know that."

Blade. Not Remy.

"I went up to her, you…and put my arms around you, like you did with me earlier that day. But she pulled back, pushed me away. Told me that it was after curfew and if I didn't get back to my cabin, she was going to report me."

Oh… God. He was killing her without pulling the trigger. He'd known all along that the truth, his truth, would do so.

"And she…" Remy's tone of voice completely changed. It was like another man was sitting there as he tightened his grip on the gun, turning his fingers white, as he continued with, "And she…just turned away. I couldn't believe you, of all people, would do that, Morgie. That you'd *hurt* me like that. I was so…mad." His voice changed again, making him sound like a little kid. "And…and jealous. And…mad. And I picked up a fallen branch, swung it at her and ran."

She might die. She knew that. Played it out anyway. It

was her job to get it all on tape. She was finally bringing her sister justice.

Maddie. Who'd already conquered death. Because of Morgan.

"It was an accident, Morgie," the young voice said. "I didn't know until all the commotion before dawn that she was even hurt bad. I snuck outside, hiding, scared to death they'd know it was me, and that's when I saw Shane go into Blade's bunk and come back out again. He told me later that morning that he'd been happy to hear that Blade had done it, because he'd been afraid people would think it was him, because he'd been with her out there after the party."

And Remy had sat with her, hearing her scream at Blade, and hadn't said a word.

She had it all. Everything she'd said she was living for. Everything she'd had to have before she died.

Except...she'd been wrong about that, too.

She hadn't had a life with Blade, yet. Hadn't borne his child.

Remy lifted the gun off his leg, let it fall again, said, "And now, Morgie, it's all come full circle. We're going to get it right this time, me and you. We're going together. Here. Now. Right where it all really ended forever ago..."

Murder suicide.

He turned, and she caught a glimpse of the barrel of his gun pointing at her as she pulled her own.

She felt a blow even as she heard the shots.

And barely noticed the loud splash as body weight hit water.

He hadn't been in time.

The gun had gone off.

Blade had his man. Held Barton's arms so tightly behind the other man's back, he figured Remy's shoulder was out of the socket. And still the man thrashed in the water, fighting him.

He'd seen the gun go flying. Hadn't pulled his own. He had no authority to shoot.

He had to get to Morgan. Blade hadn't heard a second splash. Couldn't get a look at the log to see if she was splayed across it. Or how badly she was bleeding.

Please, God, and all fates that be, let her be alive.

Let her hold on.

The FBI agents would have heard the shot over the wire. They'd be there...

"Move again and you're dead." He heard hatred in the voice, saw the gun barrel pushing into Barton's head. And felt the man's muscles go limp.

"Don't loosen your grip, Blade," the most beautiful voice in the world said next to him. The same one that had just threatened to blow a man's head off. But in an entirely different tone.

"I have no intention of letting this bastard go," Blade said, his grip tight even as he weakened with relief. And a gratitude unlike anything he'd ever known.

Less than a minute later, a swarm of agents was upon them, and handcuffs were placed on the wrists dangling from the arms he held in a death grip. Morgan's gun disappeared from the man's head. And she told him, "You can let go now."

She might think so. He knew differently.

Dropping his hands from the dangerous man's body, he reached instantly for the one person he wanted to hold on to for the rest of his life.

Holding her by the arms, gently, as the river flowed

around their ankles, he searched her head, her face, her clothes, for signs of blood.

"He missed," she told him. "Because of you."

He noticed she wasn't pulling away from him. So he held her hand as they climbed up on the bank, and as they walked back to the caravan of cars. And as they both answered questions. He got in the car first, to head back to Rocky Springs, and when she slid in beside him, she didn't stop sliding until her shoulder and thigh were touching his.

They were two peas in a pod. Needing each other.

He could be misreading things.

He didn't think so.

And was glad when he heard Kelly Chase on the car's audio system, reminding Morgan that Madison's death was not on her.

"If I'd dealt with his attraction the moment I'd felt it…"

"No, Morgan," Kelly said again. "You sister made choices, as did Barton. I'd like you to call me tomorrow so we can talk more about this."

Morgan's okay was witnessed by Jasmine, her new partner, Kelly Valentine, and Walt, the agent in the back with him and Morgan. Blade was going to hold her to it.

There was no chance for the two of them to speak. No time when they were alone together. He had to give his statement separate from hers, but it was all formality. He'd been through it all so many times before, he recognized that law enforcement was just crossing every *t* and dotting every *i*. They had it all on tape. Just needed clarification of the end there, the part that they'd heard but couldn't see.

Remy lifting the gun, Blade lunging…

And suddenly, after a grueling morning…they were free. Jasmine offered to take Morgan back to Detroit with her. To drive her to get a rental vehicle until she could purchase a new one. Before Morgan could answer, Blade made his own offer. He'd left his truck at the precinct when they'd skipped town before dawn the day before.

"Come home with me."

Nothing else. No promises. Just that.

Her nod didn't promise anything either. They were simply two souls who'd been through trauma together. Leaving the precinct to debrief together. At his home on the beach.

Morgan was mostly silent on the drive to his place. They'd both been talking for the past hour. Had been over everything multiple times.

He didn't have a lot to say, either.

He offered her a glass of wine when they entered his house through the garage. She accepted and followed him out to the deck after he collected the bottle and glasses.

He sat in his normal chair. A rocker next to the side table. She took the other one. A match that had never had a mate.

He poured.

She held her glass for a toast.

He tipped his to it, still with no words. Was fine to keep it that way if it kept them together.

"To us," she said as he heard the clink.

He liked it. *To us.* So simple.

Yet said…everything.

"We know nothing about each other's daily lives." He tried to be reasonable, when his entire being was urging him to scoop her up, wine and all, and take her upstairs. For a few days at least. With breaks for food. And maybe playing on his private beach.

Time to sit at the water that had saved their lives and be thankful…

"If you're telling me you need time, just say so, Blade. I'm not going anywhere."

He glanced over at her.

"Not ever again," she said, staring him straight in the eye. "I know everything I need to know about you and about what I want and need. My heart, my soul, they know. The rest...it will come. And while it does... I'll be right here, welcoming it all in."

There was so much. Where would they live? Was she willing to move to Rocky Springs? Give up her life in Detroit? Her job was mobile. His was not. But he could start again. Did she still want kids? Was she...?

She was watching him. Sipping wine. Smiling. But when she saw him studying her, her expression grew serious. "Do you want a life with me in it?"

"More than anything on earth." Again, the answer was so simple.

"Then we'll figure out the rest."

"I want kids," he blurted, just too cautious to believe full-out.

"I'm ready."

"I'd like to live here."

"I was counting on that part. And thinking I'd limit my jobs to in state."

He smiled then and she asked, "What? You don't think I can? Or will?"

Shaking his head, Blade said, "I don't doubt you can do whatever you put your mind to, Morgan."

"Then what?"

"I've spent the past seventeen years of my life preparing for the worst. I'm finding that I'm not quite sure how to accept the best."

She left her chair then, but only to slide down onto his lap, wrapping her arms around his neck as she said, "Then that makes two of us, Blade. I'm still pinching myself. Saddened. And yet...feeling happier than I can remember feeling, too. Which feels...weird."

"Weird." He nodded, then tipped her chin with his finger. "I'm thinking maybe we spend the rest of our lives helping each other figure out how to live with daily happiness," he told her, feeling smarter than he had in a long while.

"Can we start by going upstairs and getting naked again? In a bed this time?" She sounded nothing at all like the Morgie he'd known.

And everything like the Morgan she'd grown up to be.

He was in love with both. Another truth. Just...there.

"You grab the wine," he told her, waiting for her to have both glasses in hand, and then, with her securely in his arms, stood.

Carried her into the house and up the stairs.

They'd fought their demons. Had kept their promises and found their truths.

Which had led them right back to the one place they'd both known, even as teenagers, that they'd needed most to be.

Together.

Forever.

* * * * *

HARLEQUIN
Reader Service

Enjoyed your book?

Try the perfect subscription for Romance readers and get more great books like this delivered right to your door.

See why over 10+ million readers have tried Harlequin Reader Service.

Start with a Free Welcome Collection with free books and a gift—valued over $20.

Choose any series in print or ebook. See website for details and order today:

TryReaderService.com/subscriptions